Will Kate risk
everything
for Nick?

Illegal Love

LEANNE LOVEGROVE

Illegal Love

Leanne Lovegrove

DEDICATION

To my darling, Scarlett who teaches me every day how to be a better person. I love you, Mum.

CHAPTER ONE

A girl dressed in a crisp, new uniform chased after a flyaway hat. Kate Penrose reached above her head and caught it. 'Oops, sorry,' she said to the parent she elbowed. Kate smiled and handed it to the young student. 'Here you go.'

'Thanks, Miss.' She skipped off to join her friends gathered in the quadrangle of Trinity College Girls' School on the first day of the new year.

Where's Angela?

Kate searched for her friend's familiar face as she nudged her way through the growing crowd. No chance of her recognising anyone else as this was her first day at Trinity, too.

Like the students commencing high school today, Kate felt a buzz of nervous excitement. She clasped her hands together in front of her to prevent their fidgeting and to calm her dancing stomach.

Everything will be okay. She released her hands and wiped her clammy palms down her skirt, hoping no one noticed.

'Hey, Kate!'

Kate waved and she relaxed. Angela! Angela Zimmerman was her dearest friend and a fellow teacher at Trinity.

'Thank God you're here. I'm a jumble of nerves but excited all at the same time,' she said and pulled Angela in for a tight squeeze.

'Don't worry. You're going to be great. The kids in year seven will love you.'

Next to them, a group of students who hadn't seen each other all

1

summer, squealed and jumped up and down in greeting. Kate and Angela moved away to a quieter spot near the edge of the square. The wind picked up and Kate swiped away the loose hair that whipped her cheeks.

'I know, you're right, just first day jitters.'

Angela leaned down close to her chest squinting. 'Your name badge says Mrs. Penrose, and,' Angela held up Kate's hand, 'you're still wearing your wedding ring.'

Kate pinched her lips together and drew in a breath. 'Yes, Angela.' She counted to ten and kept her hand in her friend's grasp. 'That is my name.' She smiled to soften her words. 'And, it's only been three years. It would be strange to start a new job with a new name on top of everything else. Besides, it brings me comfort to wear my ring.' She knew her reassuring smile to Angela was weak. With her free hand, Kate caressed the euro coin, her lucky charm, in her skirt pocket. No way would she reveal to Angela that she carried it around, too.

Her friend had always thought she was stronger than she was.

Angela stepped back, repentant but her grip on Kate's hand tightened. 'It will all become so quickly familiar. You're a great teacher, so committed and caring and this school is lucky to have you. You don't need any help, you've got this all on your own.'

'Mrs. Zimmerman? Where's C Block?' a student asked Angela and she walked away to assist, waving farewell to Kate as she left.

Alone, Kate looked around. The aged, terracotta buildings shaded the area creating a grey dome over the parents, students and teachers gathered underneath. Kate pictured the former nuns navigating the long passageways. She could almost hear the hymns they might have sung. At the voices in her head, she pushed her shoulders back and her chest puffed out as fierce determination gripped her. She stood in an historic space. Like those before her, she, twenty-six-year-old Kate Penrose, might teach students who become prime ministers, global leaders or perhaps ground level nurses, or valued community citizens. Goose pimples erupted on her arms at the possibilities.

But ghosts didn't roam the campus today. An important milestone was celebrated. Kate watched a small number of parents who may not have agreed it was a happy day. They dabbed tissues to the corners of their eyes and tried to squeeze in one last kiss. In rejection, their beloved offspring turned their faces away. Others, eager to finally be out of their parent's grasp, hurried away without a backward glance. A couple still clung to their mother's skirts.

Mixed amongst the parents were the teachers. Not only did they carry their official clipboards, they wore distinctive name badges and had their pens poised. But it was the serious expressions they sported that stood them apart. Ready to jump at the first recalcitrant child. Or perhaps, it was the realisation that summer had ended and it was back to work for another term. Some teachers counted down from the very first day. Kate determined not to be like them. She was elated to be at Trinity and her smile didn't falter. She was ready for the challenges ahead and couldn't wait to get started. Despite her nerves.

In front of her a child tripped on the cobblestone pavers and fell, landing on her knees and toppling sideways. The weight of the school bag pinned her to the ground.

Kate rushed over.

'Oh, you poor love, let me help you.'

The girl lay prone like a flattened cockroach with her stick-thin legs poking out. Kate reached down, clasped her two hands and pulled expecting the girl to lift easily upwards. The girl only moved slightly before landing back against the ground with a thud. The bulging port kept her sitting in a half up-right position. Combined with her belongings, the girl was much heavier than she appeared.

Kate spotted a student to the right. 'Want to help?'

The student, taller and more robust looking, shrugged.

'What's your name?' Kate asked the girl who'd fallen over.

'Alice.'

'Nice to meet you, Alice. Let's get you up so you can start your day. The bell will ring any minute.' Now she gestured to the bystander. 'C'mon then. Help me. You grab this hand and I'll take the other.'

As they tugged Kate veered sideways. The other student leaned against her instead of pulling upwards. Kate's head connected with the student. 'Oh, sorry,' she muttered and attempted to stand. Instead, she felt a sharp tug. 'Ouch!' Her dangly earrings had tangled in Alice's hair. Dammit! If she moved she'd either rip out her earring or the girl's hair. The unhelpful red-headed student snickered. Kate glared at her. The little terror smirked and stepped backwards stifling a giggle.

This wasn't how Kate wanted to experience her first day. Let alone, poor Alice laying helpless on the ground.

Once, Kate would have rolled around laughing about this silly situation, too. Instead, her stomach churned. Closing her eyes, she inhaled and fiddled with the hair encasing her earring to release it.

'It's okay, Alice. In no time you'll be free. I'm Mrs. Penrose by the way. What class are you in? I might be taking you for year seven English.'

Kate chattered while still twisting the strand of hair in and around the thread of her ice-cream cone earrings.

'Here, Miss, let me do that for you.' A dulcet voice echoed in Kate's ear and she felt a gentle pull. Within seconds, her earring sprang free.

Thank goodness!

Kate sighed in relief. But before she could stand, a man moved to her side.

'Are you okay?' he asked. Without waiting for a response, a firm grasp to her forearm elevated her upwards.

What? She glanced at the large hand gripping her. Once on her feet, the hand remained in place to steady her balance. Warmth radiated down her arm making her fingers tingle. She looked up at the man who stood a head-height above her.

Holy shit!

'Oh hello,' she said. Her insides melted like ice on a hot summer's day.

How lame. 'Sorry, I mean, thank you for helping me. It was starting to get embarrassing.'

The man acknowledged her with a dazzling white-teeth smile. Then he leaned down and used those same capable hands to lift Alice.

Head down and without a word of thanks, the girl moved away quickly. No doubt embarrassed by the whole rigmarole.

But Kate forgot Alice. Her eyes popped open wider as she stared transfixed at the muscles rippling in the man's arms. And, those hands. Imagine what he could do with them...

Kate touched her tender earlobe.

'Are those cones hanging from your ears?'

She glanced at him, unsure if he was ribbing her or asking a serious question. Longish, messy blonde hair framed his angular face. He had a prominent square jawline with only the slightest hint of stubble. But he was straight-faced and she couldn't decide his intentions either way.

'Uh, huh. Do you like them?'

Was she flirting?

The heat from Kate's arm now crept up her neck. God damn her body for betraying her right now.

Please don't let me blush!

He didn't answer her question. Instead, he gazed right back, his ice blue eyes staring in earnest. Fireworks exploded in her tummy as he scrutinised her and her body felt red-hot.

The noisy horde around them faded. Kate had to look away, uncomfortable with his examination. Was he reading her sinful thoughts? She shifted from one foot to another before glancing up again. His pull was electric and she couldn't resist him.

His broad shoulders hugged his casual Ralph Lauren polo. His lips moved up in a sly smile. Instinctively and lost under the spell he cast, she moved closer to him as if pulled by an invisible force. She inhaled his scent.

Oh God. She breathed deeply, wanting to wrap herself up in his smell. It reminded her of a tangy citrus tart you couldn't eat enough of. And, usually, made you feel sick afterwards, its sweetness so overpowering.

'Dad! I'm off to class.' A girl dressed in the Trinity uniform of navy pleated skirt and white shirt rushed forward and embraced him.

The father whipped out a bunch of coloured gerberas to present to his daughter. Where'd he been hiding those?

'Dad! They're gorgeous, thank you,' she said and kissed him on the cheek.

Kate's hand went to her chest, covering her heart as it hitched. Her mouth dried and suddenly she felt very thirsty.

'Have a great day at school, Evie.'

Kate touched the corner of her mouth to wipe away any drool that risked escaping.

'Mrs. Penrose.'

Kate turned toward the new voice. Her vision filled with blood red lips on a pale face.

'My name is Brittany Bartholomew.'

The woman offered her hand in a limp shake ignoring Kate's enthusiastic grip. Out of her oversized designer handbag she retrieved a business card. The edges dazzled bright pink with the woman's name emblazoned across it in glittery letters matched with a photo. Kate slipped it into her pocket.

'It is so lovely to meet you. Tell me all about your daughter.'

'I'm pleased I've caught you before lessons start. I am Coco-Sage's mother. She's in your home room and I know you'll just love her...'

Kate forced herself to remain focused on the parent and her tales of the delightful Coco-Sage. But all the time she was conscious of the man to her right. They stood so close that their arms touched. His smell mixed in with the parent. The mother was wearing Chanel No. 5. Kate would know that scent anywhere; it was her mother's favourite. Mingled with adolescent hormones, the aroma reminded her of the usual pungency of a kid's playground. Not at all pleasant. She just wanted to smell that citrus tart again.

Is that what caused the prickles of apprehension to climb her spine? Something about this mother was off. She prattled on about her daughter, barely taking a breath. Kate snuck a sly glance sideways. Or was it him? What was wrong with her this morning? This guy had captivated her and she couldn't focus. What was it about him? She hadn't so much as thought about another man, any man, for, well years, and in one brief encounter, this guy was featuring in her future dreams. Or fantasies. Or both. Kate resisted the urge to smile.

Brittany Bartholomew paused talking.

'Well, hello. I'm Brittany.' She turned toward the father. He'd stood silent at her side during Brittany's monologue. Kate watched Brittany's transformation from concerned parent to vixen with a flutter of eyelashes. The man didn't react. Good for him. She liked him better for it.

When he didn't respond, Brittany prompted. 'And, you are?'

'Nick. Nick Harding.' The words came out strained as if it was an effort to speak.

'Nice to meet you, Nick. Do you have a daughter starting year seven today?'

He nodded but offered nothing else.

Okay. Weird. Perhaps he wasn't so wonderful after all.

'Yes, I have Coco-Sage. Where is she?' she said and turned this way and that. 'Coco, darling,' she said and reached over to grab her daughter in a vice-like grip. 'Here she is. My daughter Coco-Sage.'

Kate's stomach dropped. It was the redhead from before. How appropriate. She placed a saccharine smile in place. 'Hello, Coco-Sage. I believe we've already met.'

The mother looked between them. 'How lovely.' She turned to Nick. 'Where is your daughter, Nick? It would be fabulous for the two girls to meet.'

Nick made a cursory attempt to locate his daughter. 'Um, she's over there on her way to class. Her name is Evie.'

'Evie! Wait up, sweetie. This is Coco-Sage. You two can be friends.'

Kate watched Evie turn and consider her father. Her right eyebrow arched in confusion and her lips upturned in an uncertain grimace.

'Go on, honey. Catch up and meet Evie. I'm sure you'll be great pals.' Brittany embraced Coco-Sage but she shrugged it off with a frown and strode away without any further pleasantries.

Nick regarded the Rolex on his wrist.

'I've arranged a meet and greet for the year seven parents this morning at Alberto's. Won't you join us, Nick, for a quick piccolo?' Brittany paused and looked around. 'Is your wife here, too?'

'No. It was nice to meet you both but I must get to work.' Nick cast another look in Kate's direction, ignoring Brittany Bartholomew, and penetrated her again with those eyes so that her groin quivered. Then he sauntered away. Kate froze, captured by his look.

What did it mean? Her legs went weak at the unspoken prospect. *What had gotten into her?*

Brittany lost interest in the conversation then and she found a posse of more interesting mothers to engage with.

The morning bell rang and brought Kate back to the present.

She patted down the wispy hair she imagined standing out on her head and calmed her breathing.

What a beginning. If this was any example of what the year held, it was going to be interesting.

CHAPTER TWO

Nick's email notification pinged and his irritation spiked. Forcing his gaze away from the depths of the Queensland Criminal Code— a hefty tome of a book— holding it made his hands cramp, he restored his computer screen. The antiquated legislation would bore any normal person, but all his nerve endings tingled. He was close. Had almost found the missing piece of a puzzle; one he had laboured over for days. One of these defences had to fit his client, he knew he could solve this riddle. But he hated interruptions when he was working. Now, he'd lose his train of thought. Distractedly, he glanced at the subject heading of the email received.

WARNING.

The word in capital letters taunted him as it bounced off the monitor. He scanned the message for the name of the sender. An address he didn't recognise; different to last time. Of course, the dweeb who'd sent it remained anonymous and unidentifiable. The defences in front of him were forgotten and the sections of the Criminal Code he'd been pouring over, vanished. He pushed the book aside. Thoughts rushed through his mind.

An unhappy client? A reminder he'd forgotten? An overdue tax invoice?

The possibilities were endless but they were only whimsical hopes. Nick knew exactly what this was, similar to the last three he'd received.

Nick scanned the contents. A short message with only six lines.

But each word stabbed him like a knife. He read it and reread it to ensure he'd understood. And to let the meaning sink in. With incomplete sentences and poor spelling, it accused him of being a hopeless criminal lawyer. That's okay, he'd been told that before, on the rare occasion a client didn't achieve the result they'd been hoping for. It said he wasn't capable of freeing a person wrongly accused of their crimes but had let child abusers walk free. He could handle those baseless allegations. They didn't even cause a light sweat to break out. If accusations like that threatened him, they'd be no reason to get out of bed each day. It was the rest of the email that had his heart sitting in his throat.

It mentioned his family. How did this person know he had a family? One thing he took great pains to ensure was that his private life stayed private. He never revealed personal details to his clients and only a select few of colleagues. Early in his career he'd learned that you might develop a public profile as a successful criminal defence lawyer, but you did not exist as a person. Your private life remained off limits. He'd become an expert at avoiding the innocent slips of his lawyer associates, mentioning children's names or favourite past times that allowed them to be traced. He'd been smart, demonstrated enormous self-discipline and it would now pay off. Outside the office, he was unknown.

Nick shook his head. But still, what *did* it mean? It could mean anything, or nothing. Everyone had a family, right? It was a cheap shot at best. Despite reassuring himself, his mind raced to Evie: alone and defenceless at school.

On a normal day, he wouldn't think twice about the contents of an email like this. An ordinary day for Nick involved mixing it with the state's worst criminals. He kept company with white collar offenders who'd committed fraud or extortion, those charged with grievous bodily harm or murder, right down to the simple drink driver. But, lately, his days hadn't been typical. Ever since he'd acted for Max Vincenzo.

Bloody hell.

Despite the air conditioning set to freezing in his home study, his body boiled. Nick puffed out his T-shirt allowing air to travel through and cool his skin. He took a sip of water from the drink bottle on his desk. And all the time, his mind swarmed with possibilities and what ifs and what his future might look like.

If he wore his lawyer hat, he'd sensibly tell himself that Max or any of his cronies knew nothing about him. And, they sure didn't know that he had a daughter.

Nick relaxed his hunched shoulders and released a loud sigh. Like the last threats he'd received, this wouldn't go anywhere. A gutless crim getting his rocks off.

He reached for *The Daily Quest* newspaper that lay unopened on his oak desk. Officially, in amongst the salacious gossip, it reported the daily goings on in Brisbane. Would it reveal any answers to him? Flipping through the pages, he skimmed articles on recent assaults as a result of a labour rally in the CBD; the discovery of a woman's body in bushland the day before; the reopening of an old arson investigation; and of students returning to school after summer holidays. All meaningless. But there it sat on page five: a piece on the Warlocks.

Max Vincenzo, the leader of the gang, was behind bars. Nick had been instrumental in that. Despite the kingpin's absence, the group continued to unleash havoc across the city. The article implicated that their fearless chief continued to give orders from prison. Nick knew it was possible. Photographs of graffiti-covered murals leapt off the page. The gang's prominent symbol of a red rose sprawled across the urban landscape bright and bold. It covered buildings, railway tunnels and garbage bins. The expose said the streets were filled with illegal drugs whilst shopkeepers complained of intimidation and stolen loot; women alleged harassment. The newspaper source declared the Warlocks and other bikie mobs were out in force, flouting the new legislation aimed at protecting innocent citizens. Nick sat back holding the paper aloft. Maybe they'd all been wrong. Perhaps the Premier had been right. In this same newspaper the leader of their State had said that all lawyers acting for bikies were hired guns. They took money from people who sold drugs to teenagers; that lawyers were part of the criminal gang machine and would do and say anything to defend their clients to get them off and progress a dishonest case.

This statement came before the Premier and his parliament passed controversial laws, making it an offence to fraternise with motorcycle gangs. It imposed harsh penalties for known members breaching the law. The Premier had wanted people to be scared and the public to acknowledge his government as the saviour. But clearly, the Warlocks were not intimidated.

Along with every other lawyer in Brisbane, Nick had lauded the comments as demeaning, derogatory and defaming and had lobbied against the loss of civil liberties. Because, he admitted, it meant a serious dent in his burgeoning business. But perhaps if he knew what he knew now, he'd have kept his mouth shut.

His computer pinged twice more. His heart beat out of his chest as he glanced at the screen. Two new email notifications. One subject heading read— Introduction to Trinity College – from Kate Penrose and the second from his sister, Lizzie. He guessed her message would be one of those ridiculous circular jokes that she insisted was funny. Nick scrunched up the newspaper into a tight ball and slammed the lid of his laptop shut.

Nothing else mattered at the moment.

CHAPTER THREE

'Okay, first, announcements. We've had a change of staff. Unfortunately, Mrs. McAndrews, our most beloved music teacher is ill.' School principal, Mrs. Janette Peterson, addressed the assembled group of teachers at the staff meeting and whispered, '*cancer.*'

Kate sat at the rear of the mess room and flicked over the pages of the agenda.

'But, on a positive note, our newest staff member is a capable music teacher and will conduct the year seven classes. Thank you, Kate.'

Kate glanced up.

What? Whoa!

'Um, excuse me, Janette, how many classes is that, exactly? I do have a full schedule with my English and French lessons…'

The principal removed her glasses and let them hang by a silver chain to balance on her ample bosom. Her bust sat secured in a floral blouse that matched a brown, tweed skirt. Mrs. Peterson glowered at her and fingered a neat, grey curl that had come loose from its tight bun.

Oh dear. She'd spoken out of turn. She gulped down the words she wanted to say to Mrs. Peterson. Clearly, the principal of Trinity was not someone to mess with.

Oops.

Mrs. Peterson launched into a monotone of Kate's schedule whilst the room went silent. The other teachers sat with their heads bowed, twiddling pencils or swiping the screens of their phones.

Kate sipped her lukewarm coffee whilst a creeping sensation of panic rose from her gut and climbed to her shoulders. She breathed out when the principal finished and moved on to the next topic.

'Okay, we need at least six volunteers to supervise at the first term disco. It runs from six to nine on a Friday evening.'

Along with a few other staff, Kate raised her hand.

Janette wrote her name down. 'Thank you, Kate. That means you are organising the year seven music tour, are a netball coach and haven't you volunteered to be on the organising committee for our annual fun fair, too?'

Kate shrugged. Inside, her tummy swirled. Was she biting off more than she could chew, as her mother would say? But the principal offered that pencil-thin smile, a know-it-all sort of grin that demonstrated the years of her experience toward a novice, presenting herself up for slaughter. Kate remained determined. She would be successful in this position. If the school leader was in any doubt about her abilities, she wouldn't be soon. Despite her confidence, Kate held tight to that euro coin throughout the rest of the meeting.

##

'Evie, can I speak with you for a minute please?'

Kate addressed the young girl as students billowed from the room when the home bell rang.

Evie Harding balanced her books in the crook of her elbows and blew stray whips of sandy blonde hair from her heart-shaped face. She frowned as her classmates departed.

'Is something wrong, Miss?'

Kate paused. Evie had the same crystal clear and penetrating eyes as her father. Wise eyes she'd say. Despite their initial brief meeting, she'd been unable to forget Nick's eyes; so vivid and bright, they were almost fluorescent. They held a spell over her and she knew they'd pull her deep into their depths if she let them. And, somehow, Kate knew she wouldn't resist.

What was she doing? Her thoughts had meandered to Nick. She needed to focus on this student. Why was she thinking of him anyway? It was pointless, stupid. She was not interested in anyone. Not him, nor any other gorgeous man, and certainly not a parent of one of her students. Her focus was on re-establishing her career.

Evie waited. Coming back to the present, Kate smiled. 'No, nothing wrong. It's only that I've sent your parents various emails about the music tour and haven't had any response.'

Evie's shoulders sagged and her lips formed a compact smile. 'Oh, okay,' she murmured.

'Here,' Kate said, showing her a piece of paper. 'This is the email address I've been using. Is it correct? Is this the address for both your mother and father or is there another more appropriate one I should use?'

Evie inspected it.

'No, that's right, Mrs. Penrose. But there's only my dad. But, yep, that's the right address. I can mention it to him again tonight and ask that he respond.' Her voice wavered, so fleeting, Kate almost failed to detect it.

No mother? Of course, she'd assumed Evie had a mother. Kate placed her hand on Evie's arm and thought of her own dear mum and felt bereft for Evie; for the occasions that only the two can share: the laughs and tears and screaming matches. She fought the urge to pull the girl in for a cuddle. For Kate, it was unimaginable not to have her mother.

'I'm so sorry Evie, I didn't realise. Are your parents separated?'

'No. My mum died when I was small.'

Kate's stomach dropped; it was worse than she thought. 'How old were you?'

'I was two. After she died, I went to live with Dad but I've spent a lot of time with my grandparents. I lived with them in Toowoomba for a while.'

Once, she'd been tough, but now, any distressing situation had Kate reeling and uncontrollable emotions spiralled to the surface. This new Kate was as soppy as bubbles in a bath. Everything came back to Ben.

His death.

Her life being irrevocably changed.

So final.

At least she'd spent valuable time with her husband. Evie, she guessed, would have little memory of her mother. Would not know her favourite foods, smells, perfume, whether she had crazy idiosyncrasies or whether she preferred to read or watch T.V. She'd been lucky, even if her time with Ben had been cut short. But this wasn't about her. She gathered her strength and hid her own, very personal, distress.

'Goodness, it sounds like you are very loved. So, it's only you and your dad now?'

Evie nodded.

Nick was a solo parent. A single man with mesmerising eyes. Stay focused Kate and she had to force herself back to the present again. 'That's lovely.' Kate bit her lip. 'However, I need to get the numbers for the music tour confirmed. And, I should also thank your dad for his kindness on the first day of school.'

Evie grinned, her face shining. 'Yes, he's like that, so kind, always helping people. If there's a lost dog, he'll find its owner, you know stuff like that. But with his work, he fights for justice, right over wrong. Works super hard.'

Hopefully she didn't fall into the category of a lost dog. 'It sounds like the two of you are a formidable team. If you remember, ask him if he's received my messages. It's important I calculate numbers for the tour and make the arrangements, even though it is eons away. It will be upon us before we can blink! And,' she smiled at Evie, 'you are an integral member of the ensemble and we need you on the trip.' And, as Kate turned away, she said '*Plus, everything must be perfect for Mrs. Peterson.*' 'Anyway, enough about that, we'll sort it, won't we? But tell me, have you enjoyed your first month of school?' Kate grinned forcing her old self back into the present. She worked hard at being happy and had earned a reputation for being ridiculously joyful and sometimes, not everyone appreciated it, however infectious it might be.

'Yeah. It's been fine.'

The classroom door behind them rattled and they both turned. A figure lurked behind the glass panelling. A shadow of red flashed back and forth.

'Who's that?' she asked Evie thinking she'd recognise the student.

'Not sure,' Evie shrugged but her forehead creased. The student passed across the door once more. Kate saw vibrant red hair in two perfect plaits.

'Is that Coco-Sage?'

'Dunno, maybe.'

'Yes, it is. Why is she loitering out there?' Evie didn't respond but checked her watch, shuffled her feet and twiddled with her ponytail.

'Is she hassling you?'

'She bothers everyone.'

'Okay, but does she cause you any particular difficulties, more than others, say?'

'Nah. She annoys a lot of girls, but she's always following me around and making comments. That sort of stuff. But, she does that to everyone.' Evie shrugged.

A hot flare of anger ignited in Kate.

Bullies.

As a teacher, she experienced them every day. Sometimes directed at her, but usually in the playground, power plays acted out in each corner. These days it had become like a rite of passage. As if you couldn't move through your schooling without having a run in with an overbearing fellow student, particularly at an all-female school. She didn't like it.

'You do know that I'm the year seven pastoral leader and in charge of all you bright young things. So, this is important. I need to know about this. Thank you for telling me.' Kate paused. 'What to do about it, though?'

'Nothing, Mrs. Penrose, honestly. If she knows I blabbed, it'll get worse. Please.' Evie's face scrunched up.

Prickles crawled up Kate's spine as she watched Coco-Sage.

Like mother like daughter? Kate chided herself, that was unfair. She hardly knew Brittany.

'Of course. At this stage, I won't do anything to make matters worse. But let's keep in touch about this, okay? I want to make sure you're happy and enjoying school, and not constantly watching your back. This is what we'll do. Now, you'll accompany me to my office so I can provide you with another copy of the music tour note for your father and hopefully, she'll not follow and head home. On the way we can brainstorm ideas to avoid her. You know there's a range of safe options around school?'

Evie rolled her eyes. Kate laughed and mock-punched the girl on the upper arm and she beamed. It was exactly the reaction she'd desired. 'More importantly, are you enjoying *To Kill a Mockingbird*? And tell me, what do you love most about Atticus Finch?'

CHAPTER FOUR

Nick wasn't equipped to deal with this. Emotional pleading had always brought him undone, particularly from a female, and especially from his daughter.

'Dad, please. Why can't I go? I don't understand.'

For once, Nick didn't have a good explanation. Not one that made sense to thirteen-year-old Evie, anyway. What he did know, though, is that the thought of Evie in a crowd and away from his protection, made him sweat buckets. Rationally, he told himself, that at this stage, the threats, meant nothing. But the niggling fear wouldn't disappear. What if it was something? He needed to be on guard. Of course, to his daughter, he was an overprotective, unreasonable bore.

'Give me the details again.'

Evie squealed and jumped up and down on the spot. 'Hang on,' he said placing his hands on his hips. 'I have not yet agreed.'

Evie didn't listen, and she spoke so fast Nick couldn't discern the words. Her innocent face beamed at him.

He was a goner.

'Okay, I give in. You can attend the disco on the condition you stay with your friends on the premises and be available at nine for me to collect you. I'll be waiting at the front gate, don't be late.' Nick accepted the hug Evie offered, soaked it up and bottled it for later. He was sure he'd call on those reserves many times in the coming months. Evie was growing up fast. His metaphorical tight grip was loosening on her teenager self and their fingers becoming unravelled.

He didn't like it.

Admittedly, he wouldn't like it at any time, but right now, he wanted to ground her, lock her in the house and never let her leave. His own Rapunzel. Unfortunately, he didn't joke; the smile slipped from his face.

Nick hadn't been able to settle since the last email. He flinched at unexpected noises and had been hyper-alert for another message. None had arrived. Yet. The dread sat like a lump at the back of his throat, hard and uncomfortable. The unknown made him edgy and he wasn't a jittery person.

He operated best with facts and detail. The lawyer in him would not accept the messages as random. Why would a person bother to send multiple messages, if they weren't intending to act on them? Surely there would be more; there had to be. And after they stopped threatening, what then? None of this mattered to his daughter, though, dancing around the living room; the sight of her filled his heart with love but it also shrank in pain. If anything should happen to her…

Nick couldn't bear to think about it.

An hour later he dropped Evie at school and watched her enter safely, find her friends and run together into the hall. Nick moved away from the curb and parked his car in a dark side street. Exiting his vehicle, he walked the short distance back to the grounds. He entered adjacent to the school hall where excited chatter was loud above the already pumping music.

The hall sat atop a grand staircase with the main entry at the front. Of course, Nick had scrutinised the school premises before he'd enrolled Evie. He'd always been a control freak, even before this current situation. He shrugged; it paid to be cautious. He'd learned that in his line of work. As a result of his investigative skills, he'd memorised the map of the campus and knew where he was headed.

Music pounded louder as he drew closer to the obscure side of the building that housed a balcony and where extended glass doors ran along the perimeter.

The doors were all shut, but Nick pulled one to test if it was unlocked. It moved under his hand. He tried a few more and they all jerked open.

Any student could leave with little effort. Nick's right eye twitched. He didn't like this. Of course, it did mean a safe escape in an emergency. God. Listen to him. Nick acted as if he was seventy-five, not thirty-five.

He shook away those thoughts. He did what he had to. He found the perfect spot to wait and dressed in all black, he slipped into the darkest of crevices, ready. Ready for what, he didn't know. But there wasn't a chance in hell of him going home to rest on his couch. He'd stay right where he was until Evie returned with him.

***

The hall was humid from all the hot and sweaty bodies dancing together. Kate wiped her brow and her hand came away damp. Her throat was parched and the thought of the sweet bubbles of a gin and tonic sliding across her tongue and tickling her nose made the supervision bearable... just.

Time for a break; Kate gulped in a deep breath and walked onto the balcony adjoining the hall. The breeze caressed her damp skin the moment she exited. Stretched before her was a clear, black sky dotted with sparkling stars. The days were clinging to the last traces of summer.

Moisture pooled at the base of her neck. She pulled her hair up into a make-shift ponytail and enjoyed how it cooled her down immediately.

She stood still and closed her eyes. A nineties song from her childhood started playing and pulsed loud in her ears. She smiled remembering her own school dances, all those years ago.

She let her arms drop and her hair returned to her shoulders. When she opened her eyes, she squinted, allowing them to adjust to the darkness. Kate glanced around her. Boys and girls were clinging together in each corner of the octagonal terrace; their bodies merging as one shadow.

Thank goodness Mrs. Peterson wasn't on duty. The principal would go ballistic. And damn, Kate had forgotten her Bible. The one she had to use to measure the appropriate distance between the dancers, and more usually, pull them apart for being indecently close. It was a funny, yet archaic rule. She looked around her to make sure activities were not out of hand. One tall figure stood out at the far edge, reaching above the height of some bushy foliage. A flash of disco light illuminated the pot

20

plant and the figure behind it.

Kate turned and inspected the other silhouettes. None of the teenagers were that tall and everyone stood in pairs.

Odd.

She took careful steps across the balcony and toward the far railing. Apprehension crept up her spine with each stride. The figure moved as she approached. That couldn't be a coincidence, surely? She stopped, and her stomach dropped. Whilst she took her supervision duties seriously, she didn't honestly think she'd need to protect the children tonight from anyone but themselves and the danger of raging hormones. The figure sidestepped again, dodging another plant. The person came to a halt behind it, attempting to conceal themselves. It was futile. Fluorescent eyes beamed out of the blackness.

Evie's father.

Those eyes shone like the stars she'd been admiring moments before. Her pulse raced at the prospect of being near Nick again. Whilst excitement made her heart thump, her chest tightened.

What did she really know about Nick Harding?

He was well-groomed and neat, smiled so as not to appear rude but avoided conversation, appeared to care deeply for his daughter and yet didn't seem to trust her and was present yet absent at the same time.

So, that all added up to nothing, really. She didn't know the guy at all.

One thing was for sure, he was intense. But his face lit up when he smiled.

None of it added up.

Why would any ordinary parent lurk in the darkness at their daughter's year seven disco?

'Odd' was the only answer that made sense. Nick Harding was *unusual*. Prickles crawled up Kate's back and uneasiness sat square in her chest. She hoped it was merely oddness and nothing more sinister.

Who was this guy? He fought for justice? So did she and her job was to protect her students. Her sense of righteousness arrived and wouldn't be shaken. She was the children's guardian tonight. Her responsibility. It was her duty to ensure their safety did not become compromised. Before she could talk herself out of it, she marched over to him.

'What are you doing here?' Her voice came out harsher than she'd intended.

***

It was the teacher.

His heart sank. No, not now, not tonight. His shoulders sat solid, tense with the emotion of the evening. Kate Penrose intrigued him, dare he say, excited him even, but he had one mission tonight and he didn't need distraction. His ears burned red. Nothing about this situation could paint him in a suitable light. How did she see him in the shadows? With a deepening sense of dread, he understood it looked ridiculous, humiliating and at best, strange. What could he say that would make sense?

Damn it. She headed his way at a quick pace. Nick extracted his phone and concentrated on whatever page popped open. At least then he couldn't be accused of ogling young people pashing. When she spoke, he came out from behind the bush, hands up, defeated.

'I'm waiting for Evie.'

Kate screwed up her face and turned her head quizzically to one side, appearing to size up his answer. She crossed her arms and placed one foot in front of the other. Her narrowed eyes matched her tight lips. He'd underestimated her. Explanations spun through his mind, and words formed on his tongue. As an expert at keeping his cool, his clients could tell him the most abhorrent of stories and he would not elicit even a flicker or blink of an eye by way of reaction. He needed to do that now and tuned into that zone. His facial features became unreadable and he remained silent.

He watched the battle going on in the teacher's mind, her expression an open book. Her stance loosened and she uncrossed her arms. She opened her mouth but closed it again. Her reaction would be amusing except for his embarrassment.

'Okay.' Kate dragged out the word, making it clear his response was unsatisfactory. 'It's only seven-thirty, and the dance finishes at nine. So why are you so early, and why are you not out the front waiting in the main area?'

Nick built barriers around himself. He stood up taller using his height to his advantage. Her tone made him sound like an idiot. He didn't need to justify himself to her. His stubborn streak kicked in, but he was never going to reveal the real reason he lurked around like a common vagabond. Sucking in two deep breaths, he agreed on a different approach. Silence had not worked so far.

'This is Evie's first year seven dance. I'm an anxious dad. I want to ensure, like any responsible parent, that she's safe and secure and there isn't anything funny going on.'

'Funny?' The first hint of a smile appeared.

That smile almost made him crumble. Almost. Her voice and teasing smile; it wasn't flirtatious, wasn't sexy or tempting. It exuded innocence, fun and a cuteness that he found irresistible. Even the prospect that this pretty teacher could captivate him fascinated him. Perhaps in his cutthroat world of crims and arguments and endless conflict, he found her enlightening, harmless and pure. An angel might be standing before him. He swallowed his laugh before it escaped his lips because there wasn't anything amusing about his current dilemma. In professional mode, he had to pull himself together and take this up a notch. No more giving in to priceless smiles, he had a job to do and a serious problem and he didn't want her involved.

'Mrs. Penrose, I appreciate this isn't usual, but I needed to ensure Evie was safe. I've done what I thought was right. I thank you for supervising and I now realise there are numerous teachers in attendance tonight, more than enough to guarantee student wellbeing. With those assurances, I'll wait for Evie at the front entrance where it is perfectly well-lit and continue the work I was doing before I was interrupted.' Nick held up his phone as proof. He stifled a groan. This luminous young woman would think he sounded like a stuffy, pretentious old man.

Worst thing was— he did.

Glass shattered to the ground near Kate's feet and a shove pushed her sideways. Swinging fists went back and forth and a scuffle broke out between two teenage boys. Kate jumped straight between the young men whilst directionless thumps were made. Nick watched her duck twice. She was tenacious, he'd give her that. He winced as one young boy's balled fist connected with the other's jaw. Nick didn't want to get involved. He didn't. Invisible was his only aim and he was failing miserably already. He raked his hand through his hair as he watched Kate try to control them. Dammit! He stepped in and held one boy by his collar, nearly lifting him off his feet and placed a flat palm to the other's chest.

Other teachers came to assist. A male supervisor held one boy whilst Kate detained the other. Both continued to mutter profanities. Kate's hair was tussled around her face that glistened with a light sheen of perspiration. His heart tugged at the sight of her, but Nick forced himself to step back. The situation was under control and his assistance was no longer required. Now was his chance to slip away.

The distraction of both Kate and the fight meant that he still hadn't observed Evie and ensured she was safe. He'd have to hope she milled amongst the thronging crowd indoors, jumping obscenely to songs he'd never heard before.

***

Kate noticed Nick's absence the moment the balcony cleared. Where was he? A hot flare of anger ignited. Not only had they been interrupted, she still hadn't thanked him properly for his assistance on the first day of term. Kate felt unsettled— at seeing him or his strange behaviour, she couldn't be sure. Probably both, the guy was an enigma. Damn him, this man who presented as a mystery. She didn't like the peculiar. Kate liked to know what was going on and to understand a situation. Despite her eagle-eye observations, she didn't spot him again during the disco.

At nine p.m. on the dot, bright lights burned into student faces, forcing figures apart. En masse, they spilled from the hall. Kate remained inside, herding them out like cows. Some lingered, wanting the night to continue, several held onto hands of new friends, but most tidied themselves, wiped their sweaty palms down their skirts or pant legs, before the inevitable reunion with parents. Kate delighted at their innocence, the flush of blossoming love and young fun.

Once outside, she observed parents huddled in groups, their necks craning to spot their child.

Nick stood a head above the other adults as he stayed to the side with a clear view of the students. He frowned, his eyebrows joining his crinkled forehead whilst his eyes scanned the melee. Kate rolled her eyes when Brittany sidled up next to him, leaning in too close.

Nick craned his neck toward the staircase, ignoring her. Kate's heart skipped a beat; not everyone fell under Brittany's spell. Despite the few metres between them, Kate sensed Nick's discomfort mounting until he moved away from Brittany and skirted through the crowd. He hurried up the stairs, two at a time before pausing at the top.

Kate rotated left and right, attempting to spot Evie. Flashes of colour and an array of hairstyles passed her but no distinctive blonde curls. Kate saw Brittany fold her arms across her breasts, scowling with her foot stamping. Coco-Sage was nowhere in sight either. The crowd around Kate thinned as the minutes passed. Children said goodbye to friends and accepted lifts. She took the stairs back up to the hall. A couple of the staff were inside collecting rubbish. Where was Evie? Kate hoped that the next time she ventured outside, Nick would be cuddling Evie and asking about her first high school dance.

She walked toward the rear of the hall to help with the clean-up duties. A bruising grip on her arm caught her half way. She spun around and her eyes widened. Nick's grasp was too tight and she was about to object but his pinched expression stopped her.

'I can't find Evie.' His eyes hammered into hers, fear striking out of them.

'Okay, I'll help. I'm sure she's here. I'll go this way, you check that direction.' Nick obeyed and raced away. At that exact moment, Evie walked out of the girls bathroom with a friend.

'Evie!' Kate shouted.

Evie turned and acknowledged Kate, offering her an uncertain wave. Nick hurried across the hall, and Kate followed more slowly. She watched him regain his composure before coming to a stop in front of the two girls. His broad chest expanded as he sucked in deep breaths. When he eventually spoke, his voice came out even but forced.

'Evie, I couldn't find you. You said you'd be at the door at nine.' He looked down at her with his head tilted. In different circumstances, it would have made Kate melt with desire.

Evie's laugh was low and she covered her mouth with one hand as she turned away from her father, to titter to her friend in secret. Together, they ignored Kate and Nick and continued their giggling conversation. Nick's hands jerked at his sides. Even Kate wanted to give her a good shake up. Nick remained steadfast, patient, staring at her, waiting. Kate was intimidated by his demeanour and gaze; how could Evie not be? Eventually, she couldn't ignore it.

'I needed to go to the toilet, Dad, okay? It's no big deal. It is,' and she made an exaggerated reading of her wristwatch, 'exactly, nine eleven. I'm not that late.'

Watching the exchange, Kate had to agree, despite Evie's attitude. She hadn't realised the time. It had felt like over thirty minutes but less than eleven had elapsed since the lights illuminated the room. It was hardly a long passage of time by anyone's standards. Conscious they were the only people left in the hall and their voices echoed around the vast space, Kate watched them both, wondering how Nick would respond. She should leave them alone. Evie had been found and her presence was no longer required.

But, she couldn't drag herself away.

A throbbing vein pulsed in Nick's neck. What was he so worried about? Opposite him, stood his daughter, flushed with embarrassment or the fun of the night, who knew?

'Let's go.' Evie strode away ahead of her father.

Nick turned without a word and shadowed Evie as they headed into the darkness of the night.

CHAPTER FIVE

'Hey, mate. I need a drink and some company. Are you free to come over?'

'On my way.'

Nick relaxed as he disconnected. Curtis would be straight over; he was Nick's closest friend.

Nick couldn't talk to most people about his job, but Curtis was different. Friends since high school, they knew each other well and after Curtis had joined the force - whilst on opposing sides— they both dealt with the seedier side of life. They were always bantering back and forth about the legal system and those worthy of justice. Most of the time they disagreed, but nonetheless they still talked and understood each other. He was grateful for the friendship.

Nick sank into an armchair before his legs gave way. His limbs ached, like he'd run a marathon. His chest was tight, too. He emitted a deep sigh but it didn't help at all.

Half an hour later Curtis sat with him in the study, enjoying a scotch. Another thing they shared, they both liked their liquor hard. With each sip, the cloud hanging over Nick evaporated a little more.

'You working nights at the moment?' Nick held his glass up and the ice tinkled.

'Nah. Days off. I go back on Monday. Having a whole weekend without walking the beat sure is good.'

Nick nodded.

'How's Evie settling into school?'

'Yeah, good. She only tells me bits and pieces but she's made some new friends and can find her way around the campus at least.' Nick laughed. 'It's the little things, you know? She said she had trouble opening her locker, for example, and that made her late for class. But the organisational stuff is settling down.'

'She's a smart kid. She'll work it out.'

'She had her first disco tonight.'

'Yeah. I remember those days…'

'Yes, me too. But these are strictly supervised. I'm surprised they don't pull out the nuns to scare the poor beggars into compliance.'

'Sounds like every parent's wish.'

'Unfortunately, I acted like a bit of an arse, in front of one of the teachers, too.'

'What, you didn't make a pass at her did you, not in front of Evie?' Curtis' smile was broad, awaiting further detail.

'No! God, I do have some decency.'

Nick reached for the bottle, anything to avoid admitting the truth. 'It involves something else I'll tell you about, but because of this, this, other thing, I stayed lurking in the bushes at school to make sure Evie was safe and this teacher found me hiding behind a pot-plant.'

Nick looked at Curtis. Both men doubled over in their seats with laughter.

'Do you understand she probably thinks you're some sort of sicko leering at young children?'

Nick stopped laughing. 'No joke, I believe she does. I had some quick explaining to do, making up all this stuff about being an anxious parent!'

Curtis laughed harder. 'Glad I don't have kids to worry about this stuff. But it's funny. What caused you to do that? It's not like you to be weird. You're many things, my friend, but I wouldn't call you that. What aren't you telling me?'

The warmth of the alcohol faded and ice chilled Nick's veins.

'I should have shared this with you ages ago. I've been keeping it to myself. Hoping, and honestly believing that the problem would disappear. Stupid, I'm not a kid anymore. I should know better.' Nick shook his head and tilted the ice cubes in his empty glass until they clinked. 'I'm afraid this is going to be a case of you told me so.' He rubbed his hands over his face. 'And me being too stubborn to listen.'

Curtis remained blank-faced.

'It's all gone to shit, basically, over my own greed and ego. Remember about eighteen months ago, I started acting for members of the Warlocks bikie gang?'

Curtis nodded, but his cheeks paled and his gaze was intense.

Nick's stomach churned. 'In the beginning it was all petty stuff. Break and enters, assault, trespass, those sorts of crimes. I got lucky. The members I acted for were acquitted, most on trivial details, others for lack of evidence or similar.'

Curtis gestured with his hand, indicating he should continue. This wasn't news and now wasn't the time to argue about the rights and wrongs of guilty persons freed on technicalities.

'Anyway, let's fast forward. It progressed well. For a long time, I received a steady stream of business and I became the gang's go-to criminal defence lawyer. I've acted for most of them and it's a sizeable club. Over time they became bolder and more daring or I guess, I became aware of more serious crimes being committed. They assured me of their innocence and proclaimed a great sense of righteousness.' Nick shrugged. 'But, they paid well and that's unusual in my job. I was stoked. But, like you, my business partner warned me against it and said no good could possibly result from working for professional criminals and those that flout the law so brazenly. I'm sure he was more worried about the firm's reputation than anything else.' Nick slammed his hand on the arm of the sofa. 'Damn it, you know me, Curtis. I'm the man who fights for the underdog and has always paid heed to the creed that everyone deserves legal representation, even those who are guilty—'

'Fair enough,' Curtis interjected.

'But then, you remember that the leader of the gang was charged with some very serious offences— torture, deprivation of liberty, and after the investigation by your mob, murder. This took us into the big league. Do you remember how excited I was? Like a little kid. You saw me on the news most nights at the time. I loved the exposure. All publicity in this industry is good for business.'

'But. You didn't get him off.'

Nick nodded. 'That's right. No defences applied and he wasn't mentally ill and the police...You have to place this in context, it was around the time of the violent offender legislation, the Premier raging against bikies and their associations were the target.'

'I remember, the government rode to success on those laws…'

'Anyway, cut to the chase, I couldn't get him off and no surprise, Max Vincenzo did not appreciate a sentence of life imprisonment. Nor did the gang who were without a leader.' Nick smacked his forehead with the flat of his palm, as if knocking sense into himself. 'Stupidly, I thought that was it. I'd run a good defence and you know, if you're found guilty of murder, there's only one result. It wasn't like I could mitigate much against a life sentence, particularly where the offences were so violent. Plus, I'd had a high success rate. I honestly thought I'd get him off. But you can't win them all, right? And I can't accept that the Warlocks would think I had the ability to perform the impossible. More importantly, though,' Nick sat forwards and he thrummed with tension. 'He was locked away from the community. What could he possibly do? As it turns out, a lot, with the help of his followers.'

'What do you mean exactly? What's happened?'

'Well, that's it, nothing's happened. I've received email threats. Against my life. And in the last message, threats against my family.' Nick held up his hand to silence the questions he could see Curtis wanting to ask. 'No, it didn't mention anyone by name.'

'Okay. Do you actually know it's the gang?'

'No.'

'Are there any other clues?'

'No.'

'Are you still acting for them?'

'What? No!'

'Do they know where you live?'

'No.'

'Do they know anything about you personally? That you have a daughter?'

'No. I guarded my privacy diligently. I never spoke about Evie.'

'Stupid question I guess, but have you spoken to the police.'

Nick didn't answer that one, only shook his head. He kept talking to avoid Curtis' lecture.

'I know it's not relevant. But they also haven't paid their last legal bill for the defence of Max. So, on top of everything else, my firm is pissed off with me and that describes the situation in pleasant terms. It costs thousands to run a criminal murder trial.'

Curtis nodded and paused, as if he digested all that information.

'There's nothing I can add here, mate. You know my position on this and that's why you've kept it a secret. You have to involve the cops. But you won't, will you?'

'You know me too well. I won't report it to the police. Do you understand what I'm dealing with here? One of the most prolific and dangerous bikie gangs in Brisbane.' Nick's chest sliced in two as he spoke the words. 'I know what they are capable of.'

'Mate, this is too much. Deep shit. Show me the messages. You've kept them, haven't you?'

Nick stared at him. The-do-you-think-I'm-stupid look. 'My business is gathering evidence, after all.' Opening up his laptop, Nick logged in to his email account but instead of retrieving the messages from the folder he'd saved them to, he reclined in his office chair, silent.

'You've found them?' Curtis stood behind him, slapping him on the shoulder as if to hurry him up. Nick didn't answer and Curtis leaned over, scanning the screen. Nick pointed his finger at one entry, illuminated in red, unopened, in his inbox.

'YOU'RE GONNA GET IT THIS TIME' stood out in bold. Nick rose and moved away from the desk. He'd read it on an alcohol-fuelled stomach and re-filled his glass. The scotch burned his throat as he swallowed. But he didn't need to read it. Curtis' voice was loud as he enunciated each nasty word. Nick stopped himself from doubling over with the weight of the threat. The air emptied from his lungs when he heard the one word he was desperate not to – Evie. No longer able to bear his own weight, he sat with a thump. Curtis handed him another drink and he tossed it back. It helped loosen the knot sitting square in his chest.

Five threats. He'd been kidding himself, hadn't he? And, potentially put his daughter's life at risk. They were in trouble.

CHAPTER SIX

'Dad! It's been weeks since school started. I know where I'm going. You do not have to walk me to the front gate,' Evie pleaded.

'I am aware that I don't have to and am now fully coherent with the fact that you do not wish me to, but I want to escort you safely to school.' Nick stood unyielding, facing Evie, her slight body hunched over with the weight of her school bag. She inched closer to him. Nick leaned forward also, presumably ready for his good-bye kiss.

'Dad, see those cars pulling into the kerb? Those are normal kids being dropped off. They aren't escorted to the gate like a preppie. Tomorrow, I'm catching the bus!' Evie stormed off.

Kate overheard the exchange standing one metre away at the school crossing. It was hard, but she stifled her smile. Nick Harding had difficult days of parenting ahead if he did not loosen the reigns over Evie. Kate turned back to scan the horde of girls. On duty, her official job was to ensure their safety as they crossed the busy main road fronting the premises. But really, she searched for students not wearing their appropriate school uniform. Welcome to a brand new day at Trinity – here's your detention for forgetting your hat. It wasn't a job to be envied, but at least she did it with a smile.

Before she'd heard Evie, she'd detected Nick's presence. It freaked her out. How was that even possible? The guy had an aura that preceded him wherever he went. Perhaps it was because his physical bulk filled every available space around him and sucked away the oxygen out of the air. Looking over her shoulder, Kate sighed with contentment. Nick Harding deserved admiration: a Greek god respected for their form and shape. Were they not also renowned for their fearlessness? He struck her as that sort, afraid of nothing. God damn him for being here. His close proximity made her palms clammy, her mouth dry and her heart gallop. It was ridiculous, she didn't even know the guy! She detested her body's betrayal but loved the buzz it gave her. All her senses tingled, became heightened and alert. She felt alive and her smile beamed wider.

Upset, Evie had raced away. Now, Nick stood alone at the paved driveway entrance to the school. No other parent was in sight. Girls pushed past him and two or three stared in his direction with glassy-eyed looks. Apprehension found Kate. That similar sense of dread that had crept up her spine at the disco when she'd found Nick lurking behind the ferns.

No doubt about it, he demonstrated some odd behaviour. She tried to force the sinking feeling out of her stomach, but it lodged there, not budging. It brought her back to earth with a thud, dampening those heightened senses. Her elation burst like a popping balloon.

Without blinking, she strode over. She'd done a lot of that recently where he was concerned, not thinking before acting. Her feet slipped in her leather shoes at the heat of the summer morning. Nick stood behind a brick pillar watching the back of Evie as she disappeared into the grounds.

'Good morning, Mr Harding. How are you today?'

His face tightened when he turned in her direction. Kate sensed he wanted to roll his eyes.

Did he dislike her?

At least, he had the decency to look embarrassed, again. 'I'm well, thank you, Kate.'

The cheek of him becoming so personal with her!

'Is there something I can help you with?'

'No, thank you. I was just dropping Evie off.' His jaw sat clenched and he crossed his arms across his chest.

Defensive? That didn't stop him boring those penetrating blue eyes in her direction. They glowed aquamarine today in the bright sun. Always so intense; like he had a thousand issues on his mind that weighed him down. But perhaps his stare was more of a challenge then interest in her? She imagined most people would be compelled to back down at its power. Kate maintained eye-contact but yes, those eyes sure did distract her. She shuffled her feet as she felt off kilter. One moment her blood ran hot at the sight of him, the next, he caused chills to race up her spine.

'I've been sending emails to you for weeks but you haven't responded.' Kate waited for platitudes and excuses or an apology. Instead, Nick surprised her by remaining silent.

She carried on, her words rushing out too fast. 'It's about the music tour. I need you to return the permission slip and make a deposit to allow Evie to participate. It's one of the most significant events of the school year. Well, it is, if you're in year seven and a music student.'

Was he listening? Kate regarded him, trying to ascertain whether he had been hooked like most parents at the mention of the unique tour. It usually worked. Most parents believed their daughter was extraordinary and talented and would have returned the slip within twenty-four hours. Nick hadn't.

He didn't even blink.

Out of nowhere a tanned arm snaked around his torso. Brittany engulfed him in an embrace. Nick startled and shifted sideways, out of her grip. Kate took a step backwards, too, creating space between them.

'Hello, Nick. How lovely to see you again. Where have you been hiding? I haven't seen you for ages.' Brittany dragged on a cigarette before releasing a puff of smoke that drifted up and away.

Kate coughed, covering up a giggle when Nick didn't respond. He frowned and manoeuvred further out of her reach, inching along the path. Disappointment palpitated off Brittany. With her free arm, she clutched at her bright blue Hermes handbag, tugging on those bag straps while her other hand held her cigarette aloft. 'We must arrange a time for our girls to catch up. Perhaps a weekend movie, lunch or maybe a shopping trip?'

Kate looked from one to the other.

What was wrong with Nick? He stood mute and non-responsive. The man didn't even fake a smile to combat the circling tension. But Kate knew Brittany would demand an answer and wouldn't be dissuaded. With eager expectation, Brittany gazed at him with her ogling eyes and waited, tapping her foot. Even Kate became uncomfortable with the silence. Why didn't he say something?

Finally, Nick cleared his throat. 'Evie is busy most weekends with school work and, um, other activities.' It was obvious his words held no sincerity. Embarrassment hung in the air. Kate turned toward Brittany, eager to observe her reaction. Her job of pulling up recalcitrant school girls was completely forgotten; students could roam free today inappropriately dressed. Kate hoped Mrs. Peterson wouldn't notice.

'Oh, don't be so silly. Of course she has time. Even my Coco-Sage, who is engaged in a range of activities to ensure her all round well-being, has time to have fun. I'll contact you and we'll arrange something. Okay, bye then. Gotta run. I'm off to pilates followed by lunch at Gerards. Have a great day, toodaloo!' Leaving behind a swirl of smoke and perfume aroma, she strode away.

Kate's mouth hung open. Did Brittany not detect that she'd been brushed off? More likely, she'd refuse to accept it as a possibility. Kate was sure most people didn't reject a Brittany Bartholomew invitation.

Nick turned away from Kate, as if forgetting she stood there and walked off. For a fleeting second, Kate thought about running after him.

Damn it! She still didn't have his permission for the music tour. She wanted to stamp her foot as she stood alone on the path, but resisted. Every interaction with Nick Harding ended in frustration.

All girls were now safely in their allocated classrooms, the traffic had eased, and the day had taken on the beautiful lull that occurred after school had commenced. It was a peaceful transcendence. But Kate didn't feel peaceful. What had she witnessed? Was there something wrong with Nick Harding or was he simply rude and unfriendly? Sinister? Or did he simply dislike Brittany Bartholomew? She couldn't figure him out, but she did know that Brittany was one of a kind and would not give up. If that woman wanted something, she would not surrender until she'd captured it in her French-manicured hands.

Ignoring the rambunctious behaviour of her students as she entered homeroom, Kate headed straight for Evie. 'Is everything okay, Evie?'

The girl looked up.

'Yes, Miss, everything's okay.' But as if that had been the wrong answer, she said, 'the same as the other day, if that's what you mean.'

'No, no, I wasn't referring to that. I tried to gain your father's permission to participate in the music tour and he didn't provide it, or even indicate if he'd read the correspondence.'

Evie grimaced. 'I have talked to him, he's aware of it. He's not keen for me to travel overseas by myself. It's such a long way and all that, but I'm working on him. Usually he comes 'round after he evaluates it. He needs to digest the information before he's prepared to commit.'

'It's actually becoming a problem. We need final numbers and deposits have to be paid and arrangements confirmed. There's lots of preparation for these trips and it takes many weeks. We are running out of time, Evie, and this is such an important trip for you, for your music education and self-development.'

The young girl nodded.

Kate didn't mention that Mrs. Peterson was breathing down her back about preparations. Evie was a talented flautist. For the trip to be a success, she needed her to attend.

'If I need to provide permission now, well, I guess I can't go,' Evie shrugged.

Nausea settled in Kate's stomach. She wanted this for Evie but why did she care so much? If Evie wasn't part of the ensemble travelling overseas to perform, then another student would be soloist. Kate couldn't bear the thought, but only because Evie was the best, right? The blossoming fear of failure sprouted deep down. Kate wanted to bury those buds of doubt. This was an opportunity to demonstrate her skills in organising a successful year seven music tour, but it threatened to collapse around her. But Nick's face kept popping up: dare she admit that this project had a tenuous connection to the attractive parent? Or did Evie need protecting from an overbearing father, one who was suffocating and strict? Or, did she feel sorry for the girl? If honest, it was probably all these reasons. Either way, she determined that Evie would be on this music tour and her prodigal student would shine as the star she deserved to be. Kate would help this young, vulnerable girl in whatever way she could. Or at least until she figured out what was really going on. Kate refused to acknowledge the burgeoning emotion the girl's father evoked in her. She was Evie's teacher; she had a duty of care to her. She had to do the right thing, and everything had to be perfect.

##

Kate read the fifth email Brittany Bartholomew had sent that day. All contained similar information: requests that Coco-Sage be the captain of the netball team, make the A division of the debating team, be front and centre in the cheer squad performance, appear in the school musical as lead no less and lastly, be the star attraction on the music tour. Unlike Nick, Brittany had returned Coco-Sage's permission form within minutes, paid the amount owing in full for the trip plus extra for incidentals.

Did this woman believe that Kate controlled all extra-curricular pursuits in the curriculum?

She had to be kidding. Kate chewed the lipstick from her lips and tugged at her crayon pencil earrings. This parent was becoming a problem. Kate had not yet decided if Brittany's over-zealous behaviour could be laughed over in the tearoom with her colleagues or was more alarming.

She guessed she'd find out.

CHAPTER SEVEN

Nick drove his Land Rover Discovery home on autopilot. A red Mercedes had cut him off and he didn't even flinch. The morning had not progressed as planned. He'd simply wanted to escort Evie safely to school. It wasn't an unusual arrangement, but Evie had other ideas. He'd have to change track; he risked suffocating her with his fears, and the 'what ifs'.

Sitting in the cool air-conditioning of the car he waited for the electric gate to open. His guts churned. It was a new sensation. Even his most difficult legal cases didn't make him ill. Only one obsession did; something happening to his daughter. The thought twisted like a knife in his heart and his stomach protracted like he'd been hit with a closed fist. Evie had been through so much in her short life: losing her junkie mother, moving schools and having a transient early life. He'd provided for her, but had not always been present.

He slammed the door with unnecessary force as he got out. Ridiculous, that's how he'd describe himself at present. Nick Harding didn't lose control and he certainly didn't brood. He dominated others: in the courtroom, on the sports field and in general life. With steely resolve, he vowed this situation would not overtake him, he needed to stay calm— for Evie. Determined to be a better parent, he would not sway from his duties now. Resolute, more than ever, he would keep her safe.

Nine a.m. was too early for a drink, not that he'd seriously resort to drinking alcohol at this hour, but the option comforted him. Coffee would have to suffice.

Kicking the machine into action in his industrial kitchen, the metallic surfaces all around him gleamed. He fumbled, not used to the espresso maker but after pressing a few random buttons, it hissed into life. He didn't usually work from home, but suddenly it had become a permanent arrangement. His business partner had readily accepted the proposition when he'd pitched it to him. He was fast becoming a liability to the firm but he'd worry about that later, Evie was his top priority. To stay available to her, he'd continue to hide away at home. As the coffee machine spluttered, he cursed and looked to the heavens.

Perhaps he'd get Mrs. Travers, his housekeeper, to assist during the day, too. At least she could make him a hot drink without any difficulty. Nick made a mental note to ask her and to give her a pay rise for the great job she did in caring for him and Evie. He couldn't afford to lose her, particularly not at the moment. Her domestic help made his life easier and ensured not only that Evie ate healthy meals but that an adult was always at home. It was nice to have a female presence, like a grandmother, around the place, too.

After the machine finally cooperated, Nick took a large sip of his coffee. As the caffeine pulsed through his veins, he breathed in deeply and focused. Evie sat secure in her classroom and while he may not be in the office, work still beckoned. The Chalk file had sat on his desk requiring attention for three days now. Usually, he'd have read the file, police reports and other documents moreover so that it was memorised and he'd have identified the gaps in evidence. Dr Richard Chalk, psychiatrist, a new client, prestigious—in the medical world anyway— deserved his concentration.

Entering his study, he pushed a button on the remote control to open the curtain and allow bright sunshine to fill the space. Fifteen minutes in and he'd responded to his urgent emails—none that important in his opinion – an enquiry from a previous client about a traffic offence; children busted for smoking dope at school and a prostitute worried about interruptions to her business from dodgy clientele. Nothing unusual in his line of work. None of it made his spine tingle or excitement creep in. These days, it took major crimes for him to break out in a sweat.

Would Dr Chalk deliver?

The doctor did. The renowned anaesthetist had killed his wife who had terminal cancer. Euthanized her would be the word Nick used in his defence whereas the prosecution would prefer murder. His adrenalin flowed with the turn of each page and his mind drifted to his day in court, the prospect of a hard-fought legal case and getting an acquittal in a case no one considered a winner.

As the case fought for space in his brain, he paused to gaze through the large bay window to collect his thoughts in a coherent order. The windows were the feature in his study. He'd pondered many a legal battle looking through them. His manicured lawn, trimmed hedges and the glistening swimming pool always calmed him. Inevitably, it swelled his heart with contentment. He'd worked hard to achieve this house and his life. But today this place, his home, was a safe haven, a paradise where his family couldn't be disturbed.

An unusual lump of blackness caught his eye, contrasted against the green of the grass. Squinting, his eyes zeroed in on it. Was it rubbish or a clump of fallen tree? It sat at an odd angle and had an unusual shape. Usually, he wouldn't interrupt his work, but scanning the yard, he spotted various other objects scattered about. Nick shot out of the chesterfield leather chair. At full height the broad window provided a clear view of the side garden. Carnage. Shit everywhere. His thoughts splintered in all directions so that he couldn't grasp them fast enough. His once open expanse of lawn, trimmed and neat with matching hedges and blossoming flowers, was covered with debris across its span.

Brown feathers, claws…

His mind couldn't comprehend what his eyes saw. Nick raced down the long hallway to the laundry and the exit to the yard. In his rush, he stumbled, his feet not carrying him fast enough.

Nick paused, not afraid of entering, but of what he'd find. He yanked the concertina door open, smashing it sideways. Objects hung from his tall concrete fence. Except for the time of year and their colour, they might have been Christmas decorations. Nothing festive about this. He stopped at the first bundle. A dead chicken. The scene came into vision now – ten at first count, perhaps more. Feathers floated in the breeze, catching in bushes and branches and against the hardness of the house. Necks detached from bodies, legs broken, dried blood around their beaks. He craned his neck to take in the spectacle. Along the fence, the birds had been flung over and hung from rope, their necks cracked in the process. Upon close inspection, beady eyes stared back at him. He yanked on the rope, burning his palms but the animals didn't move.

Nick peered at the upstairs windows, shining back at him silently. Did the curtain in his bedroom move? Was someone in his house? Running so fast he almost lost his balance, he tore on his heels into the house, examining each room. With the first floor secured, he approached the second and did the same: opened each wardrobe door, checked behind closed ones and around corners, under furniture. The house sat quiet compared to his loud heartbeat.

Confident no intruders were in the house, Nick paused to catch his breath before running back to the paved pool area. They'd only gained access to the lawn. The objects now scattered in his yard must have been flung over his high boundary. Thank God for the expensive security system he thought he'd never need.

He rolled the wheelie bin from the garage and collected a shovel. As if possessed, he extracted each feather and loose claw and dumped them into the rubbish. The rope he cut with unnecessary force, almost severing the chickens as he did so. With almost all the waste disposed of, he came to the last bulge. It sat smaller and was a dark shade of grey, unlike the other traditional red hens. Nick's face screwed up in confusion and he had to cover his nose from the stench. Approaching closer, he gagged. A half-decomposed possum, a pest to most, its insides escaping, with flies and maggots feasting on the carcass.

Colour exploded amongst the grey fur. Blood? Another animal? Nick nudged it with the toe of his shoe, rolling it an inch to the side. A collar of bright blue choked the neck of the animal. Attached to it, sitting crooked with the bend of its body was a tag. Nick held his breath and leaned down close. It contained a green-stemmed rose with petals the colour of bright blood. The Warlocks logo.

His vision blurred. He'd known. No shock, it had always been them.

But here sat the evidence.

The Warlocks were out to get him and shit, he was scared. Bile rose in his throat. Like the wounded animals on his property, it felt like one was trapped inside him, like a demon. It clawed up his chest, biting and clamping along the way, ready to split his torso open. His fists clenched at his sides.

Nick fought to remain in control. So he moved. That dead possum was tossed in the bin without a second glance. Then, he scrubbed his fence, not once, but twice and wiped down the pavers beside his pool even though no animal had touched there. Next, he pressure-hosed his yard, soaking it with water and litres of detergent until it bore no trace of what had occurred. Not one single feather, nor the slightest aroma remained. Satisfied, Nick sank to his knees. Dr Chalk and his challenging legal case forgotten.

***

'C'mon girls, defend! Get the ball back down our end,' Kate screamed from the sidelines. It'd been years since she'd played and she'd forgotten how tense netball could be, particularly as a spectator.

'Hey, good looking! How's things?'

Kate turned to face Angela. 'Oh, hello, love! Where are you playing?'

'Over there.' Angela pointed to further afield, a spare concrete court where a bunch of girls were warming up with a fair dose of talking mixed in.

'What time's your game?'

'Any minute now, when you finish, I think. But I wanted to grab you quickly to save me a phone call later. We still on for cheap Tuesday?'

'Yes, definitely.' Kate replied. 'I'd forgotten it's Tuesday. What's showing?'

Angela shrugged, her black locks bouncing and her green eyes twinkling. 'Does it matter, we'll watch whatever, right? We chat through most of it anyway.'

Kate laughed. He friend always had her in stitches, something she'd needed over the last few years. Kate could never repay Angela's kindness. After Benjamin's death, she'd been her rock, and now, she'd helped Kate secure this new job, a fresh start and finally allowed her to get, not only her life, but her career on track. Whenever she broached her thanks, though, her friend brushed her off.

'That's what friends do.' It was the only time Angela's smile faltered, as if she did realise the lifeline she'd afforded Kate.

'Your team scored a screamer of a goal.'

'Shoot! I'd better watch, see you tonight at seven, my shout,' she

42

said as Angela turned back to her team.

For their first game, the girls had worked well together. Except, occasionally, the ball didn't get passed to certain players: those that tended to drop it or miss the crucial intercept. Coco-Sage darted in between her team mates, covering the court in her position as centre. This allowed her to direct the ball's play.

Kate squinted, paying particular attention to the girl. Coco-Sage was instrumental in each pass and often blocked a player to grab the ball. Then she directed it where she wanted whilst elbowing the opposition out of her way. Kate glanced at the umpire, shocked she wasn't pulled up for obstruction. Was there anything this kid didn't get away with?

'That's it, fantastic.' Kate cheered as Evie dropped another goal as the team's shooter. The bell dinged to signal the end of third quarter.

'Let's huddle. You girls are doing so well. You're keeping your cool and watching the ball and making smart moves. Okay, this quarter, we'll swap Gina from wing defence to the bench and sub in Emmy; Coco-Sage we'll move you into goal attack and Lucy is centre…'

'What? No. I only play centre,' Coco-Sage interrupted Kate, standing with her feet apart and legs locked. She gripped her C marked bib.

'I know you prefer centre, Coco-Sage, but it's our first game and we need to switch around to determine the best fits and how we all work together. You've done a great job so far but let's try you in this position.' Kate tossed her the GA marker. It fell to the ground, uncaught.

As the team walked to position, Coco-Sage sulked on the sidelines. Lucy walked up and collected the crumpled C bib and reluctantly, with a loud sigh, Coco-Sage attached it to her teammate's uniform, upside down. In the semi-circle, Evie and Coco-Sage didn't greet one another, but stood stiffly side by side and acted as enemies rather than co-players. After the bell, opposition players jostled for the ball, manoeuvring it around the court. The Trinity Royals Under 13 team struggled to gain traction. Three goals were taken in the first five minutes. Kate fiddled with her fairy bread earrings, twisting them so much her ears hurt. Only a few more goals and they'd be back in the game.

Lucy passed cleanly to Gemma. Coco-Sage and Evie were both in position to score a goal. Kate's back was ramrod straight. She longed for their practised play to work like magic on the court. Imagine if she coached a finals netball team. Mrs. Peterson would notice her then. The ball flew through the air in the right direction. Coco-Sage jumped up with a large lift off, arms stretched out and reaching high. Her left elbow connected with Evie's nose mid-flight, slamming into it with such force, Evie crumpled to the ground. Coco-Sage caught the shot. She aimed and the ball sailed through the air without touching the ring and sliding to victory. Kate's heart hammered with the thrill of the score. Coco-Sage danced a victory lap.

But the rest of the team crouched around Evie.

'Evie? Show me. Are you hurt?' Kate asked. With no response, she forced Evie's face upward so she could examine it. 'Ah, that's great, no blood. It's not broken or swollen,' Kate rubbed her fingers over Evie's face, checking for abrasions or bumps. Satisfied there was no damage, Kate sat back on her heels. Evie still didn't move.

'Evie, it's okay. You're not hurt. Let me help you up. There's still a few minutes left to play.' Tears spilled over Evie's cheeks that were pink and warm from playing.

'What is it?' Kate asked.

'Miss, it's her wrist, here.' Gemma pointed towards it. Kate leaned in and took a deep breath. Evie's wrist was swollen to double its size and starting to colour with a visible bump at her joint. Reaching over to examine it more closely, Kate used a feather light touch. Evie screamed and yanked her hand back and Kate fell backwards onto her bottom.

Fear clawed at her. Images of Benjamin laying prone on a similar hard surface filled the edges of her mind. Except, in her vision blood covered his face, neck and head. As she looked up, she could only see men gathered around them, talking swiftly in a language she didn't understand whilst gesticulating with their hands.

A shake to her arm pulled her back to the present. She was on the netball court with Evie motionless on the blue bitumen whilst her team mates offered comfort. Kate felt like her body lifted and floated above the scene. To the far side of the court, two girls stood away from the commotion. Coco-Sage and a friend snickered behind palmed hands.

'Get the medic,' Kate snapped. 'Quickly, Coco-Sage you go, now, and hurry up!'

An hour and ten minutes later Kate threw her mobile phone so that it landed on the plastic hospital seat in the emergency waiting room.

Where the hell was he?

Three messages.

No response.

The coffee in her styrofoam cup from the children's hospital vending machine had cooled. She sipped it and grimaced.

CHAPTER EIGHT

Nick held a scotch but didn't drink it. He'd made it by rote when he'd returned to the study. Instead, he sank into the sofa and sagged as the weight came off his aching body. He clenched and stretched each limb in turn. Whilst fit, he wasn't used to physical work.

A distant buzzing sound echoed but it didn't register as his mind tossed over what had just happened.

The vibrating started again.

His phone. Damn it!

He jumped up fast and the amber liquid spilled on his jeans leg. The glass dropped silently and the rest of its contents leaked onto the cream coloured carpet. At his desk he followed the noise and tossed papers aside until he located the phone under Dr Chalk's police statement. Swiping the screen left, it filled with messages. Three unanswered calls from a private mobile number he didn't recognise. Apprehension gripped him around his middle. Two unanswered calls from Trinity Girls' College.

Shit.

Nick's fingers trembled as he pressed return call. As he listened, Nick grabbed his car keys and headed out the door.

***

'Where have you been?' Kate asked before the hospital sling back doors had returned to position. Nick didn't notice her balled fists or high clipped pitch. He didn't notice much at all and didn't have time for Kate or her accusations.

'Where's Evie?'

Kate flung her arms in the air. 'If you had answered your phone the five times we've called, you would know where Evie is. She's in the hospital obviously, being treated. We've been here, let me see,' she held up her arm and read her watch, 'over an hour and a half. One and a half hours she's been here asking for her dad and me having to tell her I didn't know where you were.'

'What's wrong with her? Is she hurt? Did someone do something?' It took all his strength not to shake the woman to get answers.

'Yes, she's hurt, that's why we are here.' She spoke to him like he had a learning impairment and struggled to understand the words. He watched her chest rise and fall, gulping in air. Oh God, was she hyperventilating? He needed answers before she lost it.

The teacher with the preppie, tailored clothes and the red lipstick not only on her lips but streaked across her top teeth was only warming up.

A snarl curled off her lips. 'What sort of parent are you?' It came out a question but she kept on talking with no opportunity for him to defend himself. 'You can't leave your daughter alone. You escort her to school every day and collect her, basically leading her from the premises.' She nodded her head emphatically. 'Spy on her at social events *hiding behind pot plants* and yet cannot answer a simple email, return a permission slip, answer non-urgent phone calls let alone urgent ones, and are not available when she does actually need you.'

She paused. He thought it was to take a breath but she wrinkled her nose and said, 'Have you been drinking?' A look of disgust rested on her features.

Each word stabbed him in the heart; the quickest way to wound a person was to attack their parenting. People in the crowded waiting room stared. Nurses stopped tending to wounds and listened. Security lingered in the corridor. Only doctors in scrubs with more on their minds than a domestic spat, kept about their business.

'What? No!' Nick yanked her elbow and pulled her into the nearest cubicle surrounded by a flimsy cotton sheet that he flung on its rim to give them a semblance of privacy.

'How dare you! Firstly, you stand there accusing me of things

47

you know nothing about, that are none of your business, and secondly, you've ranted and raved at me and still haven't advised me about my daughter.' Spittle flew from his mouth. He needed to hit something. Moving across the space, he slammed his fist on the pathetic side table adjacent to the hospital bed. A metal dish with instruments lifted in the air and landed with a clang. An animal grunt escaped from him. He returned to Kate's side and peered into her face.

She cowered. Her eyes widened and pooled with tears. She shrunk from him as if he might strike her.

Bile rose in his throat for the second time that day. He'd made a woman shrink in fear. That was something his misbehaving clients did because they were not intelligent enough to control their emotions or their flailing limbs. They were unable to connect their actions to the thoughts in their brain quick enough. He clamped his hands to his sides. 'God, I'm so sorry. I'm worried about Evie.'

Kate pulled a handkerchief from her pocket keeping her eyes trained on him. She was too frightened to look away in case he hurt her. His mouth went dry. In the sterile environment with the overpowering smell of ammonia, he detected sweet lavender. Her smell. Kate wiped her nose and put the handkerchief back in the pocket of her pencil skirt. His heart rate slowed and he regretted his actions. What a douche!

Priding himself on his conduct, he'd disappointed himself and now he'd made a woman cry. Even with her crumpled and teary face, she was stunning. Her beauty hit him like a punch to the face. He'd thought her pretty, but he'd been wrong. She was striking. She stood watching Nick and biting her red chapped lips. One hand tugged on a coloured earring. He imagined nibbling on those pale, cream lobes, before tracing his mouth around her cheek and down her elongated neck.

Nick licked his lips. As if reading his mind, she left his side and went to the water dispenser to pull out a clean paper cup and fill it. She delivered it to him without a word.

He took a sip. 'Kate, I'm so sorry. I don't know what's come over me. I'm sorry I missed your calls. I was caught up in a, um, work situation this afternoon. It was urgent and I didn't have my phone on me.'

She nodded. 'Of course, I'm sorry, you were working. I didn't mean any of those things I said. I had no right. And, she's fine from what

I can work out. They won't tell me much because I'm not family, but—'

'What happened?' His voice was soft as butter, melting off his tongue.

'Today was the first netball game. The girls played well for their first effort. Anyway, in the fourth quarter, I swapped the girls around.'

Nick nodded, listening, waiting for the point. He had to admit though, now that he'd cooled down, he drank in her words, her expressions and mannerisms. She was cuteness personified, just like a little pixie come to life.

'...so Evie played goal shooter. She's good at it, by the way. It's because she's so tall and she has impeccable accuracy. Then Coco-Sage teamed her in goal attack. Coco-Sage vigorously attacked the ball, desperate for a goal and she pushed, accidentally, I'm sure, Evie, and she fell at a funny angle. I thought it was her nose at first and was relieved to discover that it wasn't broken, nor swollen even but unfortunately it was her wrist. She landed awkwardly on it.'

As she finished, a faint flush flashed across her face so fast, that if Nick hadn't been devouring her words, he'd have missed it.

'Sorry. Long story short, she's hurt her wrist. It's been X-rayed and the medical staff are saying it's a hairline fracture. It's minor but she'll need a light cast.' Kate swung her head to the side and her earrings dangled. 'C'mon, I'll show you where she is.' To his surprise she cracked a wide grin and her eyes danced.

Nick followed Kate down the corridor. They arrived at a zucchini green door with a glass panel. Kate gave him privacy as he stared through the smudged pane before grasping the door handle and rushing inside.

***

After the events of the afternoon, Kate could not leave before she had reassurance Evie was okay.

She waited. Swiping through the images on her phone - not discerning any but a few jumbled words - she sipped tepid tea from the vending machine. Dealing with the stress of Evie's injury, she'd forgotten her hatred of hospitals and waiting rooms. Hours spent in the hallways of a foreign emergency centre, with the language impossible to decipher, she'd never felt so alone. The fear that sat in your gut as you waited for news of a loved one - in an uncomfortable environment that was not familiar and too bright - wasn't easily forgotten. The smell of the acerbic air had stayed with her always. Because of that experience, being in the waiting room, with its clientele and noisy environs made her jittery and anxious.

Focusing on her phone, she tried to calm her uneasiness. It didn't work. Instead, she thought about Nick. His lips as his tongue flicked over them; those intense black pools, his presence as he stood over her and the pressure of his grip. She imagined his hands caressing her arms whilst goose pimples formed at his touch; his head leaning down so close she could feel his warm, honey breath.

Quite rightly, she should leave and dismiss him as an over-protective father and bully. But her intuition told her otherwise. A man under pressure acted out of character, right? When she'd peered at him as he held her, shock stared back at her, like he couldn't believe what he'd done. She'd had no experiences of abuse – is that what abusers did?

In psychology 101 from her teaching studies, she understood a display of immediate regret was normal to then be followed by remorse. Kate didn't want to make excuses, particularly for someone she didn't know. But she detected a softness, even a vulnerability that pervaded Nick's hard edges and brusque presentation.

His physicality was a no-brainer. Any woman would be attracted to him. That hair! Her fingers ached to run through its length, tousle it making it messier than it usually sat. Why did he wear it so long? His right hand occasionally raked through it, like it frustrated him and tickled his neck and chin. Or perhaps it had become a habit? In times of stress, maybe he ran his hands along his scalp.

She pictured him in his jeans and the Ralph Lauren T-shirt he wore today. Then she imagined him without the clothes. *Stop Kate!* A soft giggle released before she could control it. It felt good. Of course, she'd laughed in the last few years, but rarely. But forget laughing, the tingle in her groin, the tickle running across her thighs and stomach, that was a long forgotten, buried sensation. She ached to be touched by his large hands and gentle fingers caressing her neck whilst his hot lips converged there, travelling along her shoulders, every pulse in her body on fire.

Kate jumped up. If she didn't, she might self-combust. She needed to move, get the blood circulating to her extremities and calm the intensity going nuts in her adrenal system.

***

That crazy teacher was still here.

Nick had been in with Evie for over an hour. And, outside Kate sat, hunched over in the uncomfortable hospital chair. Except for her, the waiting room sat empty and quiet. She thumbed her phone with a faraway look in her eyes, as if she could have been anywhere.

She'd waited.

A mixture of feelings surfaced. Relief. Evie only had a broken wrist. It could have been much worse and it would heal well. With a good prognosis it became a simple sporting accident, nothing more sinister. But then, Kate. How had this woman got under his skin? She penetrated his staunch barriers in ways he guarded fiercely. His tough façade was unbreakable.

Why was she different? Was it because she seemed to care for Evie? He'd met many pretty girls before, so her captive beauty was not it. Perhaps he had to accept that explanations could not be reasoned from a textbook, an act or case law. Perhaps he was attracted to a beautiful woman who had a sense of helplessness about her and a sadness that he related to, like she had lived many lifetimes like he had and as if they both had a lot to lose.

The timing was wrong. It could not be worse. His professional life was imploding and his personal life sat in the grip of a crazy, ruthless gang of bikies.

And yet.

She had a pull on him that he couldn't resist. His smarts told him to walk away. She was his daughter's teacher, and that was it. But, the pounding of his heart faster than normal and his racing pulse meant that he couldn't, or wouldn't walk away, not for the moment, not yet anyway. He strode over, lightly touching her knee when he reached her. She gazed up at him with those large chocolate eyes.

Uncrossing her legs, she stood. 'How's Evie?'

'You know what, she's great. A broken wrist, which isn't fantastic, but could be worse, and it's not a bad break. A simple cast and the prognosis for a clean heal is good.'

Kate stretched her arms above her head. Nick glanced at the bare creamy flesh exposed by the lifting of her shirt. His mouth dried as the soft moulds of her tummy transfixed him. Oblivious, Kate rubbed her eyes, sleepy and soft. Warmth radiated off her. Nick fought the urge to draw her into a tight embrace and soak in that heat, breathe in her floral scent.

'Thank you for staying. You didn't need to, but I'm glad you did.' He touched her arm, leaving the weight of it there whilst he spoke.

Kate didn't shake him off. In fact, he was certain she moved in his direction, urging the hand to stay.

'Why are you always around? Why are you always keeping an eye on Evie? I don't understand. Aren't there lots of teachers at Trinity, but you're always present?' Nick shook his head.

Kate laughed. 'I'm her netball coach and we were at a game this afternoon. I'm her homeroom teacher and teach her year seven English, Music and French. Oh, and I'm the year seven pastoral leader.' She shrugged.

'I didn't realise. I would have if I'd been paying better attention.' Nick shook his head. 'I obviously understood you were a teacher at the school and knew Evie, but I didn't comprehend that you were so involved with her. You have certainly been there for her since she commenced at Trinity. Thank you. I'm sorry again about before. I'm stressed at work. It's a difficult situation with Evie adjusting to school and being her only parent, it's a juggle. But they are excuses. I lost it before and you didn't deserve it and I'm sorry.'

Nick forgot he spoke to his daughter's teacher and placed his hand on her cheek, his large palm covering its surface. His hand trembled at the touch and his breathing shallowed.

'Dad, I'm ready to go,' Evie came up behind them and hugged her father. Nick's hand lowered, but his eyes stayed focused on Kate. Her expression was unreadable with her wide eyes and parted lips. Reluctantly, he drew himself away.

'Okay, kiddo, glad you are up and about. You'd never know you've been injured.'

'Mrs. Penrose, thank you so much for looking after me this afternoon. By the way, Dad, where were you? Why'd you take so long?'

Nick and Kate laughed, breaking the tension and sharing the private joke. Evie's gaze moved between them, confused and her forehead creased.

'I'll tell you all about my complex and interesting legal case of Dr Chalk, shall I?' Nick teased.

Evie rolled her eyes and groaned. Nick steered around Evie now the centre of attention and kissed Kate on the cheek. Close to her skin, he drank in her light, lavender smell, and stored it up for later.

***

Kate went out into the night air, grateful for the coolness of outside after the stuffiness of the hospital. The darkness surrounded her like a cloak. Touching her cheek, the light touch of Nick's lips remained there. Her limbs were heavy now and each step became an effort as fatigue gripped her.

Pulling out her mobile phone, she rang Angela. 'Hey. My afternoon didn't turn out as expected. Can we ditch the movie? I need a drink…'

CHAPTER NINE

'Thanks so much for changing our plans. Did you want to see that latest Star Wars movie?' Kate smiled at Angela across her tiny kitchen.

'Um, it's the most popular movie this year, and will probably be the highest grossing, so yeah, it's worth seeing. It's called *Rogue One* by the way, in case you need to talk about it in an intelligent way.' Angela's laugh filled the cosy space. 'You've saved me anyway. Todd wanted to see it and was cranky with me for going with you, so you've done me a favour. But enough about that, how's the injured student?'

Topping up their glasses with more chardonnay, Kate filled Angela in. 'Have you met the dad?'

'No. This year I'm teaching senior school. Man, it's going to be tough; year eleven maths is a challenge. Why?'

Kate smirked.

'What? What is it? Is he a raving lunatic that we need to report to the authorities?'

Kate's grin grew wider.

'Oh, okay, he's good looking, is he?'

Kate nodded, and Angela snorted through her fingers and took a large gulp of wine. But by the time she returned her glass to the table, her face was drawn.

'What is it? What's wrong?' Kate sat beside Angela and placed her hand on her knee.

'This is the first time we've done this since Ben died.'

'What do you mean? We've caught up plenty…'

'You know what I mean. Laughed about a boy, talked about a good-looking man, relationships, the other sex. I don't mean to ruin the mood when we were having fun, it's just that I'm pleased for you.'

Now, it was Kate's turn to be subdued. She could allow this diversion back to the past to overtake her and dwell there, or she could choose to remain in the present. Split seconds passed. 'Don't get too far ahead of yourself. I'm not talking marriage!' She pointed her index finger at Angela and the tension broke.

'I know. But even to be having the conversation. You're amazing, Kate and so strong, given what you've been through.'

Kate hugged her friend, her lifeline, and shed quiet tears into her shoulder. After a few moments, Angela shrugged her off.

'Keep drinking, we're getting way too melodramatic. Tell me about this father.'

When the Chinese take-out arrived, they launched themselves into the comfy sofas of the living room. Over another bottle of wine, they discussed Nick Harding as if he were a school assignment. They analysed his physique and personality until they thought they knew him best. When the conversation might have been exhausted, Kate would say, 'but did I tell you about the time he hid behind the pot plant,' and they would break into hysterics.

Occasionally, Kate fingered the unopened container of sweet and sour pork and rolled the cardboard flap between her thumb and forefinger. That dish had been Ben's favourite. She poured an extra glass of wine, and then drank it herself. Angela didn't comment; some habits were hard to break.

Hours later when Kate lay in bed, sated with too much chow mein, and good company she relived the conversation with Angela. Between the jokes, she'd asked Angela her impression of Nick given his strange behaviours. Ever-sensible Angela had replied that a single parent of a teenager with a high pressure job would be under constant stress. And perhaps he didn't have any help.

One thing they had agreed on; he was delicious. Descriptions had not been enough for Angela. Like the adolescents they taught, they Googled him, finding his firm's web page.

'Yeah, I put two and two together and realised he's a lawyer.

Evie says he fights for justice and tonight, he mentioned a legal case.'

'He looks like that guy from Outlander. What's his name? Sam Heughan, but his hair is not as red. Such a babe!' her friend had exclaimed. Kate's belly ached from all the laughing. As she drifted to sleep, Kate dreamed of Jamie Fraser and not surprisingly, she slept well.

***

Brittany Bartholomew lingered near the school refectory. A sea of blue and white converged past her, the cherub faces covered by school hats but wearing broad smiles as they made their way through the passages of Trinity. Brittany was late, but she couldn't head to the P&C meeting without a last cigarette. She stood out amongst the neutral colours with her lollypop dress and white sequined heels. As always, her blonde hair was styled, today in a perfect French bun.

The other parents and volunteers would wait for her anyway. As the chair of the fundraising committee, they couldn't commence without her. She smiled. She was an efficient and good chair and it was a perfect role for her. With little effort, she was adept at getting people to hand over their money. Brittany's mind wandered to the first item on the agenda: the house soirees. As she took a deep drag of her cigarette, she spotted Kate and Nick standing together a hundred metres away. She forgot the soirees and instead leaned back against the brick wall to conceal herself. She pulled down her Chanel sunnies in a further effort at camouflage.

Anger uncurled within her, like a building storm. For weeks she'd been trying to engage the adorable Nick Harding and he'd resisted her. Today he was talking to that stupid teacher.

Again.

Brittany's forehead creased as much as the botox would allow it. How could he find that frumpy, boring woman who wore those stupid, child-like earrings, attractive? She inhaled on that cigarette as his smile sparkled in Kate's direction. Nick must have teased her because the silly girl laughed, her head titling back. Oh, she was good, her head lowered coquettishly, flirting from under her eyelashes. Brittany watched Nick soak it up.

His rejection was raw but, now, instead, a shimmer of excitement shot up her spine. Of course, she was thrilled anytime she saw Nick. He was beautiful. Brittany wanted to touch those pectoral muscles that were defined under his shirt. She wouldn't mind if his large, strong hands explored her body either. She tingled all over at the thought.

But that was for another day. Today, her stomach did somersaults as she watched the exchange between the single parent and school teacher. Such fodder! Suddenly, everything became crystal clear. How could she have been so blind? Something was going on between Evie's father and Kate Penrose. Without checking the school policies, she *knew* this would be frowned upon. Of course, it would. As a devoted parent and member of the school community, Brittany would make certain to find out. It would be the duty of a responsible parent, after all. And she was the perfect woman for the job.

Brittany extracted her phone. She had to quell her disgust at the smiles, laughs and soft touches the two exchanged. Clicking furiously, she took more photos than necessary. The prize shot was one of Nick leaning in close as if kissing Kate. The next frame clearly displayed the real action; he'd in fact only tilted in close to speak into her ear. Brittany deleted that one. She smiled like the Cheshire cat. Her day had suddenly got a whole lot better. If she couldn't have Nick, she'd be damn sure that mousy teacher didn't either.

***

Satisfaction thrummed through Kate's veins. She was up to date with the National Curriculum and hummed as she walked out of her classroom at the end of the school week. Spying three or four pairs of skinny legs below an open locker door, she slowed her steps.

'You're a loser, that's what you are.'

Loud voices rang out as she approached and she paused, listening.

'That's why your mother's dead, you know, because she couldn't stand the sight of you…'

'What's going on here?'

Caught by surprise, four heads spun in her direction. One head did not turn, instead continuing to observe the ground with her back to Kate, the girl's body obscured by the locker door. Wide open mouths greeted her while hands moved quickly behind backs.

'Coco-Sage, what is behind your back?'

'Nothing, Miss,' the girl trilled in a singsong voice matched with an innocent grin.

'Deidre, I'll ask you. What is behind your back?'

'Nothing, Miss,' she parroted.

'Okay, that's fine. Instead of showing me, you can take whatever it is you're hiding to the office and show the principal instead.' The fourth girl jostled the others and held out a school sports bag.

'Whose bag is this?'

'It's Evie's,' Coco-Sage said.

'Evie? Is that you? Come out of there please.'

Evie emerged, failing miserably to conceal her tear-stained face. A lump lodged in Kate's throat. She reached forward and snatched the bag.

'Why are you holding this?'

Silence. Staring at them with her sternest teacher face, Kate waited. Coco-Sage's friends were neither as canny nor disobedient as her.

'It has…'

'It was…'

'We were trying to clean it for Evie. It's dirty you see,' Coco-Sage jumped in, interrupting.

Kate examined the bag. 'Where's it dirty?' she said tipping it the side to manoeuvre the zipper open. A gush of liquid escaped, splattering her shoes and emitting a disgusting odour.

'Argh!'

Putrid sour milk poured from the school bag. Peering inside, Kate noticed the contents were covered in the off-white liquid. Coco-Sage laughed wickedly. Her friends had the sense to remain quiet.

Kate's words were laced with steel. 'Deidre, Rebecca and Audrey, you may go.'

At that, Coco-Sage's bravado dropped. She scowled at her friends as they scurried away scot-free. They might pay later, Kate realised. For ten minutes, she berated Coco-Sage. The girl couldn't defend herself as she stood and listened to a lecture on appropriate behaviour towards others. Her expression moved between snarly contempt to remorse when she realised there was no getting away with this one. Kate would make sure Coco-Sage delivered a replacement sports bag to Evie next week.

With the worst of it over, Coco-Sage walked away with a

confident swagger. Kate stood with Evie who hadn't muttered a word during the exchange. She tidied her locker, one-handed with her wrist still in plaster, and walked, head down, with Kate. Along the way Kate threw her sports bag in the garbage. 'I'm going to drop you home. It's late now. How come your dad wasn't here to pick you up?' Kate was shocked that Nick hadn't collected Evie. Wasn't this the behaviour he was specifically trying to protect his daughter from? So, where the bloody hell was he?

The man of mystery vanished at odd times.

'We were working on a group project and had to complete homework together. Audrey's mum was supposed to drop me home. Coco-Sage isn't even in the group.' Evie gave a weak smile, all the pluck squeezed out of her. As an afterthought, she added, 'Dad'll have a fit when he finds out my lift evaporated.'

'You should tell him about these girls.'

'Mrs. Penrose, do you realise that if I tell my dad, he will be up here at the school demanding the situation be dealt with and he'll speak to Coco-Sage's parents. She's the ringleader. Those other girls follow her around. Do you realise how much trouble that will place me in? The whole grade will hate me.'

Kate smiled at the dramatic retelling. 'You know what? I reckon your dad would have a fair chance of sorting this out, don't you? He looks like a person who gets things done.'

Evie reciprocated the grin. 'Yeah, he is, but that's the problem. He won't let it drop.'

'Okay, I get that too, but what about discussing strategies with him?'

'You and I have done that. I got caught out today. I need to be more careful.'

'Doesn't help, I guess, when other girls turn on you too, and gang up with Coco-Sage.'

'Everyone is scared of her.'

Kate rubbed Evie's back.

'I'll read up on the school policy and ask around. Maybe there are tactics I haven't thought of. Trouble is, she's a formidable force, isn't she?'

'Yep.' Evie sounded resigned.

'And so is her mother,' Kate added.

They were in Kate's car now. 'Better tell me where you live.' Whilst a cloud of despair hung precariously low over Evie, she brightened during the short car journey. Trying to keep the girl distracted, Kate's mind didn't turn to the fact that she was about to see Nick.

They pulled into an elaborate circular drive where high concrete walls surrounded the property. Was this a home or a prison? Did she spy barbed wire atop the fence? Her stomach tightened into knots.

Nick was in there.

'I'll have to jump out and type in the code so the gate opens,' Evie said as if there was nothing unusual about having a security system. Didn't people with alarms need protecting? Weird.

As the wrought iron gates swung wide, she caught a glimpse of the house beyond through majestic oak trees that lined the driveway. At the end of that curved drive sat an enormous white stucco building. The house had two stories, a four-car garage and white columns framing a grand entrance. Everything was neat, straight lined and tidy. It reminded Kate of Tara out of *Gone With the Wind*. Was Nick her Rhett?

Kate held her breath.

The Harding's were seriously rich.

Her car rolled to a stop. 'I might leave you here now that you're safely home. Your dad isn't expecting me, so I'll…' But as she spoke, a two-panelled timber door opened, and Nick stepped out, barefoot and wearing casual blue jeans and a white T-shirt.

Kate bit her bottom lip.

Oh my.

He had large feet, too. He approached her Peugeot. Kate clung to the steering wheel ready for a quick getaway. His hair was mussed, like he'd been raking his hands through it, or…

Nick opened the driver's door.

'You're Audrey's mum?' he said without a flicker of amusement.

'No, no, umm, no, I'm not, of course, you know that,' she stammered.

'Then what are you doing here?' he said not unkindly, but with no accompanying smile.

Kate glanced at Evie and caught her wide and pleading eyes. They hadn't discussed what to tell her father. Kate wouldn't lie, but how could she tell Nick about Evie being bullied when Evie wouldn't? She smiled up at Nick. 'It's a funny story. I was coming out of my classroom and the girls were ready to leave, and I offered to drop Evie. You know, to make it easier for Audrey's mother being busy and all.' Better leave the explanation simple and not embellish either of them in a web of lies. Nick's body relaxed and he loosened his hold on her car door.

'Evie could have rung me. I would have picked her up. She knows that.' He glanced in his daughter's direction. Evie hung back, near the car with her school bag on her back.

'I was leaving anyway.'

'Thank you, once again, for looking out for Evie.' He finally smiled at her. 'You're like her fairy godmother.'

Kate released her grip on the wheel and sat back. 'Oh no, not at all.' Discomfort settled in. Was that what she was doing? She had taken Evie under her wing, but the term fairy godmother had too many connotations with motherhood and she wasn't Evie's mother.

'Would you like to come in?' Nick asked.

CHAPTER TEN

Hell yeah.

'I'd love to,' she heard herself say. But immediately, her stomach dropped. Why had she agreed?

Too late, Nick opened the car door wider and motioned toward the house.

No! She wanted to shout, I meant no. She wanted to drive out of there and as far away from Nick Harding as possible.

He waited. Hiding her trembling hands, she managed to exit the vehicle. Nick closed her door and let her enter his home ahead of him. They entered into a bright and spacious foyer.

Evie squealed, 'I'll leave you to it. I'm starving and I promised I'd ring Arabella! Thanks again for the lift, Mrs. Penrose!' She strode up a grand staircase, lost to the upper level and appearing not at all disturbed by her teacher being in her house.

Kate watched Evie disappear up the stairs. Ornate in stature, the staircase was wide with deep off-white granite steps with artwork lining the walls to the second level. Large gold-gilded framed paintings that belonged in a gallery hung amongst smaller, more delicate pieces. A couple were in bold colour whilst others were drawings in black and white. Kate was sure she recognised some of them.

'I love your paintings.'

'Thank you, it's a hobby of mine.' It appeared to be much more of a serious collection, than a hobby. Kate loved beautiful things. But it was such a grandiose statement upon entering a man's home. And, so unexpected.

'Come through, and grab a seat, please. Even though it's beautiful outside by the pool, it's cooler in the house. Can I offer you a drink? Coffee, wine or something else?' He checked his watch. 'Nearly five o'clock on a Friday afternoon, it must be time for a drink?'

'I'm driving but perhaps one, and then a coffee?'

Ah, God, did she say that? Was she insinuating that she'd stay for hours? She went to bury her head in her hands but Nick ushered her into another airy and light room. No paintings in this one, just muted-white walls with showroom furniture.

Nick walked over to a bar in the corner.

'Would you like champagne?'

'Are we celebrating something?'

'Maybe.' He didn't add anymore.

Kate's spine tingled. He delivered her bubbles in an elegant tall flute but held a short stout glass in his other hand.

'You aren't having one?'

'No. I don't drink champagne. I like scotch.' He held it up as proof.

'Hard day?' They were talking in monosyllabic sentences. Were they able to hold a proper conversation?

'Cheers,' she offered in customary greeting when he didn't answer her question. He held up his own drink but didn't comment. Instead, he flicked a switch on what resembled a remote control and blaring Jimi Hendrix vocals filled the room.

Kate startled and held tight to her glass.

'Sorry about that. I was playing it loudly before and I forgot to turn it down.'

She laughed but it caught and died in her throat. Within seconds, the noise changed to soft acoustic guitar, soulful yet jazzy.

'Beautiful,' was the best she could do. Words stuck on her tongue. It was wrong to be here in his living room, to be with another man, intimately, sharing a drink. And yet, it felt so right. She'd be reluctant to leave if a fire broke out. To calm her rattling nerves, she drank the champagne too quickly. Nick retrieved the bottle and refilled her glass and she didn't object. Other than the background music, silence filled the room. This striking Andronicus before her didn't attempt to fill it with small talk. Had she misread the cues? Was he simply being nice on Tuesday?

'So, Evie called you Mrs. Penrose. Are you married?'

The question threw her off guard. She hadn't expected it. It was so personal and to the point, but of course, it made sense. But, shouldn't he have asked that the other day before he kissed her? Oh God, maybe she had read the situation completely wrong. Maybe he was simply being kind. He did act chivalrously. She rebuked herself for being so stupid. There was nothing to do but answer the question. 'No, I was.'

'Are you divorced?'

Talking a deep breath, she steeled herself before answering. 'No, my husband died in a car accident.'

Nick's face revealed the sympathy she hated. It was a normal reaction, but still, the aftermath of such a tragic tale inevitably ended in meaningless words and uncomfortable pauses.

'I'm sorry. You're so young, you must have married early.' It was more a statement than a question.

She nodded. 'He died on our honeymoon.' Why did she say that? Kate took another large gulp to stop herself from revealing more.

'Oh, shit, that's terrible. When did this happen?'

'Three years ago. I was twenty-three.' She changed topic. 'You didn't work today? I mean, you're at home?'

'No, I did. I worked here today. I have a home study with everything I need.'

'Oh, of course, I'm sorry, I didn't mean, you know it's none of my business. I get the impression you work hard.' She gestured weakly around her at his massive home with its beautiful decor.

'Yes, I have worked hard over the years. I love my job.'

'That's great, me too.'

Awkward. She needed to leave. Unable to string a coherent sentence together, he'd believe she was an idiot. Becoming uncomfortable and hot, she needed to recover the situation. She took a slow, deliberate sip of her drink to buy time and gazed up to watch him. His mouth focused on her lips as they sipped and swallowed. Her tongue darted across her dry lips.

Okay.

'Um, talking about work, we need to discuss the music tour. I happen to have the permission form in my bag. You need to sign it, it's overdue.' Kate fiddled around in her bag to extract the paper. Handing it over, a freeze entered the room. Nick's face had set steely, his lips thin and closed, and his shoulders held solid.

She held the sheet aloft. Nick didn't take it.

Kate sighed. She was tired of this game and confident from the alcohol.

'What is your problem with the tour?' She rambled on. 'It's well organised. I am in fact the organiser in co-operation with a professional company that arranges these types of camps each year as their core business. It's a small group of twenty girls, selected by the school and the itinerary is almost finalised. It's a great opportunity.'

Nick half nodded. Was he convinced?

'Is… is… it the cost?'

Laughter erupted from him.

'I'm sorry I didn't mean to insult you. I didn't imagine it was the money, but hey, who am I to know, you might be in financial trouble. Maybe that's why you're always so tense and serious…'

Oops, she veered off track with that.

As she looked up through her lashes, Nick stopped laughing.

'Am I always so solemn?'

'No, you laughed just now. But I guess, most of the time you are rather grave and you don't talk much.' Again, he nodded. Kate fiddled with her Eiffel Tower earrings, worried she'd made a faux paux, when all she wanted was Evie on this trip.

'I'm sorry. Yes, you are probably right, I have a lot on my plate…'

'So you keep alluding too. Anything I can help with?'

He smiled at her with such genuine warmth, the world illuminated. The edges of his lips curled whilst his eyes twinkled.

'I guess, that's a no then as you aren't taking the offer seriously. I do mean it. Perhaps this trip can give you time out, with Evie away for two weeks you might be able to attend to your business.'

***

Nick squirmed. The last thing he wanted was Evie out of his sight; it was too dangerous. If the Warlocks got wind of the fact his daughter was alone on a school trip, he couldn't trust them to keep away from her, even if she was overseas. Yet, Kate, sweet, adorable Kate sat across from him saying all the right things. This was an amazing opportunity for his young daughter. Any normal family would jump at it – a chance to play flute overseas, perform, experience the culture of Vietnam, volunteer and contribute to their impoverished society – all sounded like a dream: for normal people. If he didn't give her permission, he would be disappointing two people now, not only his daughter.

This was one passionate teacher. He admired her pluck. If being honest, he liked a lot more than that. Okay, he'd admit it to himself, but this couldn't go anywhere. She talked on, about bus trips and food and schedules. The sound of her voice dripped like honey, soothing and delicious. Her quirky earrings swayed with her enthusiasm, arms flailing in description and her bright red lips moving fast.

He took the paper and signed the form and placed in on her lap. She stopped talking.

'We're having homemade pizza tonight. Want to join us? I can't claim it as my own creation. My housekeeper, Mrs. Travers made the bases and provided the ingredients. I'm simply putting them in the oven. But pizza is one of Evie's favourite dinners. We'd love to have you.'

Pure delight danced in her eyes. He pushed down the fear in his own. It was dinner with a friend; his daughter's teacher and innocent fun. Kate was a good conversationalist and he'd spent too much time alone. Her company ignited something within him, an excitement that scared the hell out of him.

He did not for a second believe all this self-talk. Deeper, more intimate thoughts kept surfacing every time he glanced at her. At least with Evie present, he'd have to be on his best behaviour.

'I'd love to stay,' she said, interrupting his internal dialogue.

Nick was in trouble, he knew it. But that didn't stop him from striding over and kissing her, where she sat, taking her by surprise. Like a fumbling teenager, he aimed for her cheek, but Kate moved at the last moment and the corners of their lips connected. He kissed her again, pausing as he felt her chin lift to meet him and he held his lips on hers, lingering. A delightful shiver of wanting pulsed through him. By the look on her face, she'd felt it too.

Best keep their distance through dinner.

***

As they sat for dinner, the telephone rang.

'I'll get it.' Evie jumped from her seat and raced out of the dining room.

'Dad! It's Auntie Lizzie.'

'Okay, thanks, sweetie. Tell her I'll ring her back after dinner.'

'That's my little sister, Elizabeth or Lizzie as she prefers to be called.'

'Where does she live?'

'Toowoomba with my parents. She's only twenty-five and has two great loves-design and horses. I gave her free reign in decorating this place for me.'

'Ah, that's make sense. This house is amazing; a designer home just like in a magazine. I did wonder, though. I mean, you're a single dad. Shouldn't you have casual digs with dirty towels on the floor and empty shopping bags lying around?'

Nick laughed. 'When I could afford it, after all the years of struggling as a junior lawyer, I wanted something big and bold and to show off, actually. The house on this property was old and rundown. I tore it down and constructed this,' he waved his arms wide. 'Lizzie did a great job decorating and created the statement I wanted. Even though sometimes I think it's a bit feminine with the white walls and pale blue furnishings. But it's beautiful and peaceful. I love it.'

'Me too.'

Evie ran back into the room and sat at the table. 'Aunt Lizzie says hi. But she's going out so she'll talk to you later about coming down to visit in a few weeks.'

Nick nodded.

'Evie. Your Dad has given permission for you to attend the music tour.' Evie, with a mouthful of margherita pizza, tried to squeal but the sound got gobbled up. Instead, she jumped out of her dining chair and raced around the table to hug her father from behind.

Nick accepted the embrace and beamed back at his daughter with a broad smile.

After she'd finished chewing, she sat back down to continue dinner. 'Oh, I'm so excited! That's unreal. I don't know how you did it,

Mrs. Penrose. You must be very persuasive. The last conversation Dad and I had about the trip, he asked me a million questions that I couldn't answer. Thank you.'

Nick soaked up the words and watched Evie in her delight and the matching happiness radiate off Kate. He'd done the right thing. No point dwelling on it or getting worked up.

A loud thwack to the roof echoed through the house. Immediately above their heads.

'What's that noise?' Evie asked.

Nick sat bolt upright, a slice of pizza halfway to his mouth. He dropped it back down onto the plate. He listened but could only hear his pulse beating in his ears. Nothing. But then it came again. Another hard whack against the roof tiles. He stood up and his chair scraped louder than he'd intended. Both Evie and Kate turned to him; two pairs of eyes stared upwards, wide and quizzical. He needed to stay calm.

'I'm sure it's nothing. Maybe a couple of possums having a fight up there or maybe a tree branch has come loose and fallen onto the roof. I'll go and check it out and you two keep chatting about the tour.'

The moment he was out of their sight, he bolted up the central stairs, two at a time. He heard Kate say something about rickshaws and Evie giggling in response. At least they were not alarmed.

At the top floor he went to the spare room and opened the window. He climbed through it and onto the first floor roof that extended over the far end of the house. With height to his advantage, he'd see the second level roof clearly from there. He let his eyes grow accustomed to the darkness, the stars and vivid, silver moon his only assistance. His gaze scanned the roof. A couple of square red bricks lay up there, scattered a couple of metres apart. As he stood there, another sailed over his head, barely missing him and landed with a clank in front of his left foot. Nick snatched up that brick and turned, ready, his arm drawn back and in position. He held it there, braced for more. *Stop, don't.* The voice echoed in his head. Nick knelt down out of sight in case another block came flying. He concentrated on his breathing and calming himself the hell down.

No more bricks came. Slowly, he climbed onto the window ledge and reached up to extract the two bricks. Luckily they landed near the guttering. Holding them in his hands, he sat on the lower roof, waiting. Ten minutes passed. He had to get back otherwise Kate and Evie would worry. Back in the bedroom, he examined the bricks hoping they'd give him a message or a clue. Nothing. Ordinary, plain house bricks. Nick shoved them under the spare bed. He took slow steps walking back downstairs trying to compel his body to act normal.

With a big smile plastered to his face he said as he retook his seat, 'It's not Halloween is it?'

Evie laughed. 'No, Dad. That's in October, months away.'

'Okay. Must be some random kids being stupid. They threw a couple of bricks onto the roof. Lucky they missed the windows, otherwise I'd be chasing them down the street.' His joke fell flat but he covered it with pretend mirth.

Kate looked at him. 'Shouldn't you call the police?'

'Nah. Don't want to get the kids in trouble. It's only a bit of stupid Friday night fun.'

'Little buggers,' Evie said.

'Yep,' and Nick dove straight back into his slice of pizza even though it roiled around in his stomach as he ate.

'I'm stuffed. Thanks for dinner, Dad. Thanks for joining us, Mrs. Penrose. I'm going to head up. I have homework to do over the weekend,' and she looked pointedly at her teacher.

'Best get to it, then,' Kate mocked.

After she'd left, Kate started piling plates. 'It's late, I should be going, too.'

Nick's mind raced fast. He needed to ensure whoever'd been out there was not still hanging around. 'Can you help me with the dishes?' he asked. The words sounded lame to his own ears. When had he ever cared about cleaning up?

'Of course.'

They started clearing the table and Nick threw away the leftovers. 'I'll take this rubbish out. Won't be a sec.' Nick pulled out the rubbish bag and tied it up. Once it was swept into the wheelie bin, he raced around the outside of the house. He walked down the drive and opened the gate. There weren't any cars on the street and no sign of life. He waited a few more minutes. It seemed okay. His stomach knotted at the thought of Kate leaving without his protection. How could he pull this one off without raising her suspicion? He didn't know.

When he arrived back in the kitchen, the benches were sparkling and the dishwasher hummed. 'Oh, I'm sorry. I didn't mean for you to do that all by yourself.'

'It's fine. A thank you for dinner.'

Kate gathered her handbag and commenced walking toward the door. Nick sweated. What lay out there? Nothing he prayed.

He turned off the automatic sensor light and they stood on his doorstep in darkness. Together, they walked toward her car. Kate turned to him, expectantly, her gaze fixed on him. Man, he couldn't act all romantic now. He needed Kate in her car and speeding away toward the safety of her home. Kate bit her lip. Nick felt his defences crumbling. He leaned down, cradled her neck with one hand and kissed her, full and hard on the mouth. His force caught her by surprise and she took a step back with one foot. Having regained her balance, she placed one arm around his middle and pulled him closer.

Nick wasn't feeling it. His mind raced in different directions. But a hint of her lavender smell overtook him and he felt himself losing control. In the distance, he heard a car. That was enough. He pulled his lips away from her and raised up abruptly. To ease the blow of ending their kiss too soon, he leaned back in and pecked Kate on the cheek. But he opened her car door quickly. The message was clear, and Kate understood. Nick couldn't look at her as she hopped in and started the engine. He did watch her car as she meandered down his drive and until her rear lights had turned onto the street.

If Evie hadn't been home, he'd have screamed his frustration out loud and into the darkness.

CHAPTER ELEVEN

Debris was scattered throughout the foyer and into the office spaces beyond. Nick stepped over broken glass, walked between upturned chairs and criss-crossed through the patterns of colour spray-painted into the wool carpet. Ironically, the reception to McLaughlin Grant Lawyers resembled a crime scene. Nick hung his head. Shame spread through him and his heart sat heavy in his chest.

He'd sunk to his knees when he'd received the telephone call from his partner. But this, this made him want to puke.

Staff hovered in the centre kitchen, all wearing grim faces and tight expressions. Somewhere, a phone rang out unanswered. Silently, he walked past them and avoided eye contact. He didn't know what to say.

Coward. It was his fault.

Nick found Rob Grant in his corner office. Despite the chaos of the office around him, his pinstriped suit remained free of creases with its starched lines and good quality fabric. One cufflink sat unbuttoned.

'I'm so sorry, Rob,' Nick said as he touched the elderly man on his back. A gesture he'd made a hundred times before, but today, it felt tainted and wrong. To his surprise, Rob didn't stare back with an expression of 'I told you so'. He was too honourable for that. Puffy, black bags sat under the man's eyes, though, giving away the true ramifications of what had happened.

'Mate, I had to call the police. I couldn't wait. The staff were frightened. The police have been to lift fingerprints and gather as much evidence as they could. Nothing was stolen. Obviously, your bikie friends didn't want our office equipment, and of course, the pathetic little amount of petty cash wasn't of interest to them. They wanted to destroy and send a message, I guess.'

'Rob, I truly am sorry.'

'I know you are. You don't have to keep saying it. It's not the damage; we can fix it and clean up the mess. It's our employees. What if they'd been here, Nick? What if someone had been hurt? The message these people are sending, are you getting it? Do you understand it has to stop? And, do you finally accept your association with them is dangerous?'

'Rob, please, believe me, it's stopped. I haven't done any work for the Warlocks since I lost the trial. Even if I had wanted to continue, they won't engage me. I'm of no use to them anymore. You know they briefed someone else for the appeal. They haven't been in touch since.' He looked around him. 'Not for legal advice anyway. But they are having a hard time forgetting, unfortunately.'

With his back to Nick, Rob fiddled with the photo of his family and the other private treasures he kept on his desk. Nick's heart sank; he knew this man and had been his friend and colleague for the last ten years. Rob Grant had been the guru in criminal defence when they'd met and he'd mentored and guided Nick. He'd believed in him. It was faith he could never repay. Nick desperately wished he could turn back time and listen when he needed to and take the advice offered to him.

Too late now.

Nick waited for Rob to continue. He avoided looking at him and Nick knew what that meant–an unpleasant conversation.

'You've been a fantastic addition to this firm. When you arrived you were a breath of fresh air. You brought dynamism and gusto and over the years, a wealth of fees. We've all benefitted. And for that, I thank you. I've loved working with you. You've made me young again. But, Nick, it can't go on. This can't go on.' He gestured with his arms wide indicating the offices. 'The reputation of the firm is at stake along with our future and the security of the staff we employ. You understand, don't you?' Rob stared at him directly now. His light grey eyes pleading with him to understand.

Nick nodded but couldn't speak. He couldn't utter that he'd fucked up, royally. And, now, it was over. The job he loved, sacrificed to a low-life group of scumbags who'd sucked him in and bled him dry.

'I will get this place cleaned up. You'll be ready to open back up for business tomorrow, I promise. Once the Warlocks learn I'm no longer associated with you or the firm, they'll leave you alone. It's me they're after, not you.'

'What do you mean? Has something happened?'

'No, nothing like that,' he lied keeping his head turned away so his colleague couldn't detect his deceit. Hand on shoulder, Rob offered a tight smile. There was nothing left to say. After all their years together it had come down to this. Rob sat down at his desk; as a seasoned professional, he would work through the chaos. He picked up his quill pen and considered the pile of papers in front of him. Nick was dismissed.

Clicking the door shut behind him, Nick entered the communal staff area. Candy, his personal assistant, stood cleaning down benches in the kitchen. She came over and embraced him, tears slipping down her cheeks.

'Are you okay?' she asked, despite the predicament she found herself in.

'Of course,' he offered her a smile of reassurance. 'Now, put that down. You're going home and taking all the staff with you. The office is shut for the remainder of the day. I'm going to clean this place up.'

'Oh, honey.' She always addressed him like a mother would a son. 'You don't have to do that. You must have work to do.'

'No.' He removed the cloth from her hand and placed his palm firmly on her back and guided her out of the room. Each member of staff was given the same direction and soon, the office had cleared. He left Rob to his business in the back.

Nick disposed of urine soaked manila folders, cleaned down work spaces covered with graffiti art, patched up holes in walls, pulled down broken book shelves and replaced computers ripped from their sockets and put to rights stationary sprawled like confetti. After filling at least five over-sized garbage bags, Nick was getting somewhere. Small spaces began to clear and it started to resemble the office he remembered.

He worked until his muscles ached. In less than forty-eight hours he'd worked every limb in his toned body. He'd laboured harder than he had his entire life. His thighs contracted from squatting and his head buzzed with the industrial chemicals he lathered on each surface.

A team of cleaners could have been engaged; Nick would have paid them double for their effort, but he needed to do it. His actions had caused the trouble and he had to fix it. The task gave him plenty of time to think. He knew cleaning up his previous office space would not solve his problem. But, it would help his colleagues; those he'd worked with for many years and had supported him by celebrating his wins and propping him up on the bad days. If he hadn't known it already, he did now.

He was well and truly fucked.

***

Evie had become a regular visitor to Kate's classroom. Today, she danced between the desks with excitement whilst they discussed the music tour. 'Miss, I still can't believe you convinced my dad to say yes.'

Kate watched the girl with amusement. What she hadn't told Evie is that she'd pestered Nick until he gave in, nor about the kiss that might have helped the decision, too. She'd not had a wink of sleep since. Lying awake at night, she relived the moment over and over again, like a teenager after their first date. It kept the spring in her step and her daydreams alive and not dark and foreboding. Was this hope growing within her?

'Okay, what will I need?' The young woman sat down at a desk and scribbled notes. 'Um, cool clothes because it will be hot, won't it, Miss?'

Kate paused her marking and answered Evie's stream of questions. 'You'll be getting a comprehensive list about this you know. We'll be having a briefing in the next few weeks.'

'Oh, I know, but I want to get organised. I've never been overseas before. In fact, as soon as I get home I'm going to Google Vietnam and find out as much as I can. We fly into Da Nang don't we? And then, what's the name of the place we perform the concert and you know, meet the little kids?'

'Hoi An. It's so beautiful. You will love it. There's a gorgeous river running through the town and when I was there last they had lanterns lining the riverbanks that glowed a variety of colours at night time. That might have been a festival, though, I'm not sure. But, it

74

doesn't matter, it's a lovely place anyway.'

They worked on in silence, comfortable in each other's company and each deep in their own thoughts. Evie scribbled notes, her hand flying across the page and Kate, her attention strayed to an attractive, broody man. 'Evie, how long have you lived in that house?'

'Mm. Since I've lived with my dad. He's had that house for a while.'

Nodding, Kate pretended to concentrate on the papers in front of her. 'Has it always had that level of security?'

'What do you mean?'

'I mean the high concrete fence, the security gate and how it's hidden from the street.'

Evie shrugged. 'It's always been that way. Dad's had some nutty clients over the years and he likes his privacy.'

'Fair enough. It's a beautiful house. You're lucky.'

'Did you see the pool? It's so great, a fantastic spot for parties, even though we've not had one that I can remember. Maybe I should have one this year for my birthday?'

'That would be fun.'

Evie jumped up. 'I've gotta go. Dad'll kill me if I'm late again. I told him I'm getting the bus from now on, but you know what he does? He waits for me at the bus stop! It's so annoying! See you tomorrow at the fair.'

Kate raised her hand in good bye but the young girl was already out the door. Pen still poised, she abandoned the red ticks and crosses on the English passages in front of her. Cupping her hand to her face, Kate's chin tickled at the memory of Nick's face close to hers and of his hair falling forward to cover his eyes. She sat back and wished those lips could be upon her once more.

CHAPTER TWELVE

'Hello, this is Nick.'

'Nick? Nick Harding?'

Apprehension immediately gripped Nick's middle like a vice and held tight. He didn't recognise the voice on his personal mobile phone.

He paused.

'Yes.'

'Nick. This is Scott Cunningham. You represented me in a drink driving offence last year. Well, my third actually. And now I've been picked up for driving without a license.'

'Oh, hi, Scott.' Nick felt like he talked in slow motion whilst he grappled to make sense of the call. 'This is my personal mobile, not a work phone. How did you get this number?'

'Oh, um, I can't quite remember. It was saved in my phone I think from last time you helped me.'

'No. That's not possible. I've never given this number out to clients.' Nick breathed in big gulps of air. Calm deserted him.

'Well, anyway. I'm in court next week and I'm in trouble. I've really stuffed up this time and I need help. Can you do it?'

Lawyer mode kicked in. A client in trouble. This is what he did and did well. He wanted to help Scott. Remembered him from last year. Nice guy with a family but he had a drinking problem if he recalled correctly. If someone else represented him he might end up with jail time. It really was a serious matter. Perhaps he could it?

Nick got lost in his own thoughts for too long.

'Hello? Nick? I'm in court for the first mention next week and want to engage you to appear for me.' Nick remained silent. Scott continued, 'As my lawyer.'

Like a kick to his guts, realisation dawned. He couldn't help Scott. Not now. Not at the moment. What was he thinking? He'd almost agreed.

'I'm really sorry mate but I'm unable to appear for you this time. Give Rob Grant a ring and he'll be able to assist. He's a fantastic lawyer, the best around.' Nick gave Scott his office number.

After he hung up, Nick glanced around his kitchen. He moved closer to the bay windows and gazed out, craning his neck to see into each corner. Was someone watching him? Had the phone call been a trick? Nick had a sense of being observed and his scalp prickled. Paranoia was setting in.

'C'mon, dad! Get dressed!' Evie squealed as she sped past him and up the stairs. He stood at the island bench in his pyjamas drinking his coffee and reading the Saturday newspaper. Well, he had been anyway, until the phone call.

Was it the three flat whites he'd drunk or his nerves that made his hands shake?

Dammit! Nick balled his fists to prevent kicking his foot against the low cupboards of the bench.

How did this guy get his phone number? Nick wracked his brain and didn't come up with any answers. None of it made sense and he couldn't shake the feeling of being set up. Scott Cunningham was a real guy but did he have a connection to the Warlocks?

And now he had to get ready for the fun fair. He needed to be alert. Who was he kidding? He needed to be alert every day. Going to the annual school fundraiser was the last thing he felt like doing.

The events of last week had been harrowing and now this. He felt like he'd been sucker-punched and hadn't yet been able to catch his breath. The hits kept coming.

None of that mattered to his daughter.

Nerves rattling, he pulled out his backpack. He extracted the map of the schoolgrounds and read it for the twentieth time. He didn't need to, he'd memorised it. Both his mobile phone and Evie's were fully charged and... What else could he do? Pray for the best? Not his usual style, but, hey, he was starting to get desperate.

Before leaving, he'd do one last check around the house and surrounds. It had become his routine. He'd repeat it again when they returned.

Anything to keep them safe.

***

Beads of sweat formed on Kate's brow, soaking into the band of her school-issued cap. At least the moisture wouldn't be visible through the navy colour. When she'd commenced setting up the stall in the early hours of the morning, it had been cool. Now, two hours later, the sun sat high in the cloudless sky and the rays stung her bare arms.

She stood back to admire her handiwork. Yes, she was pleased with what she saw. Luckily, she'd nabbed the fairy floss and face painting stall. At least she could have fun during the long day at the Trinity College Fun Fair.

Her booth was an outrageous mixture of rainbow colours. She'd admit, she'd gone a little crazy. Kate had decorated the entire perimeter of the square tent with flamboyant and cute patterns. Pixie faces beamed out at her along with superheros and ferocious animals. On the other side sat a large, steel basin ready for making cotton candy. The whole set up could have passed as an exhibit at a kindergarten open day.

Kate shrugged. No doubt someone would object and claim it childish. But couldn't they all have a little fun? She loved it and was sure the crowds would, too.

'Oh my gosh, Kate, your stall is fabulous,' Angela yelled as she barrelled past rolling an esky on its wheels.

'Good luck on the hamburger stand. I might see you later!' she called back.

'Let's hope everyone is thirsty, we have bucket loads of cold soft drink.' Her friend disappeared into the crowd.

The volunteer roster was fixed to the back wall of the flapping tent. Kate checked it now, even though she'd committed it to memory. She looked at the 11.30 am slot. Nick had placed his name down on her list. Even now, over two hours until his turn, her tummy exploded in nerves. Perhaps they'd be so busy, they'd have no time to notice each other? Kate blew out her cheeks and retied her novelty apron once more. In front of a hand mirror, she painted a flower on the curve of her cheek.

'Here, let me help you with that.'

A hand with neat and clean fingernails and impossibly smooth skin, grasped the delicate paintbrush. She looked up to gaze directly into the face of Nick Harding. Opening her mouth to speak, Nick roused on her.

'I can't paint a perfect red rose if your lips are moving.'

He concentrated on the fine brush strokes and she promptly closed her mouth. At this proximity, Kate hardly dared to breath. Nick stood so near, she could hear his tiny intakes of breath. Not sure where to look and trying not to be obvious, her eyes darted sideways. After an agonising wait, Nick took a step backwards and considered his handiwork. His thumb rubbed away a smudge. Did she imagine his finger lingering there? As he pulled it away, his eyes locked on hers. That stare. Those eyes. Her heart leapt into her throat.

'What are you doing here? You aren't rostered on until eleven thirty. It's only nine.'

'I have taken over the entire roster for the day.'

'What?' Kate spluttered. She can't have comprehended correctly. She walked over to check the sheet of paper. From behind, Nick reached up and ripped it off the plastic tent wall and balled it into a fist.

'What the…?'

'We don't need this anymore.' He threw it into the bin. 'Today, it's you and me.' The man smacked of confidence.

Dumbfounded, Kate stuttered. 'You have to be kidding, right?' For once, she forgot his overpowering good looks and frowned when he shook his head.

'It's much more efficient to have only two people in charge. Otherwise, money gets mixed up, you are left short when someone doesn't show and to ensure the equipment is adequately cared for.' All of what he said made sense, but that wasn't the way it worked.

'Last time I checked, I was in charge of this stall and you should have asked me. Plus, today is all about community spirit, everyone helping out and making a contribution.'

Nick was not fazed by her reaction.

'Look around,' He spread his arms wide. 'There are hundreds of stands and plenty of volunteers.' He crossed his arms in front of his chest, and grinned. It was an expression that said he was right, and presumably, always right. Kate fumed. She didn't like it. Did this guy have to control every situation? Even fundraising events at the school? Words formed in her mind and were about to burst forth, when duty called. Their first customers had arrived. Nick offered that heart-melting smile again and moved away to serve the three young girls lined up.

She'd intended to address it later, but later never arrived. There had been no cause for her to be concerned, though, about being with Nick all day. By mid-morning, they'd painted at least a dozen faces and served double as many pink bunches of the sugar treat. When their arms ached from painting, they swapped over to swirl the fluffy sticks instead. There'd been no time to make small talk. Not long after one, they experienced a lull in trade and Nick offered to fetch them lunch.

'What would you like?' he asked.

'I'm starving,' Kate said. 'What are the options? I think there's burgers, noodles, sushi…Oh, I know there's a fantastic salad stand somewhere. Let's get that.'

'Do I look like someone who can survive on leaves?' he mocked, as his eyes shot skyward at the suggestion. 'Are you a vegetarian?'

Kate laughed. 'No, I guess you don't, but they do serve other things. And, I did eat those meat and cheese-fuelled pizzas at your place the other night, so no, I'm not vegetarian. I like raw and fresh products. It's called healthy last time I checked.'

'Okay, maybe they'll do steak. I'll check it out and be back in five.'

Over half an hour later, Nick returned. 'You would not believe the queue for that place. Clearly, healthy is popular, who knew?' he asked with a shrug but his eyes twinkled. 'I must admit the menu was great. Here's your salad and I've got us sweet potato fries to share.'

'Thank you. Yum, this is delicious,' Kate said as she swiped a hot chip. 'What did you get?' She pulled the lid off her plastic salad tub.

'Yours is a beetroot and pumpkin salad with oregano garlic chicken and I've gone for the salmon with a spinach green salad.' Kate shoved mouthfuls of green leaves into her mouth as Nick set out two bottles of water. They ate in peace.

Their stall overlooked the oval jam-packed with sideshow games and rides. On the netball court, where their marquee was located, there were other vendors to both their left and right. The people passing were laughing and smiling. Kate's heart swelled in a rare moment of contentment and she revelled in the feeling.

Nick stood and scanned the crowd.

'Have you seen Evie recently?' she asked.

'Yes. About fifteen minutes ago but only because she'd run out of money. She's had a dozen rides and purchased bangles and earrings and other useless stuff.'

'Earrings?' Kate repeated. 'I'll have to check them out,' she mused. Further customers came to the stall and they took turns serving them. The more elaborate face designs could take some time. Kate talked non-stop to her victim as she pasted and drew on their faces. She laughed and joked and made everyone feel special. At the end of a tricky lion face, Nick asked, 'How do you do it?'

'What? The face. I copied it…'

'No, I mean how do you stay so happy? You're always smiling. You never stop laughing and have an endless sense of fun about you. Your eyes constantly twinkle with mischief. How do you do that? I know you've suffered great tragedy. But you make life and having fun easy. Most of the time I'm like a grumpy old bear.' Nick's smile slipped.

She didn't know how to answer. The mood turned sombre. 'The earrings help,' she joked as she swished around the koalas that hung from her ears today. Nick burst out with laughter. It was one of those chuckles that rose from deep within his belly and was contagious.

'You're one of a kind.'

After Nick served a five-year-old boy a large portion of floss, Kate asked, 'Tell me about your work? I've figured out you're a lawyer.' A dark cloud descended like a veil over Nick's features. Kate watched him cover it up just as quickly.

'Yes, a boring old lawyer, I'm afraid.'

'Really? Is your job boring?'

'No, it isn't. But it's not a popular profession and when I tell people they always respond with their own lawyer story and usually it's one of dissatisfaction. They know someone who knows someone else who's had a bad experience, that sort of thing. Sometimes, I avoid telling people. The subject can stop conversations and be a real party failure.'

Kate considered what he said for a moment. 'I understand, but surely that doesn't bother you. It appears as if nothing does.'

'I can assure you that certain issues bother me…' He trailed off. 'But if you are asking whether I'm ashamed of what I do. The answer is no, the opposite in fact. I am proud that I can give back to people in times of their most desperate need. People only go to a lawyer when they need help and something is usually out of their grasp. On most occasions it will involve conflict. Rarely, not in my line anyway, will it involve happy events like purchasing a new home or a business. The majority of my clients are desperate. They require my expertise to get them out of a bind.'

'What sort of law?'

'Criminal.'

'Wow.'

'Is that it? Is that all you can say–wow?'

She giggled. 'Sorry, that didn't sound very intelligent. I didn't expect it. But now that I know, it doesn't surprise me. You're tough. Everything about you emanates strength and resilience and confidence and, oh, you know, I guess you know what I mean.'

'Do you mean that I'm nasty?'

'No! Why would you think that?'

He shrugged. 'I do take things seriously, I admit. But my line of work means people's lives are at risk and they rely on me. Working within the law does change you as a person. There are many responsibilities – from our clients, employers, from a business perspective and then the law profession itself. Sometimes the pressure is overwhelming. And, it doesn't help that I put myself under a great deal of stress to ensure that I do the best job that I can, regardless of the case or the person or their predicament.'

Kate's view of this man increased tenfold as they talked. She'd been unsure of him and at times, annoyed by his presumptions and actions, but he was a good guy doing a hard job. 'You must conduct interesting cases.'

His smiled returned. 'I sure do.'

'You must be constantly asked to share them, are you?'

'Yes, I am.'

'For that reason, I'm not going to request any salacious details or ask if you've acted for anyone famous.'

'Good idea, and I wouldn't tell you anyway.' Nick reached over and touched her knee. An explosion of tingles coursed through her body. When his hand lingered, she jumped up and acted as if a customer needed her urgent attention. Luckily, a group of girls passing shouted out in greeting and she spoke to them. Her body still shivered knowing Nick was nearby.

By dusk they'd run out of most paint colours and had no more fairy floss mix.

Given he'd spent the entire day on the stall, Kate encouraged Nick to go and enjoy the fair. Instead, he dismantled their marquee, returned equipment to rightful owners and carted the remainder of the paints and brushes to the art department. Kate wanted to call it a day and go home to put her feet up, but Nick clasped her hand.

'Let's go and have some fun.' He pulled her along to ensure she couldn't refuse.

***

Like a man with no cares, Nick walked around the fair with his arm around Kate. Today had served dual purposes for him and he was stoked. He'd never reveal to Kate, that, despite loving her company, that had been an added bonus. The positioning of the face painting and fairy floss stand had meant prime view to keep an eye on Evie the entire day. He'd been able to spot her at all vantage points. So, she'd been out having a good time with her friends and he'd been comfortable knowing she was safe. He didn't know how he would have managed it otherwise. Nick was confident that Evie would have objected to him following her around like a lost puppy dog all day.

Besides his other obvious problems, the day had progressed better than he'd ever imagined. For more than eight hours he'd been in Kate's company. What a dream come true. Her effervescent personality was infectious and he'd had fun. That woman would enjoy anything, even the most mundane of tasks. Joy radiated off her and she helped him forget his worries. That was one thing he loved about her; he ignored everything else in his life when he was in her company; she became his focus. With Evie safe and having fun in the school grounds – the last time he'd seen her she enjoyed a crazy gravity ride – he wanted this reprieve to last longer. He dragged Kate into the line for the dodgems. He wanted them to drive together, but she insisted they operate separate cars. She'd spent the entire ride trying her hardest to bump into him. He just wanted to chase her around the ring.

When they were hungry, they shared nachos under the stars in the open eating area as the sky darkened and the moon rose. Their fingers grazed one another as they reached for the same chip. It became a game and they laughed like teenagers trying to beat the other to the yummiest cheese melted nacho. The breeze picked up and Nick slid his denim jacket over her shoulders. He was sure smoke smouldered from her eyes. The crowds were dispersing but Nick couldn't face it ending yet.

'Can I go on another ride, Dad?' Evie shouted as she raced past with her group of friends. He nodded, happy she was occupied. Nick fought the urge to embrace Kate. He wanted to hold her in his arms and breathe in her sweet, lavender scent.

'Let's have one last ride on the ferris wheel,' he suggested. She nodded. Loop after loop they swung high over the school, watching people grasp the last dying moments of fun. A sizzle and explosion of colour burst into the sky surrounding them. Kate giggled like a child as a fireworks display crackled and illuminated. But Nick only had eyes for her. He waited for the right moment.

At the top, the wheel sat stationary to disembark people from below and Nick took his chance. Reaching his hand out, he gently turned Kate's face toward his. His pulse quickened when her brown eyes widened and blinked up at him. She swallowed as he lowered his face. He met her soft lips with light, feather kisses, cupped her chin and stroked her cheek with his thumb. She met him with equal pressure and he kissed her deeper, his lips smothering hers. He prised her mouth open and explored the soft folds with his tongue. Kate groaned, and he pushed closer until he moulded against her. Her breasts brushed against his chest and arm and his breath hitched. Forcing his lips away, he paused, trying to abate his building desire. His heart punched against his chest and his fingers itched to caress her bare skin. He quivered and his pants grew tight. Thank God they were in public. Otherwise he'd touch her in places that would make her moan; he'd be unable to resist. They kissed again, neither noticing their carriage begin its slow descent. As the ride slid to a halt, they forgot about exiting. The operator coughed, not once, but twice, to gain their attention.

'A good ride, then, I take it, folks,' the man chuckled, deep and low.

Nick pulled away and his body shivered at the absence of her warmth on his skin. Kate's pink lips sat apart and he gazed deep into her eyes, only visible from the colour kaleidoscope continuing in the sky. The cage door opened and Nick grasped her hand once more. Kate accepted it without looking at him. Two fingers traced the outline of her swollen lips. She turned away and they exited the wheel and simultaneously the world went quiet. The fireworks ceased and all went black until the school oval illuminated with stark white light. The fair was over.

Evie rushed over, her cheeks flushed pink from a fun day out. Kate dropped Nick's hand as his daughter approached.

CHAPTER THIRTEEN

Brittany Bartholomew took a large bite of a dagwood dog as the oval lit up. She paused mid-chew. She'd had a craving for the greasy takeaway since they'd arrived at the fair, but that didn't mean she wanted others to evidence her weakness.

Every year as a child her family had taken her to the Brisbane Exhibition. With little money to spread across six foster children, they'd been allowed one treat, always a fried dog on a stick. Her adopted mother's choice. She'd hated them as a kid; was jealous of the other children walking around with cans of soft drink, burgers and those large swirl lollipops when she wasn't even allowed a sample bag. Tonight, she'd bought Coco-Sage all that she'd desired; her daughter would not miss out like she had. And stupidly, she'd bought herself a dagwood dog for serendipity sake.

Sighing, she dropped the dog into the nearest rubbish bin. As inconspicuously as possible, she extracted the remnants from her teeth with her fingernails.

'Hey, I would have eaten that,' Lindsay, her husband said.

'You hardly need the extra weight, dear.'

Two people descended the short set of stairs from the ferris wheel to her right. Despite the light, she squinted, not wearing her glasses. The figures moved toward her and her pulse raced. In an instant, food was forgotten.

'Look over there, dear. That woman is one of Coco-Sage's teachers. She's young, isn't she? I haven't worked her out yet. She hardly replies to my emails and hasn't confirmed Coco-Sage as class captain or more importantly, soloist for the upcoming music tour.' Then lowering her voice, she said, 'I'm not sure she's a good teacher. Seems sort of ditzy.'

'She's a pretty thing, though, isn't she?'

Brittany's scowl would have scared anyone in its path. Lindsay didn't notice.

'Who's that fellow she's with? I recognise him.'

'What, that guy?'

Now Brittany was intrigued. She moved closer to her husband, ignoring the shudder of disgust that ran through her as she touched the soft flesh of his protruding tummy.

'He's a parent of another student. The young girl is a plain Jane, poor thing. But how do you know him? Has he been in the paper?'

'Most likely. There's where I meet most people. We do cover a lot of what's happening in Brisbane, as one of the premier Brisbane newspapers.' Brittany ignored his commentary, she'd heard it all before. Lindsay stared at the couple that held hands and walked away in the other direction. Brittany squealed. Kate Penrose and Nick Harding were holding hands. Unable to contain her excitement she clutched her husband's broad upper arm. Lindsay glared at her.

'They're holding hands. I knew it. My suspicious are confirmed. This is outrageous and completely unacceptable. There are policies on this and, and—'

Brittany was so outraged she couldn't speak. But it wasn't the rage that made her mute. That fire of jealousy ignited in her chest again, making it difficult to breathe.

Lindsay stamped his foot. 'It's on the tip of my tongue, I can recall his face. The young girls in the office were drooling over his picture, claiming how handsome he was. I can remember that much, so he had to feature in a prominent article. I'm sure it will come to me.' And he continued to swill his beer and munch on a sausage roll.

'I'm sure it will, dear. Make sure you tell me when you remember, no doubt it will be interesting.' Brittany lit a cigarette to rid her mouth of the greasy film from the dagwood dog. As she puffed, she ignored Lindsay and the dispersing crowd and hatched a plan. Kate Penrose would learn to co-operate.

***

'I'll have a cappuccino please, and one of your almond croissants,' Kate ordered from the waitress.

'Geez, Kate. Why can you eat whatever you want and never put on weight?' Angela asked for a small, skinny latte and a fruit salad.

Kate shrugged. They sat downstairs in the coffee shop at the base of her apartment building. Café de Flore was her absolute favourite jaunt and she could be found there most weekends. If she sat alone, she often read a trashy magazine or one of her classic novels. Sometimes she watched people stride up and down the path on the bank of the Brisbane River.

'How did you go at the fair yesterday? I didn't see you later on?' Angela said.

'Oh my goodness. I had the best time. My stall sold out and we made a huge profit. The kids were amazing and so much fun and, did you try that salad bar? Nick and I bought lunch from there....'

'Whoa, hold up. Did you say Nick? No wonder you are smiling this morning, girl.'

Kate slapped her friend playfully on the arm.

'Is that the best you got for me? Come on, you must have something to tell. Let me live a little vicariously through you.'

'What are you talking about? You are a happily married woman. You've snared one of the best. How is Todd by the way?'

'He's great. Out playing golf as we speak with workmates. But don't change the topic.'

Kate made herself comfortable, leaning on the table with her head in her hand and relived the day by telling Angela the details. Their coffees arrived and they sipped and ate and chatted some more.

'He likes you.'

Kate shrugged. 'I like him, too. But he's an overworked single parent, so that makes him a bit distracted most of the time. And that's putting it kindly.'

'Definitely. But I sense hesitation. What do you mean?'

'I've given you examples. Like yesterday. Small things happen and I go, what the? Why take over the entire roster for my stall? Why not do a solid block of two hours and then enjoy the fair? And why not consult me? I was in charge of it after all. But, instead he kept it all a secret.'

'If he did it purely to spend the day with you, that could be embarrassing. What's he gonna say? *Oh, I told everyone else they weren't required because I wanted to spend the day with you, alone?*'

Kate laughed as Angela put on a deep voice to imitate Nick. 'That's creepy and sounds nothing like him. But yes, okay, that makes sense. He told me he's a criminal lawyer.'

'Wow, interesting. Did he tell you any sordid cases he's worked on?'

'No, I didn't ask. He says he has to answer that question all the time. But I did think of it.'

'Are you seeing him again?'

'There's no plans.'

Kate did not tell her dearest friend about the passionate kiss that had curled her toes and made her stomach dance with desire. After that kiss she'd been breathless and her groin burned hot. A red-hot flush crept up her neck remembering his desire and the passion that had burned in his eyes. It had been difficult to part when those lights had illuminated the world and the night came to an end. But of course, they were assisted by Evie, giggling and happy after consuming too much sugar and on an overload of fun. In the end, she'd made it easy.

At that precise moment, Kate's phone dinged with a message and she drifted out of her daydream. Reading it, excitement built like a freight train.

'Is that him?' Angela shrieked.

Kate read the message and didn't look at her friend. Angela attempted to snatch the phone out of her hands, but Kate was too fast.

'No, you don't. But yes, it's him. But he isn't asking me out, he's checking that I made it home safely last night.'

Angela checked the time. 'It's only twelve on Sunday. You don't have any plans today and last time I checked it was the twenty-first century. Why don't you ask him around this afternoon?'

Kate's eyes widened. 'Are you kidding? To my place? No way. That is basically an invitation to come and sleep with me and I'm not ready for that.'

'Oh, go on, it could be fun. Anyway,' Angela jumped up, 'Todd will be finished playing soon and we're off to the in-laws for boring old

Sunday lunch. Gotta go.' Angela leaned over and kissed Kate's cheek.

After her friend left, Kate spent a few more minutes gazing at the message as if Nick himself was there.

***

The door slammed shut behind Kate. She had exactly twenty-five minutes to ensure the slides she'd prepared last night on the French Revolution, worked. In her hurry to enter the classroom and get started, she didn't spy the figure lurking near her desk. Brittany Bartholomew stood ramrod straight. Papers in her hand and her checks flushed.

'What are you doing?'

'Your desk is such a mess. I was tidying it for you.'

'What? You are kidding, right?' and Kate moved toward her and held out her hand for the papers. Surreptitiously she passed her eye over the desk. As she suspected, it was spotless. Brittany held exam booklets that Kate had left sitting there over the weekend. Nothing particularly special, but Brittany did not have the right to read the work of other students.

'Why are you sorting through my private papers?'

Ignoring her question, Brittany said, 'Coco-Sage didn't receive the top mark on the French exam. She's always been the top of her class, in all subjects. Now arriving at high school and you teaching her for English, French and Music, her grades have slipped. How long have you been teaching, Kate?'

Dumbfounded, Kate stood back. Was this happening?

'Mrs. Bartholomew,' Kate decided formality was required in the circumstances, 'I'm not sure what you are doing snooping around my classroom and I'm not sure what you are alluding to in relation to your daughter's grades. You are heavily invested in Coco-Sage's success…'

'Don't you tell me about my daughter!' Brittany jeered, spittle flying from her lips. But after taking two large breaths, she calmed down and spoke normally. 'For unexplained reasons you don't appreciate my daughter's talent or natural ability. You are playing favourites, Mrs. Penrose, that's the only conclusion I can reach.'

Kate had to stop her stutter. 'What?'

'Oh yes. Evie has captured your attention, although, perhaps I'm wrong. It's not her, it's her father.' Brittany smirked at Kate as if she'd uncovered a national secret.

'You don't know what you are talking about.'

'Don't I? I'm tired of playing games and of your lack of co-operation. I'll repeat my request that Coco-Sage become home room captain.' Brittany then held up her hands and rattled off other issues she'd like addressed. Kate held up her own hand to stop the blabbering. She'd had enough of this woman.

Brittany spoke over her. 'Before you speak, you should consider this. I have tried to be reasonable and work with you, but you aren't listening. Regrettably, I have to warn you. If you do not consider my reasonable requests, I will reveal to Mrs. Peterson and the entire school community that you are having an entirely inappropriate affair with the father of a student and more so, that as a result of that liaison, you're favouring that student to the detriment of others and they are being unfairly treated.'

'Again, you do not know what…'

'And, in case you consider people won't believe me, I will show them these.' Brittany flashed her phone into Kate's face and flicked quickly between dozens of shots of her and Nick. At the angles taken, they appeared to be intimately acquainted in each photo. Their faces were held close together with smiling eyes and upturned lips. Even the sheer volume of them would amount to guilt. Had they been together that often?

Kate's shoulders slouched.

'Yes, I knew you'd see sense. Let Coco-Sage shine and we'll all be happier.' And with that she whipped out an A4 sheet of paper with her list of 'requests'.

A tsunami of rage swirled within Kate. In a split second she had to decide to risk her job; the position she'd longed for to make her life right again, and that she wanted to be a success, or fight off this overbearing and demanding parent and tell her what for. These two polarising positions fought for space in her mind as the classroom door opened again.

Mrs. Peterson walked in. Kate brightened. This could be her answer. Should she reveal the goings-on to the principal and seek her refuge, or manage it herself? Kate had never been good at acting on her feet; it was not her strength. She took a second too long to consider her options and Brittany, obviously not indecisive like Kate, grasped the opportunity for all it was worth.

'Oh, Janette, good morning. How lovely to see you. I do love that sweater. That pale pink suits your complexion perfectly. Is it cashmere?'

Mrs. Peterson beamed at Brittany and removed her spectacles to let them hang by the chain around her neck. It made her eyes shrink in size. 'That's so kind of you, Brittany. This old thing, I've had it for years.'

'It matches your pearls.' And Brittany moved forward to pet the white beads around the principal's neck as if they were bosom friends. Mrs. Peterson's stance stiffened. Despite this, the smile remained plastered on the woman's face.

'I was showing Mrs. Penrose various photographs. Perhaps you'd like to see also.'

'Oh? Photographs of what exactly?'

'Here, let me show you.' Brittany extracted her iPhone once more.

Kate's heart hammered in her chest so loudly she was sure the two women could hear it. Her mouth dried. She instinctively raised her hand to swat away the phone. Mrs. Petersen gazed at her quizzically, but without so much as flinching, Brittany maneuvered the phone away from Kate's reach and closer to the principal.

'Aren't they wonderful? I should send them through to the school and they can be printed in the next addition of the newsletter. What do you think?'

What! Kate screamed in her mind, her palms now turning clammy.

'Oh, thank you Brittany. These are such lovely memories. I know we had a roaming camera on the day, but the girls were in charge of it and the results are varied. The fun fair was a great success, in thanks of course, to the P&C who were instrumental in pulling the day together...' Mrs. Peterson kept speaking but Kate had stalled on the words *fun fair*. Huh? Her mind addled. Why are they talking about the fun fair?

'Oh, Mrs. Penrose, I didn't show you this one.' Brittany shoved the phone in her face. A photograph of her and Nick working hard at the stall glared back. Nick laughed as he swirled a long stick in the candy floss barrel and Kate sat painting a child's face.

Innocent.

'Do you like it?' Brittany asked.

When she didn't answer, Mrs. Peterson frowned. Kate nodded. Her heart rate slowed, but she knew that she continued to be wrapped up in a web that Brittany controlled.

'One further thing, Janette. My husband and I have so enjoyed being at the school and getting involved and we recognise the potential here, that in addition to all the time I've devoted to the P&C and running its sub-committees and volunteering my time – too many things to mention – we'd like to ensure the school continues to flourish and make a personal donation.'

With a quick flick of her wrist, Brittany pulled out a cheque book and a jeweled pen. Mrs. Peterson's jaw dropped open.

'That is extremely kind of you, Mrs. Bartholomew.' Kate continued to remain silent. 'Isn't it, Kate?' The principal bumped her in the arm to illicit a response. Caught up in this game, she had to play, too. In her sweetest voice, she said, 'It is so considerate of you and your husband. The generosity you've shown the school and to me personally as a new teacher here this year, has been amazing.' To match the words, she added her most dazzling smile. At the saccharine tone, Brittany pulled her head up to gaze at Kate through a strand of blonde hair.

For the first time, her smile faltered. Didn't she realise Kate could play, too? Brittany made a show of ripping off the cheque and handing it to the principal.

'Oh my. This is too generous. The school cannot thank you enough, Mrs. Bartholomew.' Janette fluttered the valuable piece of paper around. 'This is going to be put to good use, I can assure you of that.'

With the excitement, the principal didn't reveal her intention of entering Kate's classroom on that Monday morning, but instead, she left jubilant, muttering all the way about what the money could be spent on.

Brittany followed suit, flouncing from the room, her strong Chanel scent lingering after her. Kate's need to prepare for French class completely forgotten.

CHAPTER FOURTEEN

Nick didn't like his new work title: unemployed.

He wasn't worried. A long and successful career to date meant he was adequately set up. He could remain out of work for the next twelve months and be financially secure. Yet, that didn't take into account that as an over-achiever and someone who had worked hard every day, rarely taking holidays, that, to avoid going crazy, he had to be busy.

Should he take a holiday? He slapped his forehead at his own stupidity. The uncertainty of his life at the moment meant he'd hardly be traipsing overseas for leisure. The Chalk case still sat on his desk. He bundled up the volumes of paper and files and readied them for collection. Dr Chalk had engaged McLaughlin Grant Lawyers and Nick was no longer employed by the firm. Shame. Nick had wanted to help the doctor. He would have loved securing his acquittal.

Should he find another job? It sounded ludicrous, even to his ears. How could he? As a previous high-profile partner of his own practice, how could he seek a position as an employee of another firm? He knew many practices would roll out the red carpet to have someone of his calibre, but it wasn't right. Begging for a job was beneath him. Plus, would they employ him now? Brisbane had a small legal community. Would his association with the Warlocks precede him and hamper his prospects? And more importantly, how could he be sure that their harassment was finished, that they would not bother him anymore?

The blunt answer was that he couldn't provide any assurances.

So, he could not, would not, put any other law firm at threat. That meant for the time being he would not be engaged in legal practice. The resolution made his chest constrict and his gut churn. Damn it! He slammed his fist onto the desk before getting up and storming to the kitchen.

Nick worked the coffee machine, read the newspaper and then news articles on the web. He reached for the pile of legal presentations and seminar papers he'd put aside to read when he had the chance.

He read three or four, but nothing held his attention. Not even the most up-to-date forensic advances in DNA testing could excite him. And usually, that sort of development, another defence available to his potential clients, would have him tingling all over. The four walls of the study closed in on him; suffocated him like a caged animal.

He picked up the phone and dialed. 'Hey, mate. Are you on days off?'

Listening to the answer, he said, 'Fancy a game of tennis?' He needed to beat out his frustration and physical activity with Curtis would be the perfect solution. He went to the hallway closet and reached for his helmet. A short ride might clear the cobwebs, too. Maybe a brainwave about what to do with himself in the short-term would come to him as he thrashed the ball or rode too fast on his Harley.

***

Kate pulled the hood of her rain poncho down lower to cover her eyes and avoid the heavy drips onto her face. She sucked in a deep breath-his smell had gone. She'd given away most of Ben's belongings but had kept the lime-green poncho. It wasn't the same without his fragrance, but she still wrapped her arms around herself as she walked.

Kate held it together for the remainder of the day, but the effort had exhausted her. Now, alone, she allowed herself to crumble. Irritable, she'd donned the rain jacket and headed out in the downpour. Living in the sunshine state people took the endless clear, blue skies for granted and became such whiners if grey clouds hid the sun. To Brisbane locals used to ideal weather two hundred and fifty days of the year, the rain was an annoyance. But this afternoon, Kate needed to get out, despite the wet.

Luckily, she lived near New Farm Park with its abundance of walkways and paths. She loved getting lost in the narrow alleys and quaint streets that she called home.

A loud Harley Davidson rode past, its rumble echoing in the air. It made her jump and cold tendrils crawl up her spine. That noise, she hated it. Too much like those nasty quad bikes in Greece. Would it always bother her?

Kate walked on and thought of Ben. He had been her emotional stabiliser and could make her laugh after a rough day. He'd been a great listener, too. Funny, how when a person was gone, you only remembered the favourable parts of them.

Kate knew she could ring Angela or anyone in her close group of friends from university. Despite it being a Monday afternoon, one of them would go for a drink or come over for a chat. But sometimes, you didn't want to talk. How could you when your thoughts were muddled and made no sense?

After Ben's death, her only focus had been herself and her work. Above anything else, she wanted to make sure she never experienced the pain of losing someone like that again. That wasn't too much to ask, was it? And, she'd been on track. Of course, such a goal required precision planning. But, at the moment she wasn't in control. What to do? Brittany's threats kept replaying in her head. They'd festered and grown to catastrophic proportions. Kate needed this job and wanted to succeed. But more than that, she wanted to be a quality teacher—one that students admired and learned from, looked up to. At the self-deprecating talk, Kate became furious at Brittany for creating doubts.

Kate walked faster as the rain beat down and she relived the school year to date. Could she have done more? Done anything different? She'd been a target since day one. And now, Brittany was getting on top of her. She needed a plan.

Being outdoors helped. It made the troubles dissipate a little. She licked the wet drops from her lips. The only way to deal with this was to stop thinking about a strategy and formulate one. Obviously, she wouldn't let someone like Brittany intimidate her. That would be too easy. But Kate needed to play smart. Running the mother's demands through her head, she elicited that at least two were achievable. If she allocated Coco-Sage to those positions, then Brittany might back off and consider she'd won. Some of those issues were no brainers. Who cared if this kid captained the netball or the debating team? The debate team didn't affect Kate as she wasn't the coach, netball did, of course. Unless she could convince Coco-Sage that she was playing below her standard and encourage her to play up. Yes! Kate fist pumped the air. There was no need to let this situation get on top of her; there were solutions, even if she participated in a game that she didn't want to play.

Kate would act on these now. There was plenty of time before the music trip. Of course, many issues were not negotiable, and now that she had Evie on the tour, she would be the soloist in the concert because she was the best musician. The weight sitting on Kate's shoulders started to lift and she walked freer. Otherwise, she'd continue to teach and mark Coco-Sage as she saw fit and deal with the consequences. If the grades were adequate, there couldn't be any ramifications against Kate, could there?

Her phone dinged. She reached into her pocket to extract it, trying to avoid the rain. Another message from Nick. It was the third text today. He'd been a casualty of her distress. With her career under threat, her friendship with him felt frivolous. Was Nick important? It had all been relaxed and fun and she'd loved how alive she'd felt. But, now, with him trying to contact her when she had issues on her mind, well, she pulled at her jacket collar. Stifled was how she felt. And with that, came doubt.

Who was he? She didn't know. Even after the time they'd snatched together, he'd hardly revealed anything about himself. She didn't even know what the nature of his relationship with Evie's mother had been. Or his parent's names and where they lived. Did he have other siblings besides Lizzie? Nick told her what he wanted her to know. And she had a sense, right down deep in her gut, that he wasn't telling the entire story. Something was not right.

Oh God! When did she get so pragmatic? Wiping away a droplet from her cheek, she couldn't tell if it was a tear or the rain, but she knew the answer to that question. Her entire life changed the moment her husband died. With him, died a piece of her and she wasn't that person anymore. For guidance, and more out of habit, she rubbed the coin in her pocket.

Her ring tone rang out. Surely not Nick again? She looked at her phone with a heavy heart. Her mother. Disappointment swept through her. The phone kept ringing and Kate sighed. She didn't speak to her mother often as her parents lived in northern New South Wales and she didn't want to ignore the call.

'Hi, Mum.'

'Hi, darling. How are you? The weather is apparently terrible up there…' After a short but pleasant conversation, Kate hung up with her mother none the wiser about her current turmoil. Her parents had suffered so much when Ben died, worried about her when she'd lost the will to live, and now, she didn't want to worry them unnecessarily.

Passing her favourite take-away en route back to her apartment, Kate made the rash decision to get one of her usual dishes. It was Monday, but hey, who cared? In this sultry weather a pho noodle soup from the Vietnamese shop was a perfect solution. Next important decision, what T.V show should she watch? A French film or more reruns of Sex and the City? Sometimes after Ben's death, making decisions was tough. Now, with the passage of time she could make them without fuss and for that she was grateful.

Tonight was about her. Kate perched on the couch with her Persian cat, Percy, purring contentedly on her lap and watched the first series of Ally McBeal for the third time. She sipped a chilled glass of white wine. Was it an irony that the show was about lawyers? Given that she put her phone on charge and didn't respond to Nick's various messages, she thought there was no coincidence at all.

***

Nick raked his hand over his face and blew out a sigh. Why did Kate ignore him? When he'd arrived at the music tour meeting, he'd made a beeline straight for her, surprised by his enthusiasm. They hadn't crossed paths since Saturday; today was Thursday. But, she'd been engaged in a discussion with a tall lanky woman with super tight curls. Their heads were down, focusing on a sheet of paper and crossing items off a checklist. Nick lingered at the back, biding his time.

After finishing that conversation, she placed chairs in the front row, tidied the brochure table and welcomed the tour operator. She must have seen him. He'd even held up his hand in a wave that went unacknowledged. She definitely avoided him, but why? Now twenty minutes had passed and his confidence waned. On one occasion she walked past him on her way to collect a stand from the rear of the room. Unless her eyesight had failed, she couldn't have missed him. Having grown up with a close relationship with his younger sister and mother, he'd always been intuitive and thought he knew women, but in this instance, he was just plain baffled. Nothing had occurred since they'd last spoke. Excepting of course, that she hadn't responded to any of his messages. Perhaps she'd been ill? Lost in his own thoughts, Nick didn't observe the man sidle up next to him.

'I say, old fellow, you look familiar. How would I know you?'

'I'm sorry?' Nick said, confident he hadn't heard correctly.

'I'm sure we know each other. Where would we have met? I own *The Daily Quest* newspaper, any chance you've featured in there?' The man chuckled and his ample stomach shook.

Nick's gut tightened. He didn't recognize the short man in the linen suit. His collared shirt strained at the buttons to expose soft flesh and his pant legs dragged on the ground. His stale breath made Nick recoil.

'Nah, mate, I've never had any occasion to be in the paper, I'm sure you are mistaking me for someone else. I guess I look like a lot of people,' Nick said. Before the fellow could speak again, he offered a small wave and moved away.

'Nick Harding, we keep running into each other. How lovely to see you,' Brittany said as she grasped his bicep with both hands making it impossible for him to escape. Nick offered a tight smile.

'I see you've met my husband. Lindsay, this is Nick Harding, another parent at the school. His daughter is Evie and she and Coco-Sage are in the same class and fierce competitors.' Brittany's laugh sounded like a witch's cackle.

Fierce competitors? That's the first he's heard of it. Given Evie held contempt for those who took matters too seriously, he assumed it was this Coco-Sage who might be the aggressive one.

'They both have designs on being the solo flautist on this music tour. May the best girl win,' Brittany said.

'I know,' said Lindsay. 'You're a lawyer, aren't you?' His eyes squinted disappearing into his pudgy face.

At that moment Kate walked past accompanied by another teacher. Brittany placed one hand in front of Kate, preventing her passage. A flicker of disdain flashed across Kate's features before she reigned herself back in and smiled warmly. 'Hello, Brittany. How can I help you?'

'Are you announcing tonight who will perform the role of soloist during the tour?' Brittany fluttered her eyelids and her words were as sweet as sugar.

'No, Brittany. My final three choices are with the head of the music school and a decision will be made during the tour. Each girl is an exceptional candidate.'

'Yes, I'm sure but there can only be one winner.'

Nick's discomfort intensified and he grew hot. He didn't want to be part of this conversation, or near this fellow from the paper. He removed his jacket and placed it over his forearm. His short T-shirt sleeve crept up revealing the base of a rose tattoo.

'I've got it! I know who you are,' Lindsay bellowed. 'You're the lawyer who represented all those despicable bikie outlaws and got them acquitted of heinous crimes.' His voice doubled in volume due to his excitement.

Nick turned toward Kate. Her eyebrows hit her forehead and her eyes were wide.

'You acted for their leader, didn't you? What was his name? Michael? Matthew? No Max, that's right. Couldn't get him off, could you? He was a real bad egg. How could you do it? Act for those vile criminals who disregarded the law and flouted the safety of regular citizens? Takes a certain sort of bloke, doesn't it? They reward you well, though, I hear.' Lindsay smirked and nudged Nick.

'I cannot discuss any case that I've worked on, that is all confidential.'

As if Nick hadn't spoken, Lindsay continued. 'But, most interesting is the gang is still creating havoc even though their fearless leader is in prison. Do you know anything about that?'

The colour drained from Nick's face.

Usually he'd tell this greedy, rumour-mongering journalist to piss off. But conscious of Kate listening, he hesitated.

Lindsay's belly shook and a laugh followed thirty seconds later. 'If that isn't a guilty face, I don't know what is! You do know something. Give me an exclusive, we can run it in tomorrow's edition. Do you have a secret line to the gang leader? Are you still protecting him?' Now he leaned in so close to Nick that their bodies touched. 'Or are you doing his dirty work whilst he's on the inside?'

Nick used a flat palm to gently shove the guy back and out of his personal space. Kate gasped when Lindsay fumbled and almost lost balance. Nick held out his arm to steady the bloke. 'We are at a school meeting about our daughters' school trip. This is neither the time nor the place for your interrogation. But for the record, I no longer have any association with the Warlocks and I wholeheartedly dispute any allegation that I'm involved in their current criminal behaviour. My previous firm acted as their legal representatives and I'm no longer employed by them, but I can confirm that the gang has engaged new lawyers to protect their interests.'

'Why aren't you working at that firm any longer? Did you get fired for your association with those outlaws? Did your firm disagree with you acting for them? Our Premier might have been right. Lawyers are hired guns. Have you accepted dirty money—'

Mr. Robertson, the head of the music department coughed to gain attention. If he'd noticed the melee in the back, he didn't regard it. People who had turned toward the robust discussion now resumed their seats and listened to the teacher. Nick reached for Kate's hand as the people around them disbursed. She snatched it out of his grip like it burned. She delivered him a caustic look before he scampered to a seat.

***

After the meeting Kate stacked chairs and tidied the room. Most parents, probably with a range of other commitments, left quickly after it ended. The last thing Nick wanted was for Kate to feel uncomfortable, but he couldn't leave without talking to her. His safest option would be to wait outside. He leaned against the wall of the classroom, his foot against the paneling keeping his balance. As if that annoying, Brittany Bartholomew wasn't bad enough, her husband operated that blasted *Daily Quest*, the Brisbane newspaper notorious for supporting the far right and crucifying the legal profession in its coverage. Why did Lindsay and his newspaper hate lawyers?

His recognition of Nick had piqued his interest, but hopefully, upon realization that Nick Harding wasn't news these days, Lindsay would leave him alone.

'Kate?' he said her name softly as she left the room. Finally, she was alone. She turned at her name and as if startled, dropped the folders and papers she held. Nick strode over and collected them.

'Can we talk?'

'What about?'

'For starters, I guess, about why you're avoiding me. And then, of course what you heard. I need to explain.'

'That's just it, Nick, you don't need to explain. You don't owe me an explanation. You don't owe me anything. We hardly know each other. What you do or has occurred in your past has nothing to do with me. Maybe you should leave me alone.'

He'd prefer her anger, anything but dismissal. Was she disappointed in him? It hit him like a punch to the gut. 'Why? Why should I leave you alone? Have I done something to offend you?' He took her books and held them whilst she flicked off the hall light. She strode down the narrow corridor and he fought to keep up with her.

'I don't know. What is going on? I've enjoyed spending time with you. But, you know, I need to concentrate on my job. A few issues have arisen and I need to stay focused. Plus, you seem to have a lot going on…'

Nick resisted a smirk. 'Is that the best you've got? You need to do your job. I didn't realise I was preventing you. In fact, I thought spending an entire Saturday on a stall with you fundraising for the school, might be assisting.'

She offered him a slight smile.

He wasn't there yet. 'What is it really?'

Kate paused.

'Kate, I'm not sure what's going on here. I thought we were having fun.'

She spun toward him so fast her skirt twirled. 'Fun? That's for teenagers and the students I teach, for people without responsibility and jobs and, and, I don't know, other people who don't have serious things that have happened in their life. Life is not about fun!'

'Whoa, I'm sorry.' Nick held up his hand. 'That came out all wrong. What I meant to say is that I like you. That fact is scaring the hell out of me, too, but, oh, I don't know, I thought we were enjoying each other's company but that sounds like we're eighty and sharing cups of tea in a nursing home.' Nick shrugged and he couldn't stop the words before they were out. 'The thought of not seeing you again, it's unbearable. You are all I can think about. I want to spend more time with you.' He didn't say she was the only lightness in his dark world at the moment.

Kate uncrossed her arms that had clung tightly to her chest. Nick watched her throat as she swallowed. 'What was all that about tonight with Brittany's husband? *Who are you?*'

'It's a long story, but one I'm happy to tell you. I will give you each boring little detail.' Nick reached for her hand, balancing her books in his other. Conflicting emotions passed over her features.

'I guess I'm confused and not sure. Work is challenging at the moment. And the time I spend with you is so all-consuming. I feel like I'm losing myself and need to refocus, back on my work. This is more than a job to me. It's important.'

Nick nodded. 'I know. I understand, I really do. Can we grab a drink?'

Kate agreed.

CHAPTER FIFTEEN

Kate knew of a chic little bar around the corner from school. She'd not been there but the teachers in her staff room recommended it. Once seated in a plush black leather booth, she ordered a gin and tonic and a scotch on the rocks for Nick. 'It's your drink, right?'

'It's my favourite, yes.'

'What else do you drink, other than scotch?'

'Everything. I like white and red wine and most spirits. I'll drink anything.' His brow creased and he looked away. 'Tell me about your husband,' he asked out of the blue and sat back, ready to listen.

Kate shook her head so that her loose hair framed her face. 'No. Not tonight, tell me who the Warlocks are and your involvement with them.'

Their drinks arrived, and she took a sip of her gin. She thought about the words Nick had uttered. *He liked her. Not seeing her is unbearable.* Kate concealed her grin and took her turn to sit back. She meant business tonight and would not be deterred even after he'd uttered those sweet words.

'You're squeezing my balls, aren't you? As my less than salubrious clients might say.' Nick told her about the bikie gang, the members he'd acted for, the success he'd had in their representation and then when that luck had run out.

Kate listened. She relaxed and observed him and took in the details of his story. For a layperson, it all sounded above board, even if not desirable work. He had a job to do and he did it. Acting for criminals, regardless of where they came from, couldn't be considered clean work anyway, could it?

A drink driver might not assault someone outside a nightclub after one too many drinks, but they still had the potential to kill behind the wheel. And, if a person made a mistake and broke the law, they needed a criminal lawyer to defend them.

Occasionally, Nick provided brief snapshots of funny anecdotes from his clients and the defences they'd offered to assist their case. She giggled where she usually mightn't, but the alcohol gave her a loose tongue.

Despite her happiness at Nick finally opening up to her, she noted his constrained state. He chose his words carefully and constructed sentences precisely. He often looked out over her head and glanced across the way, toward the bar as if expecting someone to enter and join them. Sporadically his mind wandered and he appeared whimsical as if he couldn't believe the circumstances of the stories he told. His restrained manner set off an alarm that she couldn't silence. Was he lying?

'Did you act for them honestly?' she challenged him. He gave her that rueful smile. The one that she imagined could tear a confession from the worst of offender. Perhaps he didn't like being confronted and was more used to acting as the interrogator.

'In all the cases I have acted in, or legal matter that I have conducted, I have done so with the utmost integrity and acted to the best of my ability.' His words were strong and sprang forth with so much emotion that Kate did not doubt his sentiment.

'I know you said the other day that criminals are entitled to representation even if they are guilty, but what do you do if they are culpable?'

'First of all it depends if they are pleading guilty. If that's the case then they have confessed guilt and my job is to mitigate their circumstances and achieve the best possible penalty. For example, have their parole period reduced or there might be circumstances that will affect the courts view, I don't know, like drugs.'

Kate nodded, wrapped up in his words.

'But what you're probably asking is what do I do if they tell me they're innocent and I believe they're guilty. Because unless a client tells me they did it, who knows? That's for the court system to decide, not me, not you. But if there's evidence that comes to light that means they could have done it, there can always still be doubt and my job remains to defend them as if they weren't responsible. If it's the case that there is such overwhelming proof of guilt, it is my duty to step down and no longer act for them. If I know they did it, it's too hard to defend them and mount a proper case. But I've never had to do that.' Nick sipped his drink and let those words sink in.

'I can tell you're a good lawyer. I trust you.'

As she spoke the words, he gazed at her and stared, locked onto her eyes. A longing spread like wildfire from Kate's extremities to her core. Nick lifted his arm to take a sip of his drink. His shirt sleeve lifted, exposing the blood red tattoo. 'And, is there a story behind that?' She tilted her head toward his upper arm.

Did he freeze, or did she imagine it?

He paused.

Kate guessed he was collecting his thoughts, summoning up the precise words to frame. The dread that simmered in her gut, boiled.

'It was a gift from a client. A client, that at the time I trusted implicitly. I thought it was to be a long-term working arrangement. I did it as an act of solidarity. To prove that they could trust me. In retrospect, it was the dumbest professional decision I've ever made. To align myself to a client like that? Stupid.' Nick shook his head, disgust sweeping across his features.

Kate traced a solitary finger along the edges of the tattoo's green trim. 'It's beautiful.' *Just like you.*

She motioned the waiter for another drink, but Nick glanced at his watch. 'It's after eleven and a school night. We should go.'

'Oh gosh, it's so late. I'm sorry I lost track of the time.'

'That's okay, let's go.'

Nick paid for their drinks and opened the bar door for her as they exited. When they reached his car, he opened her passenger door.

Kate became overwhelmed by emotion, it swirled in her chest making it hard to breathe. Nick Harding had her back, he protected her; in his presence she felt like the most important person in the world. Even Ben hadn't been a romantic. Hadn't been chivalrous and so, so *gallant*.

At her apartment building, he insisted on delivering her to her door. Conscious of each movement, she stumbled up the short set of stairs. His arm clasped hers to right her balance. Nick removed the keys from her hands and opened her door.

'Do you want to come in?' She didn't recognize her own voice.

Nick shook his head, even though she detected an effort in refusing.

'It's late and you have to work tomorrow.'

'You too,' she said.

'Yes,' he responded.

Nick stared at her so that her tummy quivered and she had to reach for the doorframe to steady herself. He leaned in and kissed her with the lightest touch of his lips. Kate needed more. She pulled him closer with her hand on the back of his neck and gave him no choice. Their lips converged and their tongues explored. The burnt sugar taste of the rum exploded in her mouth. Nick placed a trail of kisses from her earlobe, along her chin until he reached those full, inviting lips once more.

In the end, he pulled away first.

'I'd better go otherwise I will come in.' He turned on his heel and walked down the carpeted hallway. Kate watched him until he exited through her glass doors. She retreated inside, licking her lips for the taste of him.

Confident she wouldn't be able to sleep, she flicked on the kettle and prepared herself a chamomile tea. Placing her hot drink on the coffee table to cool, she pulled open a drawer in the retro sideboard of her dining area and extracted a box. Kate plopped into the lounge and immediately sank into its softness. She opened the lid and extracted its contents.

Silent tears rolled down her cheeks. Kate trawled through photographs of her honeymoon: happy snaps posing against Greek ruins, clear blue oceans, in museums and selfies enjoying foreign food. Her fingers traced the edges of Ben's watch. He'd treasured that watch; a birthday gift from her. Kate slid it onto her arm. It hung too loose but she didn't care. It slipped down her wrist as she raked through trinkets, wrappings and other paraphernalia she'd kept from their honeymoon. Scattered memories of Ben. A sharp pain splintered through her chest. She'd known everything about Ben, had trusted him implicitly. Nick had revealed himself tonight but she still couldn't shake the sense he held something back. Would she grow to trust him, like she had Ben? Would he become her everything? Of course, she'd known Ben for years, they'd grown as adults together. Ben had been her first love, her first kiss and the only man she'd slept with. Whilst she couldn't deny her feelings for Nick, whatever they were: excitement, hope, lust, the thought of being intimate with another man scared the hell out of her. She'd never thought she'd have to. But life throws you lemons, as Forrest Gump would say. And she'd been thrown a whole bag. Gathering up the items, she gently placed them back in the box, except the watch. She'd keep wearing it awhile longer.

Nick liked her.

It was too much for her scrambled brain to cope with and fatigue hit her like a wave pulling her under. Kate sank lower into the couch, confused memories muddled her mind, and images of both Ben and Nick intermingled. But the last picture before she drifted into a troubled sleep was of Nick Harding, not of Ben.

CHAPTER SIXTEEN

BIKIE LOVING LAWYER LOSES JOB

Notorious bikie gang, the Warlocks, is back.

In an exclusive investigation, The Daily Quest will uncover the reign that the gang still has over the streets of Brisbane.

Robert 'Robbo' Mendelson appeared in the Brisbane Magistrates Court today charged with armed robbery of a service station. Queensland Police report that Robbo held up the service station attendant with a knife and punched him repeatedly in the stomach when he refused to hand over cash. Bashing the fellow unconscious, Robbo snatched lollies and chocolate bars as he ran from the scene leaving behind small change and the attendant in a pool of his own blood.

Robbo attended court represented by Rocco Ambrose, well known for acting for the state's worst offenders.

When asked where the gang's previous lawyer, Nick Harding was, Robbo spat on the ground and said, 'That's what I think of Nick Harding. If he turned up here, he'd leave in a box.' Harsh words from Robbo before he was refused bail and taken away to the cells.

Nick Harding rose to fame when he commenced acting exclusively for the low-life gang who were wreaking havoc on the community before our Premier stepped in and introduced the controversial and tough anti-bikie association laws. Back in 2015 and 2016 when the gang had Brisbane in its grips, Harding had a string of successes in acquitting members of various crimes of violence such as torture, grievous bodily harm, assault and minor offences like petty theft, public nuisance and drink driving.

It all turned sour in late 2016 when running on an air of arrogance, Harding represented top-pin, leader Max Vincenzo. It was the first time the leader had been caught and charged despite his endless involvement in other crimes, he'd never been dragged before the law before. In spite of the outstanding legal representation, and high court antics from Harding, Vincenzo was convicted on charges of murder, torture and deprivation of liberty and sentenced to life imprisonment and lumped with a serious violent offender label.

As far as The Daily Quest can uncover, Vincenzo remains safely behind bars, but his gang has resurfaced after a brief hiatus and are causing havoc to the innocent citizens of our community. Endless complaints have been made to police over the last two months.

Robbo is not the first gang member expected to appear before the courts in the coming weeks.

The Daily Quest spoke to Harding last week and he confirmed that he no longer represents the club's interests. He verified that the gang had engaged a new lawyer but refused to comment on whether he had any current association with Max Vincenzo or other members of the club.

Rumours are running rife that Harding has come unstuck. It's reported that he's lost his employment with well-known criminal law firm, McLaughlin Grant. When contacted, the firm substantiated that Harding no longer works there. Our search result did not reveal that Harding has gained employment as a lawyer anywhere else in Brisbane.

Has Harding gone to the dark side? Has working with the underworld turned him into one of those bikies that he worked so hard to help? Despite the scathing comments from the Warlocks saying they'd cut Harding up into little pieces if he crossed their path, doubt remains about the lawyer's current association with the club.

Nick couldn't read anymore. The only positive about this scaremongering pile of lies, was that the lowlife paper didn't mention his daughter. The negative, amongst many, was the photograph that Bartholomew had printed to accompany the article: Nick and Kate holding hands and looking intimate. He recognized it immediately. It had been taken at the fun fair as they left the Ferris Wheel. Their faces flushed with excitement as they gazed into one another's eyes. In other circumstances, he'd love the photo. They were like any young couple having fun. But when publicly aired for all of Brisbane to see and accompanied by an article filled with lies and innuendo and connecting him with the Warlocks yet again, it spelled disaster.

Nick wanted to snap the paper shut and rip it up into tiny shreds to the point he could no longer recognise the image or read the words. But, he needed the paper as his camouflage and lowering it now, let alone destroying it would mean the whole airport could spot him.

Blood ran through his veins making his senses alert. He slapped his thigh; he'd been right. He'd had a lot of internal debate about following Evie to Vietnam on this school trip. His gut led him and it sensed danger. He could not have remained home for ten days, so far away from his daughter. And now, Kate had been implicated, too. Her photograph was flashed across page three. And the danger in that was the Warlocks would now connect her to him and that was all types of bad.

The coffee and sandwich he'd eaten roiled in his stomach. That bastard Bartholomew! It confirmed Nick's cynical view of journalists – they pieced together stories with no factual basis. What was the point of this article? The paper could have reported on the offence committed by the bikie member as its own news piece, but no, they had to make a connection with him. And now he'd tainted Kate with the toxin currently poisoning his life.

Since Evie had started school, he'd done a shit job of keeping a low profile. And his ultimate failure was implicating those around him. Nick slunk back in the plastic food court chair. At least in Vietnam, they'd all be temporarily removed from this situation. It wouldn't be hard for the gang to track down Kate and that would lead to where she worked at the school and where Evie attended and perhaps, that a large ensemble of year seven students were on tour in Asia. Would the Warlocks venture that far? He didn't think so. Unless they had contacts in that part of the world, but wouldn't they have better things to do than wreak revenge on him?

Soon he could stop hiding behind papers and pot plants. How ludicrous his life had become. Evie's plane was due to depart any minute. Whilst he would have preferred to be on the same flight as the school tour, even in his most creative of imaginations, he couldn't work out how to pull that off. No, he'd booked the next flight out. He wouldn't be far behind them after they'd landed.

What then?

CHAPTER SEVENTEEN

The heat engulfed him as soon as he got out of the taxi and the humidity clung to him like a blanket. Nick hadn't travelled to Vietnam before, but boy, it was hot.

Evie, at thirteen-years-old had already become an international traveller. Nick smiled at the thought. After extracting his small suitcase from the boot of the compact taxi and wiping the sweat from his brow, he gazed up at the Royal Riverside Hotel. It lived up to its name as he spied the murky Hoai River flowing freely behind the building. He wasn't sure about the Royal part, but none of that mattered, it was the location he cared about. He glanced sideways to next door.

The Riverside Oasis Resort sat where it should. The melon-coloured structure was the reason he'd chosen this hotel; Evie stayed there. It might have been smart to create further distance, but hey, he didn't always do the most sensible thing as demonstrated by him standing in Hoi An and hauling his luggage up the granite steps. His heart was in the right place, even if his brain wasn't.

Laughter and raised voices caught his attention. To his left a bunch of girls huddled together waiting for a mini-bus that was pulling into the Oasis circular drive. Nick spotted Evie, smiling and fanning herself with a pamphlet. He ducked behind one of the formal white pillars bordering the steps to his hotel's entrance. He'd be seen if anyone turned in his direction as his bulk could barely be concealed behind the narrow column. Nick strained around the concrete to gain a better vantage. Where was Kate?

Moments later she exited the hotel carrying a clipboard and a lanyard around her neck and all business-like. Her trademark beaming grin was in place. She observed the girls and shoved her notes into her tote bag. His heart did a little pitter-patter. Evie and Kate looked so happy. But where were they going? Having memorized the itinerary he knew they were not scheduled for an excursion this afternoon. He grimaced but quelled his growing anxiety.

Dropping his bag, he motioned the porter to keep it safe until he returned. Nick stepped sideways back down the steps to gain the taxi driver's attention. Thankfully, he hadn't driven away. Using snatched English, the driver understood that Nick wanted to follow the bus idling next door. The elderly Vietnamese driver smiled, nodded and said, 'okay' but his eyes were clouded. Another crazy tourist he no doubt thought. In truth, Nick felt like an idiot. He hadn't worked out exactly what he'd do in Vietnam. Did he expect to follow Evie to each activity? He didn't think so. Once he was sure she was safe, he intended to back off. But he'd only arrived and this was unexpected and had caught him off guard.

He'd settle in, soon.

***

It was a tiny concert space, but the band sprawled across the timber makeshift stage. The platform took up the width of the hall, leaving only narrow aisles on each side. It may well have been Carnegie Hall or The Royal Opera House at Covent Garden, such was the excitement of the students. They'd worked hard and were ready. It was the pinnacle of the tour and happened on day two. Kate had questioned that decision early on. As the signature event shouldn't it be the swan song, the girls' great farewell and occur on their last night? Others, much more experienced than her, had chided, and said, it was better to hold the event earlier in the trip. Even now, Kate understood the wisdom of that. With the buzz being over tonight, it would allow them to focus on the other cultural aspects of their experience.

Forgetting all that for now, she placed the girls into position and reminded them of the order of pieces. As the soloist Evie would play two pieces without accompaniment. Coco-Sage had sulked at the news ever since it had been announced. Kate hadn't dared turn on her phone or check her emails. She didn't want to read a barrage of correspondence from Brittany. Best to deal with that after the show, or maybe even back home.

Resplendent in their school uniforms, the girls were ready. Most of the day had involved rehearsal and in only five minutes, it would begin. Principal, Mrs. Peterson had flown over especially for the concert and would return to Brisbane tomorrow. She beamed from her prime position in the front row. Tickets had been sold tickets to the general public, but as far as Kate could make out, most of the captive eyes belonged to the students of the local schools. All students sat with their classmates and this broke the audience up into colour. The students from Hoi Ping Public school wore their brown dress uniform with matching shoes. The Green Shoots International School was dazzling in their blue blazers with maroon ties and yellow stripes, similar to the Hogwarts dress code. Those students didn't have a hair out of place and their multi-cultural teachers stood at the end of each row to knock on the knuckles of those misbehaving.

And then there were the ramshackle leftovers from the local orphanage sat strewn across the floor and into any available space. They sat up the straightest and with the biggest and brightest of smiles. Less than half the group wore shoes. Their clothing, whilst clean, was worn and threadbare. But they already leaned forward in attention to listen to the music and gaze at instruments they'd never seen before.

Once Kate was confident her students had music sheets open at the right place, their instruments in working order and were comfortable and ready, she retreated, moving aside a faux velvet curtain to make her way off stage. She intended to steal a seat or stand to the edge of an aisle to soak up the show.

She took the stairs down from the stage. Only a few short steps and she was at the back with ample room to enjoy the spectacle. The whirring overhead fans did little to ease the suffocating heat trapped in the room. Kate cooled her face by fanning the show brochure and looking around her. A few spare seats in the back row remained free but Kate stood. She rolled back and forth on her heels, a flutter of butterflies in her tummy. People pushed past her to catch those last available spots. Kate watched them step on toes and mutter apologies as they moved to the middle of the row.

Then she saw him.

Nick.

Their eyes connected but his face turned away immediately. He sat at the end of the row, closest to the far aisle. Kate blinked and closed her eyes. She had to be mistaken; she was tired from the journey and time difference and the frantic pace they'd kept so far. She peeked one eyelid open. He was gone. Of course. She blew out a breath. She'd been wrong. It was someone who looked like Nick. She'd thought of him so often these last few days she must have conjured up his image.

Mellifluous sounds commenced drifting down from the stage as the curtains released and the opening number commenced. It was haunting and dramatic and captured Kate's attention entirely even though she'd heard the piece a hundred times before. Despite being drawn to the music, she checked back to the seat where she thought she'd seen Nick. Perhaps he'd reappear? But now, it sat occupied by an elderly Asian man wearing glasses. There was no confusing the two.

It had been him, hadn't it?

Or did she simply wish Nick Harding was here?

Kate sipped her gin after removing the ice cubes. After having done her research, she was pedantic about not drinking the local water, including the excruciatingly cool ice. She did not want to get sick. For luck, she caressed her euro coin.

The cool liquid immediately dropped her body temperature. The blazing sun had turned her skin pink and even though the heat of the day had dissipated, perspiration still clung to her skin, making it glisten. She drank quickly and her glass was soon empty. She left it on the tall, oak table she and her colleague sat around. The local Hoi An bar had an American theme and in amongst the timber–oak bar, cedar tables and pine walls were collections of sports memorabilia. Photographs adorned the walls in their stars and stripes with their white teeth and wholesome grins. A sizeable tourist crowd had gathered on the mid-week night.

Gina, the tour operator, turned to her and said, 'The concert was a huge success, Kate. Congratulations. The crowd adored Evie when she played the solo. She was a great choice, so beautiful to watch.'

Kate lit up. It had been worth it. She pushed aside the niggle of tension that knotted in her spine at the thought of Brittany Bartholomew.

'It was great, wasn't it? All the girls lifted and they performed so well. No one made a mistake. They held their nerve. And, in the end the pressure wasn't too great because the crowd was so happy and easy to please.'

'Oh, and I filmed it, too,' Gina said. 'Let's watch it one spare evening.'

'Great idea.' Kate agreed. 'I'm so pleased that Mrs. Peterson flew in to catch the performance. She wasn't disappointed.' Kate wished Janette had found her after the show and expressed her pleasure at her hard work, in addition to that of the girls. It was, of course, all about the students, but hey, she'd worked damn hard! In any event, mission accomplished. If events on this trip now turned sour, at least the concert was a runaway success.

'I'm heading to the bathroom,' she said.

Gina looked at her watch. 'I'm due to meet a friend here in a few minutes. A fellow operator who's in Hoi An at the same time. We don't get to catch up much. Is it okay if she sits with us? Nigel is on duty with Louisa back at the hotel so we might as well make the most of our free night whilst we can.'

'Of course,' Kate said. Then she pushed her way through the crowd, passing posters of Michael Jordan and Serena Williams. Leaving the bathroom, she made out a quieter bar at the other end of the establishment. The pub narrowed with a few cramped booths aligning its edges. She headed there for her next drink, away from the crowd and to grab herself a few quiet moments. Kate thanked the barman and turned away to take a deep, long sip of her drink before heading back to Gina.

But then she saw him.

She rubbed her eyes until they blurred. The figure hunched over his phone and sitting alone in one of the secluded booths looked remarkably like Nick Harding. A tangled mess of longish hair covered his face. Her stomach tightened whilst little fireworks exploded inside her. Her excitement bubbled like a child on Christmas morning, but then as if she'd received a gift she didn't want, her enthusiasm burned to a dull astonishment.

She strode over and positioned her drink at the edge of his table and placed her hands on her hips. 'What are you doing here?'

He looked up and pushed strands of hair out of his eyes. He glowed red and sank back into the vinyl seat. But instead of blabbering apologies or explanations, he reached across the open space between them and grasped her around the waist and pulled her close. Their lips met and Kate instantaneously forgot her surprise at him being in Vietnam.

She indulged in the taste and feel of his lips, but placed her flat palm on his chest and pushed him backwards. 'Nick Harding. You always do the unexpected.'

'That's a good thing, right?'

Even though it was difficult, she ignored his devilish grin. 'Your daughter is on a school music tour. One that you gave permission for and if I'm not mistaken, you were present waving her off at the airport in Brisbane. Now, you are here in a bar in Hoi An. You were at the concert tonight, weren't you?'

He nodded sheepishly.

Turning serious, Kate responded, 'You know that I'm taking good care of Evie, don't you?'

'Yes, I do. It's not that.'

'What is it, then?'

At that moment Gina walked past on her way to the bar. 'Oh, hi Kate.' Gina glanced between them.

'Hey, Gina. I've met someone I know and I'm going to sit here for a while. Has your friend arrived? Is it okay if I leave you guys to it?'

'Sure thing.'

Nick's cover was safe with Gina having never met him before. Kate sat down and nursed her drink. Nick reached for the glass in front of him, but it was empty. He signaled to the barman for another. 'What are you drinking?'

'Coke.'

His eyebrows raised in question, but he ordered her one, anyway.

'Start talking, Mr. Harding. Otherwise, I'm actually going to think there is something wrong with you because you have followed your daughter overseas on a school trip. I suspect there's a lot you aren't telling me.'

Kate had meant it to sound flippant, but her words were harsh and she immediately wanted to retract them. Her mind was going crazy with thoughts. He likes me; he's a lawyer who's acted for a bike gang and he's here in Vietnam. Nothing made sense.

Nick slouched and sank into himself.

Kate panicked at his reaction. 'Is something wrong? Is that why you're here?' She reached across the table and placed her hand on his.

'No.' He shook his head. 'No, nothing is wrong. I am here to ensure Evie is safe. I want to make sure she's okay. Honest truth.' He did a girl guides' salute and mock-smiled at her.

Kate took a gulp of her drink. 'Nick, I don't believe you. I do not accept that a man such as yourself has any reason to follow their daughter across continents to ensure her safety on a school trip. Might I say, off topic, that these trips are the most over-regulated productions. If a child goes missing it would be a miracle. If they become sick we have the largest health policy in the world–I can produce it if you wish, and there are strategic plans for each conceivable mishap. So, no, I don't buy it. But, you know what? That's okay. I don't need to buy it. You've obviously got stuff going on.' Kate waved her free hand around in the air, indicating who-knew-what. 'And that is your business and you don't owe me an explanation. I don't want to know or become involved. Okay?'

Her lips were loose. She hadn't expected to bump into Nick. Kate thought she and Gina would have one or two quiet drinks to wind down and debrief and she'd be early to bed. This had thrown her off course. Plus, her mind was already an addled buzz. But honestly, she didn't want to know. Whatever it was, it frightened her, hell, Nick Harding scared her because of the way he made her feel. Him being here was enough for her to deal with.

***

Nick knew his story sounded strange, but he'd found Kate. Of course, Evie was safe and that was why he was in Hoi An. He would not forget his objective. But he'd longed to see and hold Kate again. And here she was.

'I didn't do a great job of hiding, did I?'

Kate laughed. 'No, a terrible effort in fact. Perhaps you wanted to be found?'

It was a joke, but Nick didn't smile. 'I didn't intentionally put myself in your path.' He shrugged. 'I didn't know you'd be drinking here tonight. In fact, I thought you'd be with the girls all the time.'

'I am here to work, you know that. But with four supervisors, three teachers and the tour operator, we agreed that we'd take turns with supervision at night. During the day we're all required on deck as we travel around, but once the students are back at the hotel, two adults present is sufficient. These sorts of trips are exhausting, so it's necessary to have some downtime. So, I do get some time off.'

'Of course, I understand. I'm really glad you found me.' Nick reached across and found Kate's hand. 'Should we order another drink?'

'Let's have a coffee.' Nick agreed and signaled to the waiter.

The moment a young girl delivered their coffees and placed them on the table, music blasted around the bar. Whilst they hadn't been watching, a band had set up on the stage in the far corner of the venue.

They both laughed out loud.

'Not quite what I was thinking,' Nick said.

Talk was impossible. They smiled at each other and drank their coffees. After a few minutes, Nick gestured with his hands to Kate in a way that asked if she wanted to watch the band.

Kate shook her head and leaned in close. 'Too noisy.' The band played Bruce Springsteen's Born in the USA and the members jumped around as they strummed their guitars.

'Okay, let's go,' and Nick started to slide out of the booth.

Outside it was still balmy. Stars covered the dark night sky. Nick grasped her hand and they walked slowly along the edge of the road as it had no footpath. Cars sped past and he held Kate close. At the end of the circular drive to her hotel, behind some tall palm trees, Nick paused and gazed at her. She took a step toward him and they kissed. It was brief but deep. Afterwards, he rested his head on top of hers, and breathed in the sweet citrus scent of her hair. He didn't want to let her go.

'I have an early start tomorrow.'

Nick lifted his head and nodded. 'Goodnight.'

'Good night,' and Kate walked away.

'Kate,' he called. 'Can I see you tomorrow?'

She smiled and nodded.

CHAPTER EIGHTEEN

'These lanterns are beautiful, girls. I'm not sure how they'll fare getting back home in your luggage, though,' Kate said as she held up a mint-green one with a traditional Vietnamese lotus flower adorning it. 'Gorgeous, Melodie.'

'Thanks, Miss.'

Gina had organized an afternoon visit to a local vendor who'd shown them how they made the beautiful and traditional cloth lanterns; a specialty of Hoi An. Tonight, Gina had shown them how to make their own paper versions. Now, a variety of coloured and decorated lanterns sat drying around the communal room of their hotel. With the session finished, the last few girls wandered off to their bedrooms. Kate walked around picking up scraps of paper, sticky tape and glue pots.

She yawned. Unable to sleep last night, she'd lain awake, thinking of Nick. That man had crept under her skin. One moment she thought he was an exciting enigma, the next, she sensed danger deep down low in her belly. Her intuition screamed at her. It said runaway fast. Kate knew she should. But her heart sang and she felt lighter than she had in years. Her senses buzzed, and her hand ached now that Nick no longer held it. Kate placed those fingers against her cheek. Did the spicy scent of his cologne still cling to her jacket? She inhaled the scent when her phone buzzed in her pocket.

She'd promised Nick she'd see him today but that hadn't been possible. It was her turn for duty tonight and she'd been on the go since seven am that morning. They'd exchanged a few text messages and she spied him near the entrance to the temple they'd visited that morning. Deception was not his forte, clearly.

With the room all clean, she headed to her quarters. Along the way she confirmed all the girls were in bed where they should be. 'Night, see you early in the morning.' Some of the girls groaned in response, others waved her away happily.

In her room, she sank down onto her bed. Her feet were thankful. She quickly typed out a response to Nick who'd asked what she was doing. Almost as she pressed send, he rang.

'Are you telling me that your lying alone on your bed?' His voice was husky.

'Mm, I might be.'

'That is a travesty. You should not be lying alone.' His voice deepened further. 'I should be with you.'

'Yes, now wouldn't that cause a scandal. Teacher found in bed with parent on overseas music tour. I can see the headlines now.'

'Ah come on…' he teased.

'Did you like the Temple?'

'I did. I spent most of my time observing Evie who didn't seem to be paying much attention to the tour guide, but rather chatting and laughing.'

'Well, the tour was a little long and detailed, so I don't blame her.'

Nick laughed.

'It's day three now Nick. Are you going to ease up? Aren't you satisfied yet that she's safe?'

The line went quiet.

'I am satisfied, and yes, I'll ease up. It is ridiculous that I'm still following her around.'

'Are you serious?' Kate couldn't believe it.

'Yes. I promise.'

'Wow, that's impressive. Well done. I'm proud of you.'

'Shucks, thanks,' he responded.

Kate told him about the rest of their day. Nick told her about all the food he'd been eating. 'Oh my gosh, that sounds amazing.'

'Have you travelled to Vietnam before?' he asked.

'Yes, years ago, I came here with my parents during one school holidays. I must have been, I don't know, maybe fifteen? Yeah, now that I think about it, almost the same age as these girls.'

'Did you love it?'

'Yes. But I was young and brave then.'

'What do you mean?'

'Everything in my life is classified as before Ben and after Ben. That trip was before Ben.'

'Ben was your husband?'

'Yes. Honestly, I was terrified of coming on this trip. I haven't travelled since Ben died and, I don't know, because it happened whilst we were overseas, I've been frightened to try it again. As if travelling overseas signified tragedy, and danger. I'm constantly frightened of another accident occurring. Constantly frightened full stop. I know it's weird but I've carried around this sense of dread in leaving Australia. As if being at home provided me with sanctuary or protection. Stupid of course, because he could have easily died at home of a similar accident.'

'It's not stupid at all. But you've done it, Kate. You've come here, you've left Australia. You should be really proud of yourself and how brave you've been. I imagine after something like that occurs in your life, it's all about small steps. And celebrating those.'

'Yeah, you're right. It is a massive milestone for me. And now that I'm here, I'm completely comfortable. Thank you.'

They were silent for a minute.

'I have tomorrow night off,' she said.

'Do you?' Nick's voice rose in excitement. 'Does that mean that we can see each other or do you have to stay at the hotel, just in case?'

'No, I can leave. Louisa and Nigel will be here.'

'That's the best news I've heard all day. What should we do?'

Through her bedroom window Kate watched the sun descend behind the nearby low, mountain range and the world went dark. It was late. She yawned three more times but she didn't want to stop talking to Nick. They planned tomorrow evening. When she eventually hung up, her hand cramped from holding the phone and her ear burned red.

Nick was right, she'd done well being here and she was proud of herself. But he didn't talk anymore about his reasons for being in Vietnam. A swell of fear still stirred within her. Nick Harding kept a secret.

How bad could it be?

***

Like a figure in a gangster movie, Nick stood partially concealed behind trees outside the entrance to his hotel. He wore dark clothing and a cap despite the night sky. If his intention was to avoid looking suspicious, he'd failed.

'You're taking this whole subterfuge thing seriously, aren't you?' Kate joked, but the sight of him had her nerves jangling.

In response, he leaned in and kissed her full on the mouth. Instead of her anxiety escalating, it dampened; it was the effect he had on her.

'Good evening,' he said when he drew breath and grabbed her hand. 'Let's go.' He held her around her waist during the short walk. People milled on the paved walkways and in narrow alleys. Tourists were out enjoying the warm temperatures and the cultural and exciting nightlife the town had to offer. Locals squatted in front of houses, shops, temples and restaurants, and talked and drank and enjoyed the cooler climes after the harsh heat of the day. A musty mixture of wet dirt and fragrant spices filled the air.

Cars were forbidden in the old town so they walked easily without fear of honking horns from motorbike riders or the crazy local drivers. The paved streets were like a maze, leading them around secret corners and revealing hidden alcoves and quaint trinket stores. They followed the crowd and walked along the river that flowed through the town's middle. As the stars filled the sky, hundreds of lanterns illuminated the riverbank and across the bridges that spanned the water. They stopped to soak in the view.

'It's so pretty, like a magical wonderland.' Kate sighed. 'The colours are incredible.'

'Those lanterns are one of Hoi An's most famous products. Have you seen them at the stalls?'

'Yeah, I have. They're impossible to miss because they're everywhere. I must buy some as gifts before we leave. My mum would love that vibrant yellow.' As they stood admiring the lanterns and the mirror image it created in the flowing water, Nick hugged Kate from behind. She snuggled into his front, conscious of all his curves and bumps. She placed her arms over his to lock him in place and all the

124

while his heart beat against her back. They stood being entertained by buskers trying to ply their wares or sing for coins. As Nick's hands rested on her soft stomach, it rumbled.

'Is that your tummy?' he asked.

'Yes,' Kate said laughing. 'I'm hungry.'

'Let's get dinner then.'

After checking out only two restaurants that lined the river bank, Kate chose a traditional yet charming shop of simple décor with a dozen tables lined with checked cloths. They located a table outside on the wide path near the water where they could people watch and soak up the beautiful setting of Hoi An. The air was electric.

'How did the girls go today?'

'We went to the orphanage. It was an awesome day even though a little heartbreaking. Has Evie contacted you?'

'She's sending a few messages and photos. I'm so grateful I gave her an international sim card now that I'm not following her every move. It means we can stay in touch. Here's a photo she sent me today.' Nick pulled out his phone and flicked through the images until he found it and showed Kate.

'Oh, I remember that child. He took a real liking to Evie. Evie had such a lovely manner with the kids; she was so patient. She played and entertained them with games and gave them gifts. Only one or two of the students remembered to bring small tokens for the children. The kids went nuts when they were handed out and they were, you know, only little rubbers or pencils or sweets. It was a great exercise for the girls to visit where these children lived and observe what little they had.'

Nick listened and nodded.

'Evie was teary after we left. She said she wanted to bundle up all the children and take them home to live with her, that she couldn't stand the thought of them living in the orphanage without a mother and father. She said it reminded her of her own mother.'

Nick's face paled and his smile disappeared. 'It churns my guts to think of her being sad about her mother.'

'I reminded her, of course, that she had you. These children don't have anyone so they are much worse off. But they are well cared for. She felt better after that.' And after further thought, she added, 'Does Evie remember her mother?'

'No. She was two when Autumn died. The only memories are photographs and there aren't a lot of those either.'

'You didn't take many pictures back then? And, Autumn is a beautiful name by the way.'

'I wasn't with Evie's mother when she died. We were in a relationship when Evie was born. We reconciled when Autumn found out she was pregnant but it didn't work. So, Evie lived with her mother until she died.'

'Was she unwell?'

Nick paused and retracted his hand. He had placed it over Kate's when they sat down. 'I guess you could say she was sick. Self-inflicted sickness.' He sat back in the plastic chair now. 'She was a drug addict and overdosed.'

Questions bounced around on Kate's tongue but the waiter came to take their order. They both ordered a traditional Pho soup with noodles and an ice-cold local beer. The waiter returned immediately to serve their drinks and a plate of rice paper rolls.

'How did you meet Evie's mother?'

Nick sat back with a half-eaten roll. 'During my law studies, I worked at a pub. It was close to my uni. I started as a glassie, then became a barman but eventually moved into security. I worked a lot; mostly nights. I'd work all night from Thursday to Saturday and study during the day. I'd work other evenings too, but the pub closed earlier during the week. Working regularly on the door meant you got to know repeat customers. Drunk women would talk to us and often butter us up, of course, to be allowed entry to the pub.'

Kate smiled. 'I'm sure you absolutely hated the attention.'

'Actually, it wasn't easy.' He put his hand up in defeat. 'Okay, I admit it sounds great, but it was tricky. Anyway, it's off topic. One woman always paid attention to me, bought me drinks and stuff like that. I didn't respond at first but she never gave up. Until I was in my last year of university and had my sights on finishing at the pub and getting a real job. I don't know, at the time I wanted to have fun after studying so hard, I guess, so eventually I agreed to have a drink with her and then we had dinner and started dating. She was fun and had lots of energy and knew where to go and what to do in Brisbane. Autumn was different. A free spirit.'

'Mm,' Kate murmured.

'Yep, she was different in all respects. Anyway, we went out, had fun but then things weren't so enjoyable anymore. When we met, she was clean but she struggled to stay off drugs. We never did them together but she'd turn up to a date and her eyes would be bulged and red or she'd be sleepy or worse, hyperactive. It was odd behaviour and because I'd never witnessed drug-affected people before, me being a good wholesome boy, it took me awhile to work it out. In the end, I gave her an ultimatum, she had to get clean or we were over. I helped her attend rehab and she was able to manage her addiction again. But drugs take a hold of people and I'm not sure it's possible to ever be free of that addiction, of the power of the drug. Anyway, long story short, she couldn't keep it up, didn't have the will power, wasn't able to hold down a job. By this time she found out she was pregnant. I had finished uni and had my whole life ahead of me but had a pregnant druggie girlfriend.'

'What did you do?'

'I secured a job as a first-year lawyer. It paid nothing but enough for the rent on a flat. She moved in and I tried to keep her off the drugs but the relationship didn't work. She moved out and I guess, that's where it all went wrong. She had Evie and I helped her out when I wasn't working and gave her financial support. Back in those days, I gave most of my money to her and basically couldn't do anything. I was poorer than when I was a student. I thought everything was okay, I was confident Evie was being cared for and safe. But I was wrong. To pay her drug habit she started prostituting herself because, of course, I wouldn't give her money for drugs. I turned up one night to visit Evie and found Autumn with a client and Evie asleep in the next room. We had an explosive argument. She agreed to stop, get off the drugs for good and find a job and we'd get someone to look after Evie. Evie was eighteen months old by this stage. Anyway, by the time Evie turned two, Autumn had overdosed on bad stash. I was suddenly the full time carer of a two year-old baby.'

'Holy shit, Nick.'

'I know.'

They paused as the waiter asked if they would like another drink.

'What happens then?

'Like every other kid, what did I do? I ran home to my parents. As a family we sorted it out. My career was in its infancy. I worked long hours and often got called out on weekends to the watch house to bail someone out. My parents agreed to take Evie in and care for her. It was never a long-term arrangement but she ended up staying there until she turned eight. Even to this day, she loves my parents, adores them and my sister, too.'

'What happened when she was eight?'

'My father had a stroke and understandably my mother had to care for him and it was too hard on all of them, and of course, it wasn't their responsibility to care for my daughter. So I brought her back to Brisbane, found full time help and managed it.'

'How old were you by then?'

'Thirty and definitely old enough to take care of my responsibilities. I regret not having her back long before then. She is everything to me.'

Another beer arrived with their food. Kate took a large sip of her drink. She glanced at the local people passing by with their wide grins. Most Vietnamese people had very little. How did you learn to be happy with nothing? Along with her students, Kate too, was amazed at their contentment. Often sharing ten people to a home, preparing simple food and working day and night, they still smiled and acted as if they were most blessed people in the world.

Evie hadn't been the only one teary today. Kate, too, could have snatched up one of those orphans and taken them home. Her tears were caused by the gulf that sat in her stomach. The hole left unfulfilled at the lack of her own family. When Ben died, that dream had died, too. Being an only child, she dreamed of a large family, a home filled with noise and chaos. Not that there'd been anything wrong with the order and quiet she'd grown up with.

Nick touched her hand. She'd drifted off to other places. Kate smiled and bought herself back to the present 'Evie is very lucky to have you. You're a great dad.' And she meant it. 'I guess we all need to learn to be grateful for what we have. I'll show you some photos from today.' They flicked through her mobile phone. Nick moved his chair around to sit beside her and heads down, they examined the roll of photos. They looked at the images, ate and drank. Nick moved his hand to her thigh.

Kate's heart raced faster. She lost focus of the photos as she only concentrated on his warm hand. His fingers sat so close to her groin, she squirmed with the pleasure of it.

'I know you once enjoyed travelling. Where's your favourite holiday destination?' he asked.

Kate told him of her love for all things French because her parents had taken her there when she'd been small and she remembered the romance of it, the colours, the language and particularly the smells. It had been an exciting elixir for a five-year-old. 'That began my love affair with the French language.'

'You'll have to speak French to me sometime.' His voice deepened. And then, he continued, 'Plus, I found a fantastic French patisserie around the corner today. I was searching for a coffee. I'll take you there; you'll love it.'

'That sounds wonderful. But what about you? What's your favourite overseas spot?'

'I'm always working so don't travel much. I often consider skiing in New Zealand or Canada or maybe soaking up the sun in the Greek Islands. Doesn't everyone want to go and swim in those crystal blue waters and drink a shot of ouzo whilst overlooking those famous blue domes? What island is that?'

'Santorini.' Kate stood and wiped her clammy palms down the front of her dress.

'Excuse me,' she asked a waiter as he zoomed past. 'Can you tell me where the bathroom is?'

The day before Ben died they'd spent a glorious, carefree few hours on Santorini catching buses and walking and exploring the hills that housed those blue domes Nick dreamed of. Standing at the basin sink in the bathroom of the restaurant, Kate washed her face with water. Its icy coldness shocked her and pulled her up sharp. She'd dreamed of the Greek Islands, too, before she'd travelled there. Kate shook her head so her hair sprang free of its ponytail and sat slick against her moist neck. No matter where she went, who she spent time with, memories always came back to haunt her.

Would it get easier?

She was rattled, that's all. Nick sparked emotions in her that left her confused and happy, yet uncertain. Once, not long after Ben had died, she would have fled this scene, gone back to safety and security and avoided the fear.

Kate stood tall. She would not flee anymore. Nick Harding was a great guy and a magnet, the force of which drew her to him. She looked in the mirror and fixed her hair back in place, wiped gloss across her dry lips and marched back outside. She refused to be defeated anymore.

Nick gazed at her quizzically when she returned. She stood at the table and drank down the last remnants of her beer.

'Should we go for a walk?' Nick fixed up the bill, refusing to let Kate contribute and helped her with her cardigan.

She stared at him. 'Why do you do all that?'

'Do what?'

'Pay for everything, help with sweaters, pull out chairs, open doors...'

'Because it is the right thing to do. My mother taught me to be kind to people, but to treat women especially well.'

'I like your mother.'

'She'd like you, too.'

A young rickshaw boy trailed them as they left the restaurant. At first, they both ignored him until Nick suggested they give it a try.

'The poor kid probably needs the money and why not? We can enjoy a ride back and rest our feet.'

Kate agreed. She settled herself into the worn old carriage. It swayed as Nick sat next to her. Once seated he reached for her. Kate didn't resist him but the ride went too fast. They'd barely caught their breath in between kisses when they'd arrived back at the hotel. Nick paid the young boy and Kate waited. As the rickshaw sped away, they stared at each other. Nick's eyes smoldered in the glare of the moonlight. Now or never she thought. Kate reached for Nick's hand. He took it and they walked away, together, to his hotel room.

CHAPTER NINETEEN

Kate's shoes dangled from her hand as she scurried across the quadrangle as the sun began to peek over the nearby hills. She'd intended to sneak back to her room in the darkness, but she'd fallen asleep in Nick's arms and hadn't woken until the first glimmer of dawn had infiltrated the curtains. She'd spent the night with Nick Harding and could hardly believe it. Another fear conquered. Something else to be proud of and plus, it had been amazing.

Glancing around as she walked, she didn't worry about running into anyone at this early hour. But as her foot touched the second stair on the short climb to the foyer entrance of the Oasis, the glass sliding doors whooshed open.

She came face to face with fellow teacher Nigel Harris. He wore a seventies style John McEnroe headband, barely there running shorts and a Bonds singlet.

Kate froze.

'Ah, good morning Mrs. Penrose. You've had a good evening then.' He actually winked. 'Do you wish to join me on a quick sprint along the river before our day commences?'

Kate tried to read his expression but he wore a genuine smile and seemed happy to be awake and about to exercise at this ungodly hour of the day. She waited for the interrogation to begin and when he remained silent waiting for an answer to his invitation, she didn't offer up any explanations or excuses. 'I would love to, Mr. Harris, but I need to have a shower and get ready for the big day we have planned.'

'Yes, of course,' he said. 'Another time then.'

'Have fun,' she said as she hurried into the building.

***

'It's agony having to wait two whole days until I see you again!' Nick swept her up off her feet and swung Kate in an embrace. She giggled like one of her charges. Once back on terra firma, he produced a single stemmed sunflower.

'Thank you,' Kate said.

Hand in hand they walked to the Hoi An night market.

'This place is a whole new town at night. It's incredible: the noise, the vibrancy, the people. But it's the colour that dazzles. By day it is terracotta, muted browns and earthy colours and textures with the stone buildings and paved walkways, but boy, oh, boy, at night, she comes alive, doesn't she? It's like the old town sits dormant all day waiting to explode with life each night.'

Nick nodded. 'Yes, that's so true.'

'It enchants me, puts me under a spell,' she gazed at him then and said, 'it makes me happy. Or maybe, that's being with you in such a magical place.'

'You captivate me.' He said to her and pulled her close. For a split second they were the only two people on the crowded street. They'd paused under a particularly fluorescent orange lantern but people jostled them at both sides and the momentum zipped them along.

Kate walked on with her head titled upwards, toward the sky. Illuminated lanterns were strung from shop fronts and across the narrow alleys capturing them in their glow as they traversed the stalls on the perimeter of each side of the road.

'There are supposed to be up to 50 vendors along this 300 metre long street set up specially for the markets. If you look between the buildings, you might glimpse the Thu Bon river through there,' Nick said and pointed.

'You sound like a tour guide.'

'That's because I have had plenty of time to read up on the sights of Hoi An. And I knew this would be special.'

In amongst the stalls selling souvenir t-shirts, there were traditional fans, silks, all measure of brass and silver trinkets and, of course, the lanterns. Food stalls set up on the cusp of the paths, placing their narrow trolleys and carts in the smallest of spaces between other sellers. Their meats and raw products were on display.

'We've eaten some delicious food since we've been here, but not street food. Tonight is the night, Nick Harding. We need to try some.'

'I read about these sizzling pancakes called Banh Xeo, or something like that. I'm not sure how it's pronounced but Hoi An is famous for them. I'm sure that guy over there is making some.' Nick walked toward the man's simple set up, dodging people as he went. He turned to Kate and gestured for her to follow. When they were closer, they could see the man add a couple of prawns, vegetables and noodles to the hot pan and pour the rice flour mixture in afterwards. The crowd surrounding him awed at the sound of the sizzle and the steam billowing from the skillet. The Vietnamese man soaked up the attention offering a broad toothless smile as he skillfully worked his saucepan.

Nick gestured to the man that they'd have two. And he immediately poured and mixed and flipped the specialty until Nick was handed two crispy pancakes.

Kate dove straight in. 'Oh my gosh, this is delicious.' They ate as they continued to walk along. Kate paused at a stall. Nick watched her bend over, studying the items for sale. As he leaned closer he saw that the shelves in front of them were filled with earrings. There were flags, psychedelic shapes, Russian babushka dolls and a variety of food types.

'Pick some out, Kate. I'll buy them for you.' He said to her as she poured over the products. She finished her pancake and licked her fingers clean before wiping them on her skirt so that she could pick up and more closely examine some pairs.

'I don't want any that I can buy at home. I want one of these traditional Vietnamese styles – what do you prefer, the hat or rickshaws?'

'I'll get you both.' And he took them from her and paid the owner. He didn't even haggle.

'Thank you. That's really kind. You don't need to buy me things. I can buy them for myself.'

'I want to buy you things.'

A couple of tourists walked between them in a rush to their next purchase. Nick moved closer to Kate and said, 'Why do you wear those sorts of earrings? I mean, why not diamonds or pearls or something?'

'Because 'before Ben', and she indicated the inverted commas sign with her hands, 'I was fun. I wanted to be a fun teacher and be relatable. Learning should be enjoyable, right? I wanted to make it memorable for my students. You'd be amazed how much discussion these generate and despite those grown-up thirteen-year-olds thinking they're babyish, they love them! I particularly like wearing crazy pairs on exam day. It helps the students loosen up a little. And sometimes, only occasionally, I might even wear a themed dress.'

'You can't be no fun 'after Ben',' and Nick made the same gesture in the air, 'because you're still wearing them. I think fun Kate still exists, she's just been lost for a little while. But she's in there, wanting to come out.'

Kate held up the small bag with her new purchase. 'I think I've been doing a lot of pretending. It's easy to put on silly earrings to make myself think I'm the girl I used to be. But perhaps I'm slowly coming back. And you might have something to do with that. Thank you,' and she stood on tiptoes and kissed him.

They continued walking on. 'Do you think Evie would like this?' He held aloft a stunning deep navy limestone bracelet.

'That is beautiful,' and she examined it in Nick's hands. Then she smiled up at him, 'but you'd have some cunning storytelling to make up if you bought that for her! Silly. You've forgotten yourself.'

Nick cottoned on and realised his mistake. 'I'm letting my guard down. And that's all due to you,' and he reached around her waist and tickled her.

'I'm going to buy this for my mother instead. I'm loving this shopping! We've been to pretty much all the cultural spots of this mid-section of Vietnam this week, but no shops. This is fantastic,' Kate said as she purchased the bracelet.

Exhausted from shopping, they kept walking to the Japanese Bridge. 'More colour,' Nick murmured in her ear as he cuddled her. 'Let's rest a bit and soak up the view.' Nick sat down and they faced the bridge that sat across a span of water.

'I guess you know the history of this monument, too?' she teased him.

'In fact, I do. Would you like me to inform you?'

Kate shook her head. Nick moved closer to her so their legs

touched. Kate's reflection glowed green from the lamps that lit the base of the bridge.

'So, is it okay for you to be away from work? You don't have a big case on at the moment?'

Nick's stance stiffened. Should he come clean or continue the web of lies he always seemed to be spinning?

In that instant, his metaphoric happy bubble burst. He'd done well on this trip so far. He'd eased up on his surveillance of Evie and did not follow her and the school group around religiously like he had at the start. Occasionally, he'd admit to a deep longing of wanting to find Evie, hold her and make sure she was safe. He learned to ignore those feelings satisfied she was in Kate's company.

But more than that, he'd stopped obsessing about the Warlocks and the danger they might cause him. It was only momentary, of course. At home in Brisbane, where the threat was real and apparent, it wasn't possible to let it go. But here, he'd relaxed for the first time that he could remember in a long time. How to relax was something he'd forgotten, even before the Warlocks. Something in him had shifted. His hard edges were softening. The threat to his and Evie's safety remained real, but he was beginning to realise that there was more to life than the way he'd been living.

Kate watched him.

'What? Do you have holiday brain? You can't remember, or maybe you don't want to think about work. Sorry.'

Nick shook his head but didn't look at her cute, pixie face staring up at him. 'No, it isn't that. At home, usually, all I do is work. I have worked non-stop for more than ten years. You know when I said I don't travel, well, I really don't and that's because I never take time off work. This industry is vicious. I've always known that but once you remove yourself, even briefly, you can see it for what it really is. As the star in our office, I was too frightened to be away from my desk in the event the next big case came in and I missed out. Plus, I never wanted to miss a court date. Represent my client, get them acquitted. But if I'm honest, I never wanted anyone else to steal my glory, the success of winning. I think I've thrived on that feeling.' All of what he said was true. But a niggle taunted him; was an omission a lie? He needed to tell her all about his life. Soon.

Kate placed her hands in her lap, her face usually so bright and open, turned solemn.

'Anyway, enough of that. No, I don't have any work to worry about at the moment. It is a very unusual feeling but something I have quite been enjoying. Who knew there were so many hours in the day to fill in when one isn't working?' He tried to lighten his tone.

Reaching over he grasped her hands in his. 'I have learned something about myself. Incredible at my age, huh?'

'It all sounds rather glum to me,' Kate responded. 'I can relate to serious. I believe I have an important responsibility in teaching the next generation and making them the best they can be. But, I do know, and this is something I think my parents have done well, is that you cannot work twenty-four-seven, Nick Harding. It makes for a very boring person. Not to mention stressed out.'

'And that is why we are here…'

They both laughed. Kate spoke first, 'Not exactly, but I know what you mean.'

Nick beamed back at her with a matching smile.

'Now, how about you tell me about this beautiful Japanese Bridge.'

***

Kate found herself scurrying back across the quadrangle between the hotels again the next morning. She was alert for Mr. Harris and his early morning exercise routine this time and paused behind the large palm trees. In the distance she saw Mr. Harris already jogging down the path that curved beside the murky river. Given the all clear, she bolted for the entrance. Once back into the sanctity of her room, she dawdled through her shower and getting dressed. God, she was exhausted! But felt so alive at the same time. Kate couldn't help it, she counted the hours, the minutes sometimes, until she could see Nick again. Today she would wear the new earrings he'd bought her and she'd think of him each time they dangled and most likely got caught in her hair. Under the spell of Nick, she rubbed a dainty spot of lavender essence on each wrist. Another gift. She craved him like an addiction. He was hypnotic. It both scared the hell out of her and made her heart swell. This sense of seduction, of not being in control of her emotions, frightened her. *Just live in the moment, Kate* she repeated over and over to herself.

Perhaps one day she'd learn how to do it.

CHAPTER TWENTY

'Please, can we stay in tonight? Let's get room service and relax.' The words burst out of Kate's mouth the moment Nick opened his hotel room door.

Nick didn't argue. 'Of course. In fact, I was going to suggest it. I don't mind what we do as long as it's together. Plus, I have a surprise.' Nick pulled her in close and they kissed hello.

'How exciting!' Kate sat on his bed. 'Our last night together here in Vietnam. The last night of the tour. I can't believe it's over.'

'Me either. But wait there and close your eyes.'

While Kate had been with the girls on a bicycle tour of the local area, Nick had arranged a French feast from the patisserie. Despite his best efforts, he hadn't been able to take Kate there. As a coffee and morning spot, the French patisserie could only be visited early in the day and Kate was with her students. The young male barista named An was delighted when Nick wanted to purchase so much of his fare.

'I give you special price,' An had said. And with the baker's help he'd chosen their most decadent pastries with glazed strawberries and custard and chocolate eclairs. Except, tonight they would indulge with sparkling wine instead of coffee. An had recommended a bottle shop that Nick suspected was his cousin, or brother or friend.

Nick shuffled around the room making the preparations. 'Okay. On the count of three, open your eyes. One, two, three.'

Kate squinted. At the first sight of a fruit tart, she squealed. Then she spotted the *meille fieux* and the long, slim chocolates and jumped up and down on the bed making it squeak.

'Stop! It's too early in the evening, don't upset our neighbours.' Nick laughed and Kate stopped moving.

'This is amazing, thank you. Do you like French food?'

Alongside the sweets sat petite baguettes and gourmet cheeses that gave off strong aromas of mildew. 'Of course. What's not to love?' he shrugged. 'And besides, it's a treat for you. I guess I can be forced to eat camembert cheese and pastrami baguette washed down with French champagne and strawberries!'

'I love it. *Merci.*' Instead of eating Kate leaned over to Nick and gathered him into her arms. Nick popped a champagne-soaked strawberry in his mouth and fed it to her.

'Stop it!' she said as he pulled back twice preventing her from taking the fruit. But when she finally grasped it, Kate held on to it, not wanting to remove her lips from his. Together they collapsed backwards onto the bed and sat cross-legged and pulled the platters of delights toward them.

'This trip has been perfect. The only way it could have improved is if we'd spent all day every day, together.'

Nick agreed. 'It's been great. So much better than I'd ever expected. This is our last night,' he repeated.

'I know,' Kate's shoulders hunched. 'It's all over.'

'It's not all over, is it?' Nick asked quietly. He couldn't believe he was uttering those words. But he meant them. He placed his hand over hers and Kate stared at him. He knew he wore his intense scowl with his features scrunched and his eyes squinted, the *I don't want to be messed with* look. People mistook it for intimidation.

'No, it's not over. This is just the beginning, right? Of course, we won't be meeting secretly in hotel rooms and sneaking around snatching kisses. Or will we be pashing at the school gate?'

Nick's face crinkled and his shoulders relaxed. 'Perhaps not at the school gate, but maybe everywhere else. How does that sound?'

'That sounds perfect.'

Nick was determined to be kissing Kate back in Brisbane. But they hadn't discussed the future. Nick fought off his melancholy; tomorrow they would fly home on separate flights. They would see each other at the airport and pretend he wasn't familiar with the curve in her hip that met her thigh or the small mole at the base of her spine. Of tomorrow, when he wouldn't be spending the night with her

The break in Vietnam from the train-wreck his life had become had served him well. He'd had time to rationalise and think. To regain some of his equilibrium. The Warlocks weren't forgotten but he'd pushed the problem away. But like an irritating rash, images of Max Vincenzo kept popping into his mind. The thing that bothered him now was his omission to tell Kate. *Do it now,* he willed. He always found an excuse. Like right now: he didn't want to spoil tonight with the truth.

If Kate had similar thoughts, she didn't voice them. He watched as she devoured a cracker slathered with cheese. A crumb sat at the corner of her mouth and her tongue darted out to scoop it up. His muscles hardened. Perhaps it was the way he gazed at her, or the slight shift of his body, but she leaned over and kissed him. Then she sat back and raked her eyes boldly over him. He wasn't having pure thoughts as he pulled her body back into his embrace. She spoke French into his ear; her breath hot against his skin. He didn't have any idea what she said, but it drove him wild.

Nick Harding would worry about tomorrow when it arrived.

***

Kate's intuition told her Nick fought a war inside his head. Emotions flashed across his features: happiness, worry and undeniable lust passed through his expressive eyes. She had learned in their evenings together that Nick Harding was a deep thinker. Whether that be his job as a lawyer, or his intense personality, he did not partake in trivial. There was no idle, only full throttle, like *Top Gun.*

She had been introspective, too. Nick had consumed her thoughts. When she sat at the orphanage surrounded by needy children who deserved her attention; on the bus as it maneuvered narrow country lanes en route to their next attraction; as the girls squealed and jumped into the hotel pool and whilst she slept, he invaded her dreams. Her body ached until it felt his touch once more.

The future excited her.

Angela had summed it up when she'd spoken to Kate on the telephone. She'd said she was smitten. If honest, Kate knew it had become more akin to obsession, that frightened her. But she could balance it, couldn't she?

Kate believed in Nick.

She knew he had more to share, but so did she.

Could this be the beginning of something wonderful? For the first time in three years, Kate wanted to move forward. Motivated to move on, wanting it to happen, like a child wishing Christmas came the next day.

A future seemed possible and she saw Nick in it.

CHAPTER TWENTY-ONE

Hours after Kate left his bed, Nick lay amongst the tumbled sheets and inhaled her scent. It clung to his skin, the pillows and lingered in the air. He wanted to bathe himself in it. He was well and truly done for. Not a minute passed that he didn't think of Kate. Was this it? Real love? At the moment life wasn't proceeding as he'd planned. His carefully constructed hard work wasn't paying off. But he declared to himself that he would fix the situation he found himself in. He would keep Kate and Evie safe. Unsure of what his future work life looked like it was difficult to make promises to himself. But, he'd work more sensibly and create a proper life for Evie where he was present and hopefully, if Kate agreed she'd become part of that future. The Warlocks would not defeat him.

His thoughts drifted back to her. Right now she'd be rounding up girls, sitting on suitcases to stuff them shut, searching for lost items and shouting out to hurry up. Nick killed time until he too, needed to pack and head toward the airport. His flight was scheduled for one hour before the school, and he'd have to get up and get organised, soon.

Perhaps he should enjoy one last breakfast at the French patisserie and thank his new friend for last night's feast. Nick dreamed of the strong coffee and the sugar-laden treats as a loud bang landed on his door.

He sat bolt upright and jumped out of bed and raced to the door in his boxer shorts. He raked his hand through his hair before swinging the door open.

'What? Whoa. Are you okay?'

A Caucasian woman stood in his doorway with blood matted in her hair, and eyes that were coloured with hues of yellow and blue. Her stretched T-shirt slipped off her right shoulder and a mud stain covered the left knee of her jeans.

Nick gripped the door handle with one hand until his knuckle turned white. With his other, he reached for her. She flinched and the hairs on the back of his neck stood on end. This wasn't right. 'Who are you? Are you hurt?' he asked.

'Don't worry about who I am. You don't need to know. I am a message. This is what they are capable of. This is what they do to people who don't do as they are told. Imagine how much they would enjoy destroying you.'

'Who?' Nick knew the answer but still had to ask.

'You know who.'

'Come in, please. Let me help you. Clean you up at least.' He said as he peered around her, down the long narrow hallway where numerous beige doors led to other hotel rooms.

'No. You can't help. You'll only make more trouble for me.' The woman stepped backwards out of his reach.

'Are you alone?'

'I'm alone. But they are watching. They are always watching.'

He tried again. 'Please. You can't leave like this.' It was the right thing to do. Adrenalin pumped through his body as if he was playing contact sport. The woman reared back further and her fright became palpable.

'No. Leave me alone. I have done what I needed to do and now I must go.'

Was she one of them? He couldn't work it out. Did it matter? Either way, the woman turned and ran without looking back. Nick watched her head toward the fire exit that led down the side of the building where she wouldn't be observed. He was ashamed at himself for the relief that rushed over him.

Nick clicked the door shut, checking it was firmly closed and rushed to gather his belongings. He needed to get out of there, fast.

***

Kate sat cross-legged on the airport seat waiting for their

boarding call. It had been a busy morning. In between packing and exiting the hotel, one of the students had fallen ill. It'd been a while since she'd cleaned up vomit! The smell of antiseptic lingered on her hands. She knew Nick would be hidden somewhere, in a coffee lounge or at the far end of the concourse, but that didn't stop her from checking out the crowds as they meandered past hoping to spot him.

Instead, she caught up on her emails and social media. There were a few messages from her parents asking about the trip and how she was coping with a group of young women.

Her sweet parents. Like her, they'd been worried about this trip, about her venturing overseas again. She shot out an email and attached a tacky shot of her dressed in a traditional Vietnamese round hat whilst standing in a rice field. She reassured them it had all gone well.

No sign of Nick. That was to be expected. She sent off a quick message to Angela to update her on the last few days of the trip then shut down her personal account. She opened her work inbox. There was the usual inter-office banter: invitation to drinks to celebrate someone's birthday; a special ceremony in the hall to commemorate a school anniversary; students checking about forgotten assessments and homework and reminders about overdue lotto money for the staff syndicate.

Interspersed amongst the official Trinity College communications were two messages from Brittany Bartholomew. Kate's mouth went dry.

They weren't insidious from the message line but a lump formed in her throat when she clicked them open. No words, only an image of her and Nick appeared. Brittany used more photographs from the Fun Fair because this one showed them laughing and shovelling mouthfuls of food as they sat at the stall during the day. Kate remembered the detail of that day but couldn't recall Brittany snapping shots of them as they ate. It was a ridiculous photo that said nothing except that they'd operated a stall together at the fair. That was old news.

At Kate's lack of response, Brittany sent a further message. Another photograph accompanied by a brief note. *This is one of the images I will be delivering to Mrs. Peterson this week.* Clicking it open, Kate gasped.

At first glance it appeared to be an image in Vietnam. She peered closer to the screen and blew out her breath. The bright lights in the foreground could have easily been the lanterns of Hoi An. Definitely a cropped image but not of them here. She was being paranoid. And now she was frustrated. After all the ground she'd made on the trip, both personally and professionally, she refused to let Brittany intimidate her.

Kate uncrossed her legs and sat up. She had achieved great things on this trip. She'd conquered her fear of travelling and leaving home. That was a major feat and she was buoyed by her own success. But more than that, in these brief ten days she'd started living again. It felt like a whole new world had opened up, one that had always been there but she'd shut the door and had firmly kept it closed. Grief had kept her in its grip for too long. And, her bruised and broken heart had started to beat again.

A troublesome parent was insignificant to these accomplishments. However, she wasn't naïve enough to think that Brittany was going away anytime soon. She made a vow though, she could deal with Brittany and maintain her achievements. Kate would also keep the door to her life open.

She experienced a deep longing for Nick. She wanted to see him, cuddle into his bulk, and talk.

In amongst all of these thoughts, Kate missed the three telephone messages from her parents.

***

Nick was uneasy. He'd not settled since the unexpected arrival on his doorstep that morning. Was Kate safe? He needed to see her and find out. Nick had travelled across countries and still the Warlocks wouldn't disappear. All that self-talk seemed humorous now. One contact from the Warlocks and he felt like he'd been transported back to the beginning.

Returning home, back to the eye of the storm, worsened his fears. Evie had talked non-stop on the short drive from the airport. She glowed with excitement about the trip and he loved hearing her stories told from a teenage perspective. With a sense of satisfaction, Nick understood it had been right to send her on the trip. Evie had grown and matured over the brief period. Nick was thankful, though, when she scooted upstairs to glue herself to social media and catch up with the goings on since she'd been away.

Mrs. Travers had piled his mail on the kitchen bench. He flicked on the coffee machine and sorted through the white envelopes. Next to them sat his newspapers, unopened and discarded from his time away. A sense of dread landed in his stomach. He'd have to go through the papers and ascertain whether anything else was printed about him whilst he'd been away. He dumped the letters back on the bench, happy that they didn't contain any surprises. After making his coffee he headed to the study. It was a habit. It's not like he had any work to do. Pushing shut the door with his foot, he pressed all the necessary buttons on the remote to blast out his favourite music. Today, Eric Clapton. Absentmindedly as he booted up his computer, he turned on the answering machine to listen to the messages. Hardly anyone called the home phone, but in case.

The phone beeped indicating more than five hang-ups. Turning down the music, he thought he'd heard wrong. Nick kept listening. Curtis' booming voice came on the line asking to catch up. He said he'd resorted to leaving a message on the answer phone after Nick had failed to answer his mobile. Okay. The phone did work. He let it play on after Curtis' message and there were at least another three hang-ups with no message. Nick changed the sim card in his mobile from international back to local and it came alive with activity.

Nick checked his messages. A few missed calls from his parents and sister and an old law colleague. No unidentified messages. Something didn't feel right but he couldn't explain it. To satisfy himself, he went on a tour of the house and gardens. Nick walked into each cupboard and small space, around the pool, the lawn and garage. He walked the perimeter of the fence, conscious of course, of another incident not that long ago. His fences were clean today. A sigh of relief.

Nick remembered the wheelie bin sat on the curb and Mrs. Travers wasn't due back until tomorrow. He opened the gate and retrieved it. Turning left and right, he saw nothing unusual and put the bin on its rear wheels. Nick did a double take. The garbage had been collected but the bin weighed heavier than it should. Nick didn't react but walked back inside his yard and the gate shut behind him. He opened the lid and dry-retched. Oh God, the smell. He yanked the lid harder than necessary and peered inside. Nick jumped back. Something round, hairy and black lined the bottom of his bin. A head? It couldn't be a human head. Bile rose into his throat and he fought to keep it down. The shade from the trees lining his drive made it hard to see so he moved the bin into the direct sunlight. Without reaching in to retrieve whatever it was, he angled the bin to see better.

A cat. He spotted the long, slim tail curled alongside the body and ears that pointed into a triangle. Nick let go of the bin and fell to his knees. It was hard to catch his breath. What would he have done if it had been a human head in his rubbish bin? He couldn't follow that train of thought.

He stood up.

Another dead animal. Not okay but not as bad as he originally perceived. However, he had a poor dead tabby to dispose of, and it was another whole seven days until garbage collection. Not one to prevaricate, he decided to bury the cat and get rid of the evidence. And the odour. As he turned toward the garage, he spotted something sticking out of his mailbox. His box was encased in his concrete fence but could be accessed from the outside. A cavern formed in his chest. If his pulse rate didn't fall soon, he'd have a heart attack.

The lid sat open, exploding out its contents. As he approached, a different putrid smell hit his nostrils. What is it with bikies and odours? He guessed it was meant to deliver a double whammy – terrorise you by both smell and sight. Tentatively, he lifted the metal lid higher to peek inside. Hundreds of flies and bugs scattered at the disruption.

Shit.

A pile of shit filled his letterbox. It smelled distinctly earthy–horse, cow or sheep? He couldn't tell. He didn't care about the poo. He cared a lot about the timing. This occurred only recently because Mrs. Travers had collected the mail during their time away.

Today.

His attackers were close, and recently. Shivers raced up his spine. They could have been here when he brought Evie home. It was that thought that terrified him. To distract himself from the 'what ifs' he got on with the job of clean up.

CHAPTER TWENTY-TWO

Kate hadn't even dumped her bags in the hallway when her phone buzzed. Extracting it from her carry-on luggage, she swiped the screen.

'Hi Mum. I've just walked in my front door. How are you? What? Calm down, of course I'm fine. What do you mean?' Her mother talked in the high-pitched voice she saved for when anxious. Placing her on speakerphone so Kate could offload her suitcase, her mother squealed, 'We've been worried sick!'

'But why?' Kate's voice came out muffled as she maneuvered a strap over her head. 'You know I've been away on the school trip. What's happened? Is it Dad?'

'No, it's not Dad, it's you. Have you read the papers? There's an article in *The Daily Quest*. We didn't see it, but Susie, you remember Susie? She used to live down here and helped your father in the shop on weekends, lovely lady. Anyway, she rang me and told me you were in the paper. I was ever so excited and went online to look it up. You can find anything online these days.' Her mother did not stop talking to catch her breath.

Kate sat down in the dining chair and listened, the phone placed in front of her on the table. 'It's an article about this lawyer who has acted for a bike gang, I can't remember the gang name right now. It was something menacing. Anyway, it discussed the increase in violent offences committed by bikies and this lawyer represented them and set them free. You can read the article, but there was a photograph of you and him together. It read as if you were a couple and that you had a link to the bikie club, too.' Her mother's voice raised a crescendo toward the end of the monologue.

It was a lot to digest. Was her mother suggesting that she and Nick had their photograph in the paper? She needed this paper. It had to be a mistake, surely, but her mother's hysteria made her think otherwise. Her mother located the subject article and sent a screenshot to her. Not a mistake.

Whilst it was small and hard to read, Kate got the gist. The photograph displayed her and Nick at the fun fair. Would the fun fair come back to haunt her at every opportunity? Damn Nick for being on her stall all day.

'Um, Mum, I'm not sure what to make of this. Yes, I know this fellow. He's a father at school and his daughter is in my class. We've gotten to know each other and did work a stall together. He's a criminal lawyer and obviously, he acts for criminals. I know that he has acted for members of a bike gang, so that's all true, I guess...' She paused to scan more of the article.

'Okay, love. Are you saying there is nothing to worry about?' Kate didn't know what she thought.

'Yes, that's right, Mum. I'm not sure what is the point of the article, but I'm not involved in anyway and the press has probably found a recent snap of Nick and used it to accompany the article.'

'Oh, that is such a relief, dear. I will have to tell your father not to worry. You are named though in the same subject as outlaw gangs. That's not nice, is it?'

Nice isn't the word Kate would choose.

'So, I'm back from Vietnam. It was a successful trip...' and Kate distracted her mother with other news. Hanging up, Kate found the article online and read it on her iPad. Despite the content, her heart jumped at Nick's handsome image. It was of both of them, happy and intimate. The photo didn't correlate to the content it accompanied though. She knew Nick had acted for the outlaw gang. There was nothing new in that. Nick had told her all about this at the bar after the music meeting. But the story insinuated that whilst he didn't act for them now, he remained associated with them.

Kate thought back to their conversation. Nick had told Coco-Sage's father that he no longer acted for them, hadn't he?

Yes, he'd acted for scary people. That was his job. She understood biker gangs were controversial with the media coverage telling us that they were taking over Brisbane and the Gold Coast and were acting unimpeded. Nick had obviously done a great job if he had them acquitted of their crimes. Perhaps they were innocent?

Kate knew Nick held a secret.

Was this it? That he was a biker or had involvement with them? Was he a criminal pretending to be a good-guy lawyer? The press said Nick was sinister. He wasn't one of them, was he? He couldn't be. These questions circled in her head and each time she dismissed them, but they returned with a vengeance. Kate grabbed a juice from the fridge and sat down in her comfy sofa.

She pictured Nick showering her with gifts, his smile radiating at her with his eyes twinkling. His looks of desire and his strong jaw when he leaned down to kiss her collarbone and lower his lips down her torso, of his kindness and the soft heart he displayed. Kate fiddled with the euro coin that she hadn't touched since early in her trip.

Nick wasn't a criminal, or one by association. She was sure of it, wasn't she?

Her phone rang again.

'Hello you. I'm back. What are you up to?'

'Todd and I are going to the open-air cinema tonight. Want to come and keep me company. I want to hear all about your trip.'

'Oh, your timing is perfect. I would love to come. Meet you there.'

Kate put thoughts of the newspaper piece aside and showered and changed and ran out the door to meet Angela.

##

'What is this movie again?' Kate asked Angela as she rubbed the chill from her arms. Whilst mild, the Brisbane winter temperatures were cold compared to the tropics of Vietnam and she'd forgotten to bring her thick cardigan. Together she, Angela and her husband Todd, sat in the open-air cinema at New Farm Park on their classic movie night.

'*Hell Ride.*'

'And why are we watching it?'

150

'Todd wanted to see it. And I haven't caught up with you for ages so I thought you could come along and endure it with me. You're quiet tonight. What's up?' Angela asked as she munched on popcorn.

Kate had learned the hard way that life was ironic. It never failed to surprise her. Angela had asked her along to this particular movie, an old film about an outlaw biker gang. They terrorised people, hurt them and created chaos and mayhem wherever they ventured and used guns like toys. The timing could not have been worse. What did it mean and what message was it sending? Kate sweated through most of it, imagining Nick either as part of the gang or defending the bikers who were portrayed as low-life scumbags. She replayed the conversation in her head when he'd told her that accused persons deserved legal representation. That he'd never had to cease acting for someone because of their guilt. She turned to Angela.

'You know Nick is a criminal lawyer, right?'

Angela nodded.

'I found out he acted or maybe still acts for bikers who have committed crimes. What about that?'

'Yuck. That would be tough. But no different to acting for a pedophile or murderer or any other criminal. But I guess I haven't given it much thought before.'

'Could you do it?'

Angela laughed. 'I'm not a lawyer and couldn't be one, but if that was my job? Maybe? We all have parts of our jobs that we don't like.'

'Really? This is different, isn't it? We might not like dealing with administration and pesky parents, but they aren't child molesters or haven't shot five people in a salon and cut their body into little pieces.'

'Have you asked him about it?'

Kate indicated she had. 'He gave me a passionate plea about how people deserve access to representation, even the guilty ones. But he didn't specifically mention that in relation to bikies.'

'Does it matter? If that is his job and he performs it well and provides a service to the community, of sorts,' Angela shrugged, 'and as long as he's ethical and professional. There is lots of media about dodgy lawyers but he seems too law abiding to do anything wrong.'

Kate slouched in the sling back chair on the grass and closed her eyes as the noise of rifle gunshots and screams rung loud in the air.

##

That night lying in bed with her iPad, Kate read, and reread the article. Then she extended her search terms and Googled Nick Harding and used all word combinations she could think of relating to bikers/gangs/criminals/law. Why hadn't she done this before? Astonished, hundreds of hits came up. He'd received significant media coverage in the past, all for representing the Warlocks. Occasionally, interspersed amongst them, were drink drivers, and minor petty theft and the odd sports star or two. His firm's name was plastered across the historical broadsheets.

She went back to the current paper. It said Nick had lost his job. The piece speculated but it made sense he didn't have employment as he never seemed to be at work. Most of it she disregarded. Had she become so besotted with this guy that she couldn't think clearly? Ample evidence existed that he spelled trouble. Or did he perform his job as Angela suggested? Her mind whirled with thoughts as she turned out the lights and tried to sleep.

When sleep finally came, she dreamed of a gun shootout in a western saloon and of rich red blood seeping out of wounds. Of knives and cursing language and of Nick on a white horse coming in to rescue them, excepting he saved the bad guys and left the innocent to bleed to death. She woke up covered in sweat. Kate gave up on sleep and sought comfort in the covers of one of her classic novels. *Little Women*. No guns or violence could be found in there.

***

Nick slam dunked the basketball. For a fleeting moment he imagined it was Max Vincenzo's skull. He perspired buckets as he exerted all his physical strength.

'Man. What is it with you?' Curtis shouted at him as they moved back to the centre after the goal. 'You're playing as if the devil's chasing you!' And as if to demonstrate, Nick shot another goal in their game of basketball.

'Hey, Curtis. Your friend can play with us anytime!' The guys on the team shouted.

'If you don't watch out, you'll be arrested,' Curtis whispered.

Nick stalled. 'What do you mean?'

152

Curtis regarded his reaction. 'Hey, chill. I'm joking. You're playing on a team of cops. So they'll either love you or want to punch your lights out. And if they hate you, look out. Not likely today with the way you're playing!'

Nick smiled. But whether it was Curtis' comment or the fact he played with law enforcers, he stopped playing like he had something to prove, and relaxed. Later, when the last of the boys had skulled the remnants of their beers before leaving the bar located near the court, Curtis asked, 'How's things? Seems like you've got something on your mind?'

'The Warlocks are terrorising me with a campaign of dead animals and shit. I don't get it, Curtis. I know what these guys are capable of. They make tough guys quake in their boots but they hit me with this minor stuff. Does it mean something? What am I missing?'

'What's happened since we last spoke?'

Nick told him.

'Is this the beginning and there's more to come? Is this how they start? I know how evil they are. The stories I've heard, some of those images of torture and violence will never leave me.'

Curtis slammed his fist on the tabletop. 'God dammit, Nick. This is minor stuff but it's gone too far. You know I could act on this now, without your permission. You've revealed details to a police officer, I might be duty bound to take this further.'

Nick let him rant. Having known Curtis most of his life, he knew his friend wouldn't dob behind his back, no matter how much he wanted to.

'What if your safety is in danger? What about your daughter?'

'Mate, I take my daughter's well-being seriously, you know that. But nothing's happened that has put us both at risk. There has been threats, yes. Disgusting and frightening messages but they have not directly approached me, or Evie. My expensive security system has kept them from the house. Best money I've ever spent. They are toying with me. Attempting to make me so scared that I will do something I regret.'

'Yeah man, I get that. It's a good theory. But the picture in the paper complicates things. What are you going to do about that?'

'What do you mean? Sue for defamation? Can you imagine? At the moment I want a low profile. I take legal action against *The Daily*

Quest and the media will be all over it. Then there'll be court hearings and not only am I exposing myself but the gang too, and I guess they won't take that lightly.'

'Okay. We've talked about this *situation* before. What's the plan?'

'I'm waiting on the appeal. Max Vincenzo has to be behind all of this trouble. The tribe wouldn't act without his orders. If the appeal is heard and fails, then the interest in me might die down. Max will be moved into a higher security facility. That will make communication with the outside world difficult. Unless of course, he has friends on the inside.'

'Are you confident he won't be successful on appeal?'

'Yeah, I am. I know this case. The evidence is overwhelming. Plus, there's the public interest factor. Community safety against bikies is one of the government's priorities right now.'

Curtis nodded. 'When is it likely to be heard?'

'Because I'm not the lawyer anymore I'm not privy to that information. I have to keep checking the law listings. I'll do that again on Monday.'

'Okay. I hope it doesn't take too long. This can't continue.'

'Agreed. In the interim, Evie's safety is paramount.' Nick hung his head.

'What?' his friend asked.

'Plus, the safety of Kate Penrose. She's the woman in the photograph and the teacher I've mentioned to you before. Will they take any interest in her?'

Curtis actually laughed, short and loud. It stopped as quickly as it started. 'Do I think that a pretty young woman that you've been associated with is safe from the vitriol of the Warlocks? Mate, you know the answer to that.'

'Plus, we've sort of got a thing going on…'

Curtis slapped him on the back but said, 'When did this happen?'

'When I followed Evie's school trip to Vietnam. She was one of the supervisory teachers and we spent time together.'

'Okay. She's hot, but not great timing. For her I mean.'

'Jesus. I know. How could I have been so stupid.' Nick slapped his forehead. Then he finished his full pint of beer in one gulp.

'Your place is like Fort Knox but what about private detail? A private security company to monitor things.'

'I mean this is ridiculous, isn't it? It's like a bad movie.' Nick shook his head. 'No. I'm not working at the moment. Something else I have to sort out, but I can ensure Evie's safety. I need to keep away from Kate, too. I will manage this. I do not want other people involved and don't want to draw any attention to myself.'

'You always were a stubborn fucker. Do you want me to move in for a while?'

'And involve you too? No, definitely not.'

'You won't stay away from the girl, though, will you?' Curtis stared at him but Nick didn't answer. Inside his mind he screamed yes, I will. But his magnetic attraction to Kate meant that he wasn't sure if he could stay away. And the thought of not seeing her made his guts churn more than usual.

##

When he arrived back home late Saturday afternoon, his house was illuminated. His senses went on high alert, again. These days his stress levels were permanently elevated. It took milliseconds for him to go from a level of calm, to frantic. He tried to keep his cool as he entered the house. He moved the heavy timber door forward an inch, listening. The only sound was squeals, high pitched like laughter, not distress. He inched the door open further. The noise came from upstairs. As he removed his shoes and padded across the foyer in his socks, a person bolted down the staircase.

Nick braced himself. A slight waif of a woman crashed into his arms. He held her tight, keeping her arms in his grip. Her long hair covered his mouth.

'Bro! You're home. Evie and I have been catching up. It's great to see you.'

When he looked at her but didn't respond, she said. 'Did you forget I was coming?'

'Lizzie?'

'Yep, it's me. Who else?'

'What are you doing here?' he said and released his hold.

'Urgh,' she said hitting him on the arm. 'You've forgotten. Remember I said I'd be in Brisbane this weekend? We talked about it on the phone. I'm down to check out a new horse. I saw an Andalusian for sale and I must have it! So, I went and visited today. It is the most gorgeous animal, Nick, but it's expensive and at the moment Dad won't budge on price. I'm arguing with him about it.'

'Another horse?' He smirked at her. 'Are you here by yourself? Mum and Dad didn't come with you?'

'No, they were keen to see you. You haven't been home for ages, but Mum had a charity lunch that she didn't want to miss and Dad said he needed to look after the cows. Plus, he wouldn't come without her.'

'It's great to see you. It's been too long.' He embraced his sister, holding her tight longer than necessary.

She pulled away, gazed at him quizzically. 'Is something wrong? Can't I stay this weekend?' She pouted. He kissed his sister on the cheek and grinned back at her infectious smile.

But of all the timing. Lizzie staying the weekend meant the prospect of someone else getting mixed up in the mess his life had become. Would he need to take Curtis up on his offer?

'No, of course you can stay. Anytime you know that, I'd forgotten. I've had lots on my mind recently.'

'You work too hard, brother.'

He ignored the comment. 'And, I've missed you, sister. Now that you're here we better sort dinner.'

'Yeah, I thought we could go to that local Italian around the corner. It was so delicious last time…'

'No, we'll eat in.' Nick cut her off. 'I'll order and do a pick up. Can you go and ask Evie what she'd like and I can be back in thirty minutes.' His little sister, with her blonde hair and impish and innocent nature didn't respond but ran back up the stairs. She ran so fast, the paintings on the walls shook.

Nick felt the world weighing on his shoulders. He had a plan. This could all be over soon. There was nothing else he could do. Nick held the balustrade lining the stairs as he waited for Lizzie to return. He wouldn't care so much for his own safety if he didn't have Evie. And now, Kate.

He reached for his phone to ring and invite her around to enjoy the Italian take-out with them. He'd love her to meet his sister. They'd be friends, he was sure. He'd punched in the numbers and his finger hovered before pressing delete. What was he thinking? He needed to stay away from her.

But could he?

CHAPTER TWENTY-THREE

'Here comes that bitch now.'

Kate paused mid-step and glanced over her shoulder. Girls milled around the school grounds. Coco-Sage stood amongst a group of friends. Who was her comment directed toward? In that split second Kate decided to keep walking and not pull the student up for her foul language on this occasion.

But then she started again.

'Did you hear she's going out with that scrag's father? Apparently, he's loaded. What a gold-digger! Plus, have you seen him? He's a babe. What does he see in *that*?'

Coco-Sage's tone cut deep. Her words wounded. Where did a presumably innocent thirteen-year-old learn to express such contempt?

Since not awarding Coco-Sage the soloist on the music tour, mother and daughter had ramped up from being troublesome to menacing. The answer to Coco-Sage's attitude—that was easy, her mother, Brittany Bartholomew reigned as the queen of condescension. The daughter mimicked the mother.

Kate turned and headed for Coco-Sage.

'Hi girls,' she said to the group with a saccharine smile in place. 'Coco-Sage can you please assist me by taking this note up to the office. It's rather urgent. Mrs. Peterson needs it before lunch is over.' Kate held out the sheet of paper. Coco-Sage delivered a scathing look but snatched it out of her hands. She made a witty comment to her friends who laughed. Kate trailed her as she moved away from them. 'If I hear that

language again, you'll be reporting to Mrs. Peterson for detention.'
Coco-Sage narrowed her eyes at Kate and stomped away.

Kate rubbed her icy hands together and decided to grab a cup of
coffee before the afternoon session of classes. Her lessons were prepared
for both French and English, so she had plenty of time to head to the
communal staff kitchen. As she entered, a group of teachers huddled
together talking.

'Hi everyone,' she said brightly. The group quietened and a
couple got up and moved away. Kate busied herself at the coffee
machine.

Adelaide Woods, home economics teacher, approached her.
'Kate, did you overhear any of that? I'm so sorry. Sometimes working in
these environments with gossipy girls and backstabbing, we forget how
to act as adults.' Adelaide stood next to Kate. 'Here, have one of these
brownies. I made them fresh today.'

'Yum,' Kate said as she bit into the square. 'This will go
perfectly with my coffee.' But what do you mean? What were you
talking about?'

'You.'

'Ouch. What did I do?'

'Honey, there are rumours circulating. I hope they're true for
your sake. I'd be jealous if I didn't have my Johnny.'

Kate couldn't hold back her smile. 'What?'

'The talk is that you're dating a good-looking parent who might
happen to have a student in one of your classes.'

'As far as I'm aware, it's not against school policy to have
parents as friends.' Kate rebuked with defiance.

Adelaide raised her eyebrows. 'At your vehement lack of denial,
I'm going to assume that's a yes. But as to policy, I'm sure having any
association with an adult who is also a parent would be a major no-no in
Mrs. Peterson's books. So, it's true?' Adelaide danced on her toes.

Kate shrugged. She trusted Adelaide, but how much should she
say?

'I have spent time with someone who happens to be associated
with the school, but I don't know, we haven't formalised our relationship
or anything. It's new.'

Adelaide hugged her. 'Oh, honey. I'm so pleased for you. How can anyone not be with your tragic past. So sad, but let's not talk about that.'

'How does everyone know?' Kate asked but she had a hunch.

'Who knows? Stories spread like wildfire 'round here, even if they aren't true. But, of course this time it is.'

'You won't broadcast it any further, will you?'

'Me? Of course not!' Adelaide tapped her nose. 'I won't, but others will and in only a matter of time, it'll head up the chain to you know who.'

Bugger.

The bell rang for the afternoon sessions.

'Gotta go. But I want to learn all about it when it becomes official. Okay?'

Mrs. Peterson stood at her door at the end of the last period. Kate hadn't even put away her belongings and the last students were still leaving the classroom. Kate's heart sank. Did she know already?

'Hi Janette. How are you?'

'I'm well, Kate. How's the class going?'

'Great. We have finally covered the curriculum left over from last term, have revised that and are moving on to the next topic.'

'What's next?'

'Past tense verbs but I'm going to use the cinema as the backdrop because the girls can easily relate to that and hopefully it will generate active discussion about movies.'

'Hm. I never did enjoy French.'

Not much to say to that.

Janette held a piece of paper and she showed it to Kate. 'This I do understand. It's English. Coco-Sage Bartholomew's assessment to be precise. Her persuasive text that you failed her on.'

Kate stiffened. 'Yes, I recall. What's the problem?'

'Coco-Sage's mother bought it to my attention when she wasn't happy with the grade. I read it and then passed it to the Head of English for a second opinion.'

'So, Mrs. Bartholomew complained about the score and asked for it to be reassessed?'

'Not exactly. She discussed it with me and asked my opinion.'

'And what is your opinion?'

'She should have passed.'

'What? Why Janette?' Kate reached for the paper. 'The topic was why school should start later for teenagers and she wrote about why she should be allowed to have a television in her bedroom.'

'Yes, I understand that. But she's followed the structure required for a persuasive text perfectly, almost textbook, I'd say and her language is beautiful.'

'I agree it is well-written but on the wrong topic. All students wrote on the subject, except her. She knew the question and chose not to address it. She has failed the criteria at the most basic level.'

'You are being prescriptive, Kate.'

'Yes, as I am supposed to be.'

'In this instance, there is merit in the paper and she needs to pass.'

'Needs to? Why?'

'What do you mean why? As I said, appealing writing, good structure and merit.'

'I can't pass her on this piece of assessment. She did not answer the question asked of her.'

'I'm not sure why you're being difficult. In this instance, the Head of English and I have agreed that she passes and allocated a new mark.'

Did Kate fight this battle too?

'And, is that the end of the matter?'

'Yes, I'm afraid so.'

Kate continued putting away her papers, pens and notebooks. She didn't look at Janette again until she had finished putting away her belongings. 'I disagree, Janette but you are the principal.'

'You are young, Kate and you will learn to understand. Experience will be a great thing. I caution you, and listen to me on this. The Bartholomew family are great supporters of this school. They donate significant money, sit on our P&C–the P&C that runs the school I remind you–and are influential in the community at large…'

'Janette, are you suggesting that we are altering a student's result based on the contributions the family makes to our school?'

'Kate, I haven't said that and you are proving to me that you aren't listening. Consider what I have said. I will feed this information back to the student.'

##

Kate dragged her feet. Usually, she danced out the door at the end of a school week. Loving her job was easy and most of the time she experienced job satisfaction. Plus, Friday afternoons – what could be better?

Students gathered on the oval for volleyball and other sports practice. A number of parents lingered in the corridors, collecting their daughters or chatting with staff. Kate passed D block where the janitor locked up for the evening. She gave him a weak wave. Up past the administration block, she headed toward the school hall and exit and passed three or four parents preparing to enter the rec for a meeting. Kate didn't recognise them. She lugged her heavy bag and lifted it higher on her shoulder to distribute the weight.

Passing the parents, she gazed up at the jacaranda tree now bare of leaves for winter. The parents had been busy chatting as she walked but had become quiet. Kate glanced back; they stared at her. She turned behind her, certain they must be focusing on someone else. But, the school yard sat empty. Confused, she twisted around to see them still looking in her direction. Kate smiled but they rotated away. She had to be mistaken and kept walking. Students were being collected at the main entrance. Drivers moving past her on the road glanced in her direction. Did she have toilet paper hanging out the back of her pants?

Students at the gate waiting to cross, ogled her. Hyper-sensitive now, she raced towards her car parked three blocks from school. Kate stared at each person she passed, most turned away the moment their eyes met. Once safely in her car, she locked all the doors. Kate's accelerated pulse made her do it.

Checking her rearview mirror before pulling out from the curb, she saw a navy blue Holden Commodore parked a few metres behind. A driver sat in the front seat but the car didn't move. She paused, waiting for it to pull out but it remained stationary. She clicked on her indicator and made to move. Across the road a red Volkswagen indicated also and she paused, letting it go first. When the road was clear, she commenced her journey home.

Driving on autopilot, her nerves sat on edge. Her legs wanted to wriggle. Irritation grew roots and spread like wildfire. She needed to go somewhere, do something. Like most weekends since Ben died, she had before her two whole free days. Why hadn't Nick got in touch? Had it only been a holiday romance? She couldn't believe it because of the way he acted, the way he treated her and the things he said all contradicted that he was only in it for the short-term. But, despite this, he hadn't telephoned.

She hadn't rung him either. Maybe she would ask if he had any plans this weekend. Turning into her street, a blur of red flashed on her driver side as a car overtook her. The same Volkswagen from outside the school sped ahead down the street.

Strange. She turned on the radio to distract her thoughts. The blue Holden Commodore sat at her tail, driving too close. Kate scrunched up her face; she must be losing her mind. It couldn't be the same car from outside of school. Kate continued to drive. As she indicated to turn into the secure carpark under her apartment building, the Commodore stopped ten metres back. Looking ahead the red vehicle parked adjacent her complex. Kate clicked the garage button and willed the door to open. She tapped her fingers on the steering wheel whilst she waited.

She poured the first gin and tonic by five. Two glasses sat on the bench, both filled with ice and alcohol. At eight, with her courage bolstered, she texted Nick to ask if he wanted to catch up tomorrow. Within twenty minutes he'd responded positively and not long after Kate collapsed into her bed, exhausted by the activity in her brain.

***

He couldn't say no. The draw to hold Kate again was too strong; an earthquake could not have kept him away. But, he'd insisted they go to the movies. A dark cinema, out of harm's way would be the perfect safe guise to meet up.

'You look tired,' he said when he first laid eyes upon her. He dragged her into an embrace and kissed her once, hard on the mouth before producing a single, long-stemmed sunflower.

'Oh my gosh, it's beautiful, thank you.' Kate kissed him again.

'Why are you tired?' he asked when they pulled apart.

'That could be either the stuff that's going down at school, or maybe the couple of drinks I consumed last night. Or both.'

'So, no alcohol tonight?'

'No. Let's go old fashioned and get popcorn and choc tops.'

Nick chuckled and it felt good. When he was with Kate he could almost forget everything else, almost. He hardly concentrated on the movie. He placed his hand on her leg, enjoying her warmth and desperately controlling his hand from crawling higher. Kate leaned in. 'This is so much better than the movie Angela took me to last week. It was an old classic. Have you seen *Hell Ride*?'

The twitch started in his neck. His hand tingled with the pressure of holding it in place on her knee. He maintained a bland expression and continued watching the screen. Kate sat so close he could smell the salt and butter on her breath. 'Oh yeah. That's a classic. Not exactly pleasant viewing.'

'No. I hated it. So violent. Made me think of you, though.'

He did turn then but now she took a sip of her drink and Nick couldn't make out her face. 'Why?' he asked. His voice sounded squeaky to his ears.

'I was reminded of that conversation we had about you acting for criminals regardless of whether they were innocent or guilty.' A fast-paced and booming crash scene made them pause as the cinema filled with the scraping of metal and the explosion of car engines.

'There must be clients you don't like acting for. Surely?'

Her eyes searched his. Even in the darkness he could feel their intensity. Was she testing him? What did she know? He did not want to be having this conversation now. 'Of course. That's only natural. But no different to you perhaps having a student that you don't get along with or who pushes your buttons.'

'Angela said that.'

She'd discussed this with her friend?

'There's a big difference. My students haven't killed someone or hurt others or stolen stuff.'

Nick didn't respond and watched the remainder of the movie in silence.

Back at her apartment, she pulled at the seams of his shirt as the door clicked shut behind them. Kate didn't speak and he was grateful. Instead they tore at each other's clothing with silent agreement. His pent-up stress and desire burst forth and he met her kiss with force. He tugged at her boots and jeans and jumper with urgency. Why did she have to wear so many layers of clothing?

Kate undid his belt buckle and traced her fingers along the rim of his jeans. Her icy-cold fingers so close to his groin made him go immediately hard. Finally, she stood before him naked. Slowing their pace, her fingers trailed up his torso to his nipples before pausing on his stubbled chin.

Nick cupped her breast and Kate groaned.

'I've missed you,' she said.

'I've missed you, too.' He smothered any further words as his mouth pressed to hers.

An hour later they lay on her bed enjoying a hot chocolate under the warmth of her doona and talked. Kate told him about the issue with Brittany and Coco-Sage. Nick wanted to seek this woman out and fix the problem for Kate.

'You can't get involved. That's so inappropriate.'

'But, I protect the people I care about. If my mother or sister were in trouble, I'd help them.'

Kate paused and gazed at him. Only then did he realise what he'd said. Did she stiffen in surprise or disgust? Given she lay naked next time to him, he opted for the former. Nick kept talking, keen to move the conversation on. He couldn't be having a heart to heart right now. 'Okay. What I can do is give you legal advice. She's bullying you and there might be tactics that can help.'

'Okay.' Kate lay back and cradled in his arms as he talked shop. When he'd finished, he knew now was the time to be honest with her but the words wouldn't come. He didn't want to give those words life with Kate. They were his problem. When he'd discovered how secure her apartment had been, he'd felt a surge of relief. Modern complexes had excellent security. Still, he might hire someone to keep an eye on her anyway. He admonished himself. Of course, he should. He should have arranged it the moment they'd arrived back from overseas. Except, he still remained hopeful that Kate could be kept out of it.

Regardless, she had a right to know she might be at risk. A right to know that those unsavory people who had committed violent crimes were currently threatening him. She had a right to know everything. Kate had a right to know who he really was. And yet, still, he didn't say it.

CHAPTER TWENTY-FOUR

CRIM LAWYER ON LOOKOUT FOR NEW DIGS.

Curtis slammed the Sunday edition of *The Daily Quest* onto the table. Nick's coffee shook. 'Who did you screw over at the newspaper? Why do they even care about you? Huh?'

Nick rubbed his aching eyes. He was tired and a headache throbbed at his temples. Was it weariness at this ongoing situation or from hours of making love to Kate last night? He wasn't sure. 'I certainly haven't been screwing the boss. He's a big, overweight man; ghastly to look at but has a fortune behind him. It makes him invincible and the courage to print whatever he wants.'

'You know him?'

'Not exactly. He's the father of a kid in Evie's grade.' Nick laughed then thinking of Brittany. 'The wife is an outrageous flirt.'

Curtis smirked.

'I'm not kidding. In my true gentlemanly style, I've not accepted her advances, but maybe I should have, and I'd have avoided being splashed all over the paper. She's a bully, too. She's not nice to Kate.'

'Yeah, but the wife's not likely to have told the husband that she's hot for you, or that she's a bully.'

'No, true. But she holds the balls, if you know what I mean. So a word in his ear about me, school, anything, might persuade him to pursue an angle he might otherwise have not. Plus, unfortunately, he recognised me one night at school. After that the first article featured. I probably pissed him off with my refusal to comment.'

'Slimy bastard. But is it true? Are you seeking new work?'

Nick slapped his thigh. 'I knew it was stupid but I'm going nuts, mate. I'm used to working twelve to fifteen hour days and now, I'm house sitting and parenting and my brain has turned to mush.'

'It's drawing attention to yourself.'

'Yeah, I know, stupid move. But it's one of the top criminal law firms in Brisbane. You'll know the founding partner, he's in the news all the time. Terrence Rafferty?'

Curtis nodded. 'Oh, yeah. He's everywhere, the cops hate him.'

'Exactly. The perfect job for me. But my chances are blown if they get wind of this trouble.'

'And what about the teacher? Have you seen her?'

Nick nodded.

'Mate, you're stuffed.'

***

'We are moving onto our next unit and you are going to love it.'

Groans filled the classroom, but Kate ignored them. 'What is the most famous love story of all time?' She addressed her year seven English class.

'Adam and Eve!'

Kate laughed. 'You are a good Christian student, Isabelle. But no, not in this instance.'

'Kim Kardashian and Kayne West!'

'Liam Hemsworth and Miley Cyrus?'

'Kate and Wills!'

The class erupted into giggles.

'C'mon, you guys. Think literature, think history, romantic love and passion. Not current pop stars.'

'Napoleon and Josephine.'

'Someone was listening during French history. Getting warmer. Well done, Charlotte. Keep going.' More growls rose from her audience as the door creaked open. Brittany Bartholomew entered the classroom and headed toward Coco-Sage's desk. At the desk, she leaned over and spoke to her daughter, handing her a notebook of some sort.

Kate stopped. Waited.

'Can I help you, Mrs. Bartholomew?'

'No. Thank you.' She kept speaking to Coco-Sage who from Kate's observation didn't care for what her mother was saying.

Kate let it go on for a few minutes. The other girls chatted and the classroom became noisy.

'Mrs. Bartholomew. We are in the middle of a lesson, can you please talk with Coco-Sage afterwards. We are due to finish in another ten minutes.'

Brittany rose up tall and glared at Kate. Without speaking to her, she exited the classroom. The door clicked shut.

Where was she, again? She'd lost her stride and forgotten what they'd been discussing. She plastered on a too-broad smile and thought back to their discussion before the interruption. When she spoke, her voice pitched too high.

'Now, where were we?'

'The most famous love story of all time. What is it, Miss?'

'Okay, yes.' Kate flicked up an image on the whiteboard reflecting Clare Danes and Leonardo Di Caprio.

'Romeo and Juliet!' the girls chorused.

'Make sense now?' Kate asked but cast a look sideways outside and Brittany stood talking with another woman.

'Urgh, Shakespeare. How are we going to read it?' one student asked.

'Read it you will, I promise and love it. There is no one else in the world that writes like him. It's pure poetry. You won't read anything more romantic.'

Outside the two voices rose in volume and laughter echoed through the open louvres. Kate focused on her students. 'Okay, who can hazard a guess at one of the themes of this play written in the 1590s? And it is a play, not a novel.'

An animated conversation played on outside. Some of the girls snickered, Coco-Sage cupped her head in her hand, presumably bored by it all but Kate couldn't concentrate. 'Excuse me a moment, please girls. Open to the first page and read the first scene. I adore Shakespeare and I know you will, too.'

Brittany kept talking to her friend as Kate exited the room. 'Brittany, I'm sorry but your conversation is disrupting my class. Could I ask you to move away into a private room?'

The other mother acquiesced and jumped forward with apologies and readied herself to shift away. Brittany held on tight to her Hermes bag, a trademark signal of her anger, Kate had learned.

'You know, Sophia. Mrs. Penrose is dating a parent. This is against school policy and I'm debating whether to inform Mrs. Peterson or not. What would you do?'

Sophia's eyes widened. 'I'm running late for a physio appointment. I'd best get going.' Poor Sophia couldn't walk away fast enough.

'Brittany, you need to stop this.' Kate controlled her voice, keeping it steady.

The bell rang signalling the end of the lesson. As her year seven students galloped past her, Kate sung out, 'Make sure you read the second Act. We'll discuss it tomorrow.' Once the entrance was clear, she went back inside her classroom to prepare for the next lesson. She had nothing further to say to Brittany.

Unfortunately, Brittany didn't feel the same and followed her.

'You think you're so smart, don't you?'

Kate stood next to her desk as Brittany approached. Brittany pointed a long pink fingernail in her direction, not quite connecting with the soft flesh of her chest.

'Kate, I wish you would listen. This is all becoming rather ridiculous. Coco-Sage is a brilliant student. All I'm asking is that you treat my daughter with the respect she deserves. By now, you are well aware of what I mean. I don't intend to repeat myself again or next time. This is it. I haven't spoken to Mrs. Peterson yet because I wanted to give you a chance. But time is up. If things don't change I will inform the head of school that you are in breach of your duty of care by forming a relationship with a parent and as a result of that affair, you favour his daughter. I have the photographic evidence. And as we both know, Mrs. Peterson loves me.'

Spittle landed on Kate's cheek and she recoiled. *Yuck*! A fire of rage surged through her and her muscles tightened. She lifted her chin. 'Yes. I think we are clear on this issue, aren't we? You want something that I'm not prepared to deliver, unless, of course, I think it's warranted. You have threatened me numerous times now with these photos but you've never acted on them. You're all talk, Brittany.'

Brittany's face turned pink as the accusation sank in. Or perhaps it was simply because Kate spoke back. The momentary pause allowed doubts to form in Kate's mind.

Had she actually said those words? Shut up, Kate!

Brittany stiffened. Kate knew she should stop, but she couldn't stem her fury. She'd had enough.

'Yes, that's it isn't it? You hope your intimidation and threats are sufficient, don't you? That people tremble when you speak to them like you do. I have news for you, it isn't working this time.'

Kate crossed her arms, defiant. Had she cracked the mystery of Brittany? Stand up to her? Brittany stepped forward and leaned in so that Kate could smell her cigarette breath. Kate's nerve started to fray as they faced each other. She stepped back to gain some ground but her foot connected with a chair and she tripped, falling backwards over the seat and landing on her back.

Brittany spat out a profanity. Kate lay on her back, the shock rendering her mute. She wanted to let rip with expletives, too, but the wind had knocked right out of her. Brittany bent down as if checking on her. She waited for the woman to extend a hand to help her up. Instead, she muttered, 'Urgh!' and stormed out.

The door slammed shut.

The whole encounter must have taken at least four minutes meaning she had exactly two minutes to get on her feet and prepped for her next class. Counting to ten, she breathed in and out and convinced herself she was fine. Sixty seconds later she stood, pen in one hand, broad smile on her face and tribal music swirling through the speakers in the room. As she stood, she placed a hand to the small of her back to support the ache that formed there.

Kate survived the day by popping painkillers at lunch. By three p.m., she walked like a stick figure, keeping her torso ramrod straight. Movement caused discomfort. At four minutes past three, she phoned Nick and walked to her car keeping an eye out for Brittany Bartholomew. When Nick answered, she burst into tears.

'What is it? Are you alright?'

'I'm fine,' she said, the words hardly discernible. Overcome at the comfort of his voice, she couldn't speak.

'Where are you?'

'I'm leaving school,' she hiccupped between sobs.

'Stay where you are, I'm coming to get you.' He hung up.

Kate hopped in her car and locked the doors. She rang Angela.

'She did what? You've got to be kidding, Kate. Are you hurt?'

Fresh tears threatened to spill over. Angela ranted about the inexcusability of Brittany's behaviour, of how it had to be reported and that she could not be allowed to get away with this sort of intimidation. Kate agreed, of course she did. Brittany's behaviour was out of line. But listening to Angela her thoughts turned to Ben. She had learned many times over that no situation could ever be as bad as losing him. Kate reminded herself of that now. By comparison, this wasn't catastrophic; she hadn't been badly injured. Instead, she became angry. How dare Brittany intimidate her? Bullies only had power whilst their tactics of belittling and cruelty hit their target. Recalling the scene, Kate stifled a tiny giggle. She'd shown Brittany she wasn't daunted, hadn't she? Even if her cheeks now sat wet. Perhaps the woman would stop, realising she wasted her time. Wishful thinking. She would probably ramp up her efforts in retaliation after the way Kate had spoken to her.

Kate sat taller in her driver's seat. Bloody Brittany. That woman wouldn't win, of course. Kate wouldn't let her. Would she alter the way she taught as a result of Brittany's taunts? No. Would she treat Coco-Sage differently as a result of Brittany's threats? No.

Would she stop dating Nick because Brittany said she'd produce photographs? No.

For proper process and to ensure the incident was reported accurately, she'd lodge an incident report form, but not to deal retribution on Brittany. Kate didn't need to cause her harm. Brittany meant nothing to her and Kate refused to dwell on it any further.

'You're right, Angela. I'll report it first thing Monday, but I won't take the matter any further. In fact, I won't be indulging in thoughts of Brittany Bartholomew or her daughter anymore tonight.'

Angela met her words with silence.

Quickly, her friend recovered. 'You go, girl.' Then in a much softer tone, she said 'You always were tough, Kate. You're amazing. See you next Tuesday?'

Kate had recovered so much by the time Nick arrived that she offered him a bright smile. He hung back, surprised as she rolled down the window.

'Um, are you okay? You were crying, weren't you?'

'Yes, because of the shock. I'm better now. It was Brittany Bartholomew again. I will not let that woman get the better of me. Plus, you've got Evie with you, haven't you? Have you picked her up from school?'

'Yep. I told her to wait in the car.'

'I don't want her to see me distressed.'

'Okay,' Nick said his words still unsure at this quick change of mood. 'I had intended that you come back to our place. Do you still want to?'

'That would be great. I'd still love your company. But I can drive, I'll follow in my car.' Kate motioned the window back up but Nick stuck his hand in the mechanism to cease the movement.

'Are you sure you're alright? You can come in our car and I'll come back to collect yours.' He kept his hand on the glass pane to prevent Kate moving it again. She started the ignition.

'I'm fine,' and released the handbrake, ready to drive away. Nick stood gazing at her from beside the car.

CHAPTER TWENTY-FIVE

Once she'd parked her car in the safe confines of his driveway, Nick strode over and opened her door. Kate forgot about her injury and moved to get out of the car. She clutched at her back.

'Are you hurt?'

Nick shut the door with force and lifted up her t-shirt. Lucky she wasn't wearing a dress.

'Kate, is this from today? You didn't tell me you were hurt?'

Pulling her top back down, she said, 'we haven't talked about it yet, so I haven't had the chance.'

'How did you get a sore back?'

'Let's go inside first.'

Nick wore his stern face but didn't contradict her. Inside he led her to the lounge, where she sat gingerly to avoid leaning against her lower back where it hurt the most. 'It actually isn't that sore,' she said.

'How about I give it a light rub with cream to ease the ache?'

'Oh, that sounds good.'

Nick disappeared and returned with a tube of pain relief cream. He shut the door behind him.

'Take off your shirt.'

Kate smiled at his officious tone.

'Where is Evie?'

'She's upstairs and she won't barge in without knocking. No one will see.'

'Except you, of course.'

Storm clouds passed through his eyes and her smile slipped. 'I'm fine, honestly. It's a bruise.' She didn't want Nick to fuss.

'Yes, I can see that. It's also tender to the touch.'

She did as she was told and allowed his large hands to massage her lower back. At touch of his fingers against her bare skin, a warm shiver raced through her. She closed her eyes and revelled in the feeling and soaked up his care for her.

'I should be hurt more often if it means that you do this to me.'

He moved to face her.

'I will do this to you anytime.' Like a magnet drawing them together, their eyes connected and she couldn't drag her gaze away.

To take her mind off his roving hands and the erotic sensation it rushed to her core, she said, 'Do you like my earrings?' She jangled them for effect. She wore the colourful Vietnamese rickshaws Nick had given her during their time away.

'I love them.' He smiled. 'How great would it be to slip away now, alone?' he whispered in her ear. Shivers raced up her spine from his warm breath on her neck.

Nick laughed. 'I take that as a yes. But we can't. Evie is going out to a party tonight, so we'll have the house to ourselves then. There'll be plenty of time.'

'Is that a promise?'

He answered by placing his soft and open lips on hers. When they parted, desire swam in his eyes and Kate wasn't sure she could wait. As she repositioned her shirt and Nick wiped away excess cream on a tissue his voice was low and husky. 'Let's get a drink and sit out by the pool. It's in the open and there's more chance of me being able to control myself.'

Kate agreed. 'What are we drinking? Scotch?'

'Not today.' Nick shook his head. 'I bought a beautiful French red duty free at the airport for this sort of occasion. Let's open that.'

'Sounds delicious. We can pretend we are in the French Riviera.'

'You head out while I grab it.'

***

The world felt right. Nick had Kate with him, safe in his secure fortress. At the moment, his house in suburban Newstead felt like one of the only places he could semi-relax.

They'd uncorked and poured the deep red wine before speaking. He was about to ask after the incident at school, when Kate spoke.

'How is it that you follow your daughter to Vietnam on a school trip, but you allow her to go to a party?'

'Good question, Mrs. Penrose. I did deliberate long and hard about this one. But this is a good friend of Evie's. I know the parents, they will be home, I've been to their house and it is close-by. I will drive and collect her and she's been informed that she isn't to leave the premises. So, overall, I feel okay about letting her go. And plus, it would be impossible to live with her if I had refused!'

Nick believed what he said, but a slight twist occurred to his stomach when he spoke the words. Fact is, he'd be uneasy the entire time she was out and until she returned safely home.

'So, what's new? How's your week been?'

Nick regarded her and took another sip of his wine.

'I am looking for a new job.'

'Yes, I meant to ask about that. I'd forgotten with everything else going on. Why do you keep featuring in the paper? And, is all of it true?'

Nick couldn't be surprised. Of course she read the paper. 'Another good question. I'm sorry we should have talked about this before. I've been distracted, too. It all comes back to that gang I told you about. Now, for some reason, *The Quest,* well Brittany's husband ironically, keeps dragging up the past. Hardly any of it is true.'

'Hardly any of it? Are you still acting for them?'

'No.'

'Are you one of them, a bike member, I mean?'

'What? Are you really asking that? Don't you know me better?'

Kate's face turned a crimson-pink. 'Yes, I'm sorry. What parts are true?'

'The job.'

'Why are you looking for a new position?'

Nick gazed into the distance and spoke without looking at Kate.

'My association with that gang has affected the firm's reputation. My partner thought it best if we sever ties. It's all amicable and we've parted on good terms.'

'And your job search? How's that going?'

Nick shrugged. 'Nothing to report at this stage so I'm taking my time to find the right fit. I could flippantly say that I'm a man of leisure, but that doesn't apply to me at all. I don't do leisure. I need to work. Some days I roam this house like a caged animal.'

'That doesn't sound at all like fun.'

'I'm doing a few stints at a local community centre, you know assisting with legal advice. They run sessions a few times a week and cry out for volunteers.'

'That's a very kind thing to do.'

'No, not kind. It's giving back. These centres have queues out the door with people desperate for legal advice but can't afford it. Who knew? Once you do get out in the world, it's amazing what you can find.'

'What are you looking for? Something different?'

'No. Nothing different. Criminal law is what I do; it's in my blood. I can't imagine doing anything else. Picture me sitting at a desk all day running through the clauses of a contract. I think I'd go nuts. Even though I'm told there are some cleverly drafted clauses that are like a maze to unpick. But I'm sure something will come up.' Nick wasn't sure about that at all. 'Other than that, I'm thinking of going to visit my parents. Evie and I haven't seen them in a while.'

'You rarely talk about your family, why?'

'No reason. I guess they never come up. And I have developed a professional routine that I never mention anything personal about those close to me when I'm working. You know, given the people I work with.'

Kate nodded. 'But I'm not professional,' she said and leaned over to place her hand on his knee. She balanced the crystal wine glass in her other hand. He took a sip of his wine and looked away to the perimeters of the property. All was quiet. His tall mango and jacaranda trees usually housed flocks of lorikeets that would squawk in the dusk light, but today the sun hadn't yet started its descent and the birds had not begun to sing.

As he turned back, Kate focused on him. Not his green trimmed lawn, the sparkling swimming pool or the mosaics that lined the space. They sat in the outdoor lounge right next to the pool. Nick perched on the edge of the grey seat, a pastel cushion behind his back. He looked away to the Japanese Geisha print hanging on the outside, concrete wall of the house. It faced the pool and he didn't often look at it. He loved that print. It was one of the first he'd purchased when he was advised to invest in art. The advice of the experts had been to invest in Australian artists and he'd done that ever since. Those paintings adorned all the white walls in his house. But this one, he bought because he liked it. Kate followed his gaze but didn't comment.

The French door swung open and banged against the side of the house.

'Evie,' Nick warned.

'Oops, sorry, Dad.' The young woman gently placed the partition into its hinge. 'Kate? Does this shirt go with these pants?' Evie wore a blush pink knitted crop top exposing her slim stomach and matched it with torn, white jeans.

'Perfectly. You look gorgeous.'

Evie touched her hair. 'Should I wear my hair down or leave it up?'

Her blonde curls bounced in a ponytail around the base of her neck.

'Definitely up, but…'

Evie's angelic face crumpled.

Nick looked between the two, trying to contain his amusement at the exchange.

'What?' Evie addressed Kate.

'You need earrings. I have plenty, would you like to borrow a pair? I have peanut butter jars, koalas or mini mobile phones…'

Evie burst into laughter. 'What are those ones you are wearing?' The girl moved closer and fiddled with the dangly decorations Kate wore.

'Oh, these,' Kate smiled in Nick's direction. 'I picked these up in Vietnam. Aren't they cute?'

'Yes, but they won't match my outfit. I'll get my own thanks; nice silver twirls should do it. But thanks for the tip.'

Evie stood back and observed them as if she only now realised that her father and her teacher sat in their pool area.

'Are you two, like, dating or something?'

Nick and Kate looked at each other.

'Would it be okay if we were?' Nick asked.

'Yep, cool by me.' And with that the teenager turned on her heels, her thoughts back on completing her outfit. 'Dad, I'm going to grab more jewellery, and then can you drop me at the party?'

Nick nodded and Evie rushed away the way she came. He rose out of the seat they shared and extracted his car keys. 'I'm going to drop her off, it's less than ten minutes away. Why don't you stay here and relax?' Nick leaned his muscular arm on the wing of the lounge and dropped his mouth to meet her lips. 'I can't wait to get back,' he murmured in her ear. Goose bumps sprinkled her arms and he drew back. 'Are you cold?'

Kate shook her head. 'No, it's you. You have that effect on me.' She smiled up at him. 'It is getting cool though, I'll head inside if that's okay.'

'Of course, anywhere. But I'll cook when I get back, so relax.'

***

Kate watched him leave out of the circular drive with Evie in his bright white 4WD. Nothing about Nick read simple. His expensive car, his bespoke house furnishings, the paintings on his walls and this house. Even his intense personality was complex. Compared to her small little unit, Nick's house was enormous. She and Ben had wanted to decorate in a French chic style, bordering on old vintage. One day maybe, she pondered. If honest, though, she'd lost any desire to work on the place. It wasn't special anymore as it wasn't a joint project to share.

Without Nick present, the spaces in his house were vast and empty and she felt lonely. As they'd be cooking upon Nick's return she pulled out one of the stools along the wide island bench in the kitchen and waited. She flicked open a magazine she found there.

He arrived back within minutes.

'You're back already?'

'Yep, I told you it wasn't far away.'

'Yes, I know,' Kate said, 'but did you double check your surveillance? Did you confirm the exit routes in case of emergency?'

Nick placed his hands on his hips. 'You're funny, Kate Penrose. I told you I've already done all that. And Evie doesn't even know so she believes I'm a hip dad tonight because I dropped her off at the curb. Now, we have more time together.'

He strode over, hugged her and produced a tall, willowy sunflower from behind his back.

'Oh, you spoil me.'

'Yes, always and I want to, every day,' he said as the strong, hard muscles of his chest almost crushed her in an embrace. Time stopped as he bent to kiss her, but he pulled away with unsated longing. 'If we don't start cooking, we won't eat and then it will be time to pick Evie up already.'

'What time is pick up?'

'10.'

In the kitchen, Nick rummaged through the fridge and the pantry and placed various items on the bench between them.

'I thought you didn't cook?'

'I can cook, but I don't do it often, and probably not that well. But we'll get by.'

'What's on the menu?'

'It's a barbeque, of course. Sausages and steak with salad. Sound okay?' He paused and quizzed her.

'Of course, don't be silly. That's great. What can I do?'

'I want to cook for you but I guess you can assemble the salad if you must.'

'Sure,' responded Kate and she collected the salad items he'd placed on the bench and a sharp knife and commenced chopping.

'But, now it's your turn.'

'My turn for what?'

'Tell me about your family.'

Kate chopped cucumber.

'Okay. It's pretty straightforward. I'm an only child and was born and raised in Northern New South Wales.'

'Urgh! Are you a Queenslander or Blues supporter? It's an important question.'

'For the State of Origin, you mean? Queensland definitely.'

'Phew! That's great, that could have been a deal breaker.' He grinned at her boyishly so that his eyes lit up.

'Mum and Dad will be NSW supporters though, so watch out.'

'So, they still live there?'

'Yes, in Bangalow. Do you know it?'

'Yes, it's gorgeous. A beautiful spot and away from the tourist crowd of Byron Bay.'

'Yeah, exactly. My father runs the local chemist and has done most of his life. My mum helps him in the store. Dad studied as a naturopath later in life and whilst he's a chemist, he's holistic in his approach and mum, she's an earth goddess. They have a hobby farm with chickens and cows and sheep. A veggie patch of course. It's a fantastic place to get away from the bustle of the city but for a young woman wanting to explore the world, it wasn't exciting enough to stay.'

'Do they mind that you live in Brisbane?'

'Yes and no. It's not far away and they understood that I needed to spread my wings. I moved away to study teaching at uni. So they've had a long while to get used to it. After Ben died I went back home for a while. It was lovely to be cared for again like a young child, have all your meals cooked and washing done. I even commenced working at the local high school thinking perhaps I should stay. They are my only family, after all, but I felt suffocated and isolated, strangely. My life, even though it had irretrievably changed, still belonged in Brisbane. By then, of course, I'd lived away from home for a number of years. It was about independence, too. I craved it after a few months.'

The meat sizzled in the pan and Nick listened as he extracted hot plates from the oven and set the table. 'It must have been so tough to lose your husband. I can't even imagine.'

'You lost Autumn.'

'That's different. I had loved her and I cared for her as Evie's mother, but not as a soul mate.'

A pause. 'Yep, it's been awful, no denying it. But I chose early on to be one of those people that wouldn't let tragedy define me. That I would not forever wallow in my loss. And whilst I've done that, the trauma stays with you and unconsciously affects your actions. Even without thinking about it, I act more securely now, and seek out comfort and safety. I realized in Vietnam that I'd also stopping living. Well, living fully. I'd avoided engaging with life. You've helped me with that. Shown me that life can be fun again.'

A knife stabbed Nick through the heart. He could not deliver the things Kate desired. The dish of warm sausages he held almost slipped. Kate didn't notice.

'Let's eat. This looks great and I'm starving. We'll need our energy, right?' she said as she touched his bottom and let her hand wander over his hard stomach and hips. Nick nodded and served up the meal.

CHAPTER TWENTY-SIX

'I guess I'd better get dressed,' Nick murmured into Kate's ear. As she lay on her side, he traced a solitary finger along the curves of her torso and across her stomach until he reached her nipple. They lay sprawled across his bed as the curtains gently fluttered in the night breeze. Nick teased Kate's nipple and then cupped her breast with his hand.

'If you keep doing that, Evie will be the last one left at that party.' Kate swallowed her moan as hard lips pressed against hers. Coming up for air moments later, they both lay back on the pillows to catch their breath.

'I could kiss you all night long,' Nick whispered.

'And, I would let you.'

A powerful swelling of emotion for Nick overtook her, squeezing her heart and making her chest ache. Kate wanted to be with Nick so much it hurt. This torrent of emotion frightened her; she'd worked hard to forge an independent life after Ben's death and becoming so attached to another man put her at risk. She rolled closer to him and looked at the man who captured her so. His beautiful naked body glistened and his hair was sleep-tousled with matching dreamy eyes. Sometimes those eyes drew her in and she didn't want to swim her way out. Nick's lips titled up in a gentle smile. For once, his forehead wasn't creased and his expression held no tension This was as relaxed as Nick Harding ever got.

'We both agree we could stay in this bed all night, but you have a daughter who requires picking up. I'll come with you.' Kate rolled out of the bed away from his touch and searched for her clothes. Her jeans were in the far corner near the door and her top and bra in the doorway.

'Will you? That'd be great. We can have a coffee when we get back. Evie seems accepting of you being here, but maybe you shouldn't stay over yet. Is that okay with you?'

'Of course, there's plenty of time.

Nick nuzzled her neck and Kate swayed off balance as she tugged on her pants. She swiped at him and pushed him away.

'Let me get dressed otherwise we'll never get out of here.'

'Okay. Okay. I'll take a quick shower.'

'Oh, and Nick?' He paused in the doorway to the en suite, his attention caught.

'Promise me you'll stay away from the Warlocks.'

Nick nodded and turned away.

***

As they parked outside the Hamilton riverside mansion, Nick texted Evie to advise that he'd arrived.

'Is this modern parenting? You don't go in anymore to collect children, but instead communicate via their iPhone?'

'Yeah, sometimes. I usually get out and meet her on the drive or yard of the house. You know me. And sometimes she takes too long and that's when I go in and embarrass her. That makes her ready to leave quick smart.' Nick chuckled then turned serious. He raked his fingers through his hair and reached over to touch her leg. 'We haven't talked much about what happened at school today? Are you feeling okay about it? And, how's your back?'

'It's been so nice to forget about it for a while. And my back feels less tender now.'

'Best approach is not to be intimidated by her. That's how she gets her kicks. You show weakness and she'll walk all over you.'

'She is already,' Kate exclaimed. 'But I was thinking exactly the same thing. So maybe, I keep teaching, doing what I've been doing and deal with the consequences. What do you think? I mean, I shouldn't be changing, should I?'

'There'll be consequences if you don't though, won't there?'

Kate nodded. 'Yes, and what I'm undecided about, is what those consequences will be. I'm scared it will risk my job, but surely a school receives numerous parent complaints. The school has to back their staff, right? I haven't done anything wrong.'

'You haven't, but I didn't get that impression from your principal. She hasn't always been on your side.' Nick shook his head.

'If I don't tackle this head on, I'll stew over it and worry more. Should I meet with Janette, the principal or another mentor teacher and get advice or report it?'

'Yeah, maybe the mentor? It's a good idea. I say that because then you have evidence that you've raised the issue, attempted to get advice and that shows you've taken it seriously. Depending on the advice given, you can follow it and that's further proof that you've tried to deal with it.'

'Spoken like a true lawyer.' Kate smiled. 'I might start with the year level co-ordinator. She's an experienced teacher that I respect and she's worked with Janette for decades. I'll do that Monday.'

'Good plan. And now, you should put it out of your mind until then.'

They sat in the silent darkness as they waited. A glimmer of the Brisbane River sparkled from behind them and the windshield of the 4WD shimmered.

'Tonight might be one of those nights that I have to rustle her up. Do you want to wait here?'

'Um, yeah, I'd better. Don't want a contingent going in to embarrass her. Plus, there might be girls from school present, so best I stay put.'

Nick unbuckled his seat belt. 'Be right back.'

Kate hadn't checked her phone all day. She swiped the screen to check her email and social media. She grinned at a photo of her uni friends holding up drinks in a bar and laughing at the camera. Posted just moments ago. She missed them but she'd entered a new world; the world she'd created since Ben's death felt distant and removed from the one she'd been engrossed in for the afternoon and evening.

Was she doing the right thing? She was going to send herself crazy always thinking about her actions.

But those worries still circulated in her mind, sometimes weighing her down. The fear of the unknown realm of Nick's life caused anxiety. But she had no concerns about him as a person. Nick Harding was chivalrous, a true gentleman, and a good person who cared deeply for his daughter and family. On top of that, he was drop-dead good looking and despite everything, he made her feel safe, unlike anyone she'd ever known.

A tiny stir of excitement burst at the base of her belly. She might just be able to get used to this 'after Ben' life. And soon, she and Nick might be out with her groups of friends having fun, too.

Kate checked the time. She peered into the shadows and watched other parents arrive and depart with their children. Still no sign of Nick and Evie. Nick hadn't messaged so perhaps he'd been trapped talking.

But then he was beside the car and tapping on the glass.

'What is it?' Kate asked as she opened her door.

'Has Evie turned up here? At the car?'

'No, she hasn't.'

'I can't find her. Her friend hasn't seen her for the past hour or so and no one at the party can remember where they last saw her.'

Nick paced.

Kate read the panic in his face. She jumped out of the vehicle and slammed the door. 'I'll help. Nick, she can't be far. We'll find her.'

He nodded and they both headed back toward the impressive three-story house, the automatic lighting system guiding their path. A few kids milled about in the front garden, reluctant for the party to be over. They stood in huddles and talked with their heads lowered. Kate didn't recognise any of them.

'Have you found her, Nick?' The host parents asked as they re-entered the premises. 'No.'

Kate left them and headed around the side. Steps led to a pool on one level, a tennis court on another and then down below, a jetty that accommodated a sailing boat. Despite the entire river frontage being lit, it was difficult to determine who might be down there. She trudged down the steps and the cool night air bit at her skin.

A dark figure sat on a low bench adjacent to the frameless glass pool fence. Kate rushed over, hoping it was Evie. A girl with short dark hair sat on a boy's lap with their faces pushed close.

'Party is over. Shouldn't you two be leaving?' Kate snapped.

'Miss?'

Kate moved closer and observed Charlotte, one of her French students.

'Charlotte? Have you seen Evie Harding? Her father can't find her.'

Charlotte stood and looked away as she spoke. 'Um, she headed down towards the water. I don't know, maybe half an hour ago.'

'Down there?' Kate pointed down the decline toward the water. Charlotte nodded.

'Thanks. Oh, and Charlotte, it's time to go home.'

Without looking back, the girl pulled her skirt straight and tucked loose hair behind her ears and headed for the steps, followed by her friend.

Thudding down the paved staircase, Kate made as much noise as possible. She feared she might find Evie in a similar position to Charlotte and didn't wish to catch her by surprise. The further she descended the slope, the more she left the house lights behind and it became darker and harder to search. Reaching the bottom, Kate paused and looked around. In front, the river lay sparkling like a jewel and bright lights illuminated the horizon. To her left sat a tall concrete fence obstructing her view of the neighbour's mansion. No place to hide.

A diminutive shed blocked her path to the right. It had bright orange round flotation devices decorating its outside walls.

A boathouse. And a great place to find privacy. Despite its small size it covered the entire span of this level and was the access point for the narrow jetty leading out to the boat. She stepped toward the only entrance and tried the door. Locked.

The boat?

Giggles rose on the wind and reached her, answering her unspoken question. Kate walked briskly out to the vessel. As she stepped one foot aboard, Nick came out of nowhere and rushed past her. His weight shifted the craft on its moorings.

How'd he get here so fast?

Kate spied them on the rear deck. The tone of voice, the long ponytail blowing in the breeze and the way she moved, confirmed it was Evie. Nick yanked the young man up and held him by his shirt collar.

'What the hell are you doing?'

'Dad!' Evie grabbed her father's arm. His strength was no match for the young girl. Evie's arms flailed towards her father as his voice rang out. Words were exchanged in the scuffle but Kate couldn't hear as the wind swallowed them. As the boat rocked, she squared her feet and grasped the side railing. Somehow the boy freed himself and he raced away down the length of the vessel. Kate steadied his walk as he approached and assisted him disembark onto the jetty

She turned him to face her. 'It'll be okay. Evie's dad got a shock because he couldn't find her. It's best if you just go.'

Without a word the boy jogged away. He climbed the steps two at a time in his haste to return to safety.

Kate stayed on the pier.

Now father and daughter were alone.

'Oh my God, Evie, I couldn't find you. What were you thinking?'

Kate heard snatched words and detected the steely edge to Nick's tone. Evie's sobs floated in the still air.

'I'm furious that you didn't answer your phone, send me a message, keep an eye on the time and have any consideration that I would be worried when I couldn't locate you.' He kicked his foot against the fibreglass seating on the deck and released a deep guttural groan.

It sounded like a wounded animal. He lowered his head and his shoulders slumped. Next time he spoke, his words were calmer. 'I am so disappointed. Go now, get back upstairs and let's go home.'

Evie pushed past him and Kate helped her back onto the jetty. Evie refused to meet Kate's eye as she stepped down. Nick didn't move.

Should she go to him? He'd overreacted, surely? This seemed to be a common trait concerning his daughter and her behaviour. Her gut told her to leave and she turned to walk down the narrow timber gangplank. The brilliant spotlights of the yard blinded her as she walked up the steps. Shading her eyes, she followed Evie.

CHAPTER TWENTY-SEVEN

Raindrops fell as they silently walked back to the car. Lightning bolts lit up the horizon and thunderclaps echoed in the air. The sky had turned midnight black, the clouds suffocating the stars that had previously blanketed it. No one spoke on the short journey home but the tension in the car sat thick and palpable. The only noise was Evie gulping in her sobs from the back seat. They paused at the entrance to the drive as Nick pounded the electric gate key. It didn't swing open.

'Damn,' he muttered and he raced out to manually operate it. His rain-soaked clothes squelched as he sat back in the leather driver's seat, but the gate swung open. The decorative driveway lights were not illuminated: the world had turned sombre to match his mood.

Before the car had pulled to a stop, Evie jumped out, slammed the car door and raced towards the house, banging the internal door as well. As the echo of her displeasure still rang out, she rushed back into the garage. Nick heard her laboured breaths and moved closer. Her face had drained of colour and her hands shook.

'There's stuff everywhere…'

'What do you mean?' Nick grasped her by the shoulders and held her tight, peering into her face.

Kate alighted from the car and stood behind them.

'I don't know. The furniture is tossed around, the kitchen is a mess of food and stuff. The lights aren't on, but I stepped over things on the floor.'

Nick froze. As if in slow motion, he released Evie and rose to full height.

'Stay here,' he said to both of them and gestured with his hand to crouch down low. Nick tiptoed through the entry into the main part of the house. His heartbeat echoed loudly in his ears. Random moonlight exposed the toppled sideboard in the hallway where the photo frames lay scattered across the tiles. His white walls were graffitied with abhorrent colour. His sofa cushions had been ripped and stuffing lay strewn across the carpet as he crept into the living area. No one was in there. Back in the kitchen he crouched at bench height and listened.

Nick craned his neck to check the paintings on the stairwell. He couldn't see that far in the dark. Of all the stupid things to think about! There weren't many objects in the house that couldn't be replaced, but his paintings, he hoped they were left untouched. A cavern opened up in his chest at the trashing of his home. His private domain and until now, his sanctuary.

A noise on the internal stairs and he reeled back against the kitchen cabinets. Nick moved around the island bench, hiding himself from the view of anyone descending his staircase.

Footsteps.

He strained to listen. One person, or more?

It was a heavy clump – the person, presumably a man, wore chunky boots. He knew the sort. They were issued to all members of the gang.

In that moment, he wished he'd relented and bought himself a gun. He'd never done it, never thought it necessary. Mostly because he was fearful it would make him like them; like the clients he represented. Right now, he thought he'd have happily held it towards his intruder and shot the goddam thing if it meant keeping Kate and Evie safe. Forget the paintings.

Was he panicking?

He prayed the two of them stayed in the garage.

The movement continued down the steps. In a few seconds, the person would reach the foyer. They'd have to make a decision to move toward the living area or the kitchen. Nick held his phone. He turned it to silent and sent a desperate, cryptic message to Curtis.

Come now, quick.

If he didn't have a gun, he'd have to make do. He reached up, carefully avoiding the cups and cutlery strewn on the bench and felt for the knife block. It perched at the end, in the corner. He found it and sighed with relief that it was fully stacked. Nick grasped the middle knife knowing it had the longest and hopefully, sharpest, blade.

What to do? Face this guy head on or wait and hope that Curtis received his message and brought help? A dark figure moved through the foyer toward the living area.

One man. Alone.

He didn't look towards the kitchen. Nick couldn't determine any distinguishing features except he appeared luminous in the dark, like a gigantor roaming in his house. His blackness merged into the shadows and Nick knew under the sleeve of that leather jacket would sit the red rose tattoo. Nick's heart rose into his mouth as the bikie headed past the living area and towards the garage.

No!

Nick raced around the island bench in the other direction. He grabbed a cupboard door and opened and slammed it shut. As he turned back, he faced his intruder five metres cross the space. Behind the shut garage door, he heard voices.

Stop talking!

This guy could not find out that Kate and Evie were alone in the garage.

'Harding. So great to see you again.'

The man knew him. The raspy voice led to an impression of a pack a day smoker.

'There's no hard feelings from me. You did a great job getting me off those grievous bodily harm charges. Imagine, I could have spent ten years behind bars. I did it, you know. Assaulted that woman, poked that gun in the poor little lady's face and made her cry. But it wasn't about stealing stuff like the police said, it was retribution. That bitch dobbed on Smith and that couldn't go unnoticed. She had to pay.'

Random pieces fell into place.

'Jonno. How are you?'

He remembered the charges. The young woman working behind the counter in the late-night bottle shop had been sliced across the forehead and down the side of both cheeks to wear permanent scars. He'd been right, it wasn't about the money, Jonno hadn't even taken the till money, he'd disfigured her and swiped gum and lollies on his way out. With no CCTV footage; the cameras destroyed without anyone noticing and the victim terrified of testifying against the attacker, the case had no legs. Add to that a police stuff up, and Jonno had walked free.

'I'm good mate. But Max, he ain't so good. He's been away for over twelve months now. He isn't happy. His new lawyer is confident he'll get up on appeal. Do a better job than you.'

'That's great. But he's in jail. What's he got to do with this?'

Jonno laughed. 'You know how it works, man. He's got everything to do with this. Doesn't matter where he is, he's our leader. And he has a grudge against you. You didn't deliver and now you have to pay.'

Nick weighed up the situation. He held the knife behind his back but Jonno would have a gun and probably, other weapons. He might, just, be able to hold his own with his fists, but he couldn't match artillery.

'Let's do this the easy way, Harding. I don't want to be sloshing your blood around tonight. It'll mess up my clothes.'

'I don't do anything the simple way, Jonno. It will be best if you leave now and we'll not take this any further. I'll clean up and never mention my visit tonight.'

'It ends here tonight, Harding. The gang finds you dispensable. You know too much, and plus, Max wants revenge.'

A squeal followed by a muffled groan escaped through the gap in the garage door.

Nick's heart jumped into his throat but he didn't have time to think about Kate and Evie. He prayed they were okay. Jonno inched forward and Nick lunged.

Man, it was dark; everything around him appeared in shadows. His arms flailed and he missed hits. How did Jonno move so fast? Nick wasn't good at fighting blind. He felt disoriented in his own home. A punch landed to Nick's stomach and he fell to the ground, doubled over. A boot to the back followed as he lay curled on the tiles. Despite the wind being knocked out of him, he jumped onto his feet and stepped backwards, trying to gain space between them. Did Jonno have X-ray vision? Each punch connected with Nick's body. A knuckle to the jaw, a slap to the head, the hits came fast. His head ricocheted back. Nick still held the knife and after a few seconds pause, when Jonno must have been assessing his next shot, Nick produced it.

The metallic blade glinted in the darkness.

Jonno laughed.

Nick plunged forward, the tip touching the man's sleeve.

Jonno retreated.

Nick advanced; this was his only hope. He didn't really want to kill the guy, only injure him enough to render him unable to fight. Imagine those headlines? He could live without that media coverage!

Jonno executed a Kung Fu like move and Nick had little chance of seeing the leg catapult toward him. It came too fast. The leg knocked against his arm and the implement dropped to the ground, rattling against the hard floor.

Nick groaned and his teeth jarred.

'What are you going to do now, huh?'

Jonno's chest rose and fell with his breaths. He might be getting tired. Making a run toward the island bench, Nick hoped he could extract another knife. Jonno, despite his apparent fatigue, sped more quickly in the other direction and cornered Nick. They stood in front of the chopping block, visible in the dimness. Nick eyed it sitting on the bench at this close distance.

Stupid!

Jonno followed his gaze. He picked one of the most razor-sharp in the bunch and held it aloft.

'Looking for this?'

Jonno poked it into the air. At this vantage point, it was only centimetres away from reaching him. And he was blocked into the corner recess of the kitchen.

In the far distance, sirens commenced their wail. Jonno stiffened. He dove for Nick who ducked low and crawled along the ground, crouching next to the bench. He didn't move fast enough because Jonno swiped his knife in all directions, hoping to land a hit. The tip scraped Nick's upper arm, tearing into his flesh.

Warm blood oozed over his hand as he covered the wound. He didn't have time to examine it as he crawled away. His blood-covered hand contaminated each surface he touched. Crawling on hands and knees Nick moved across the small space and headed into the open area of the foyer. About halfway across, Jonno crashed into the collapsed sideboard he had knocked over earlier.

'Fuck!' he screeched.

The knife twanged against the tiles. Jonno was scrambling around on his hands and knees searching for it. The man's silver rings rang out against the floor. Jonno was close to the garage and Nick further away. If he knew the girls were hiding in the garage, he'd head straight there.

The sirens got louder.

Nick breathed out. They must be at the gate. God damn this storm that had disconnected the power. The police couldn't enter his fortress unless they found the manual button. Would Curtis remember where it was? Scenarios raced through Nick's mind but still, Jonno stood before him.

Forgetting the weapon, Jonno stood up, his bulk once again foreboding in the darkness. One metre separated them. The man breathed in and out in long gulps, as if weighing up his options. A loud crash to the outside of the house, spurred the bikie into action. He ran headlong into Nick toppling him to the ground. In the scuffle they rolled one over the over until Jonno was sprawled across Nick near the base of the stairs. Nick kicked with his legs trying to get traction to push him off but it only worked to exert his energy. Jonno's torso lay across his. Nick felt cold steel against his temple. A gun. He froze. Stopped squirming and kept his limbs still. The front door splintered open and smashed against the walls of the house. His intricate stained glass shattered sending sharp shards in all directions as pieces of glass rapped against the tiles. In the darkness Nick observed people approach but couldn't make out how many or if they were police. Their feet scrunched through the debris.

Filled with renewed adrenalin at the prospect of rescue, Nick gathered all his strength and pushed upwards against the weight. He barked a loud growl. With one fist holding the gun, Jonno bashed him around the head to fend him off. Nick braced against the hits. In the fracas, a figure came up behind Jonno and put an arm around his throat. Seizing the moment, Nick grasped Jonno's shin in an attempt to topple him. But he struggled back, punching the officer and kicking at Nick still on the ground as his hands and legs remained unrestrained.

He clocked Nick in the nose with a steel-capped boot. Stars swirled in Nick's vision and the figures blurred. Nick lost focus. Then the gun went off, loud and deafening in his ear. Nick reeled from a sting to his chest and then everything went black.

***

Fingers pressed into her throat, gripping her so fiercely they choked back her scream.

White light prickled at the edge of Kate's vision and her head spun. Her heart pulsed in her ears whilst frenzied thoughts raced through her mind. If this guy was going to kill her, she wanted to hurt him first. Was she delusional? Yes, but the urge to fight back was too great. After all she'd been through in so far in her short life, this guy, whoever he was, wasn't going to defeat her.

Wriggling, she struggled against his hold and pushed her elbow into his chest. A jolt of pain shot up her arm. This man was as hard as a brick wall! The bastard laughed. Yeah, she'd really showed him.

'Good try, honey. You're a tough one, are you? You won't be when we're finished with your boyfriend. He'll be screeching like a little girl any minute now. After the Warlocks are finished with him.'

The Warlocks? The bikie gang?

His hold on her neck tightened and Kate gagged as his leather-clad arm moved to press against her face. Something sparkled in the suffused light. A ring? Panicking, her hands reached for his arm, tugging. 'I'm suffocating,' she tried to say but only garbled words came out. The man scoffed. What did he really want? To hurt her? She guessed he wanted her held captive whilst they hunted Nick.

Kate tried to piece the puzzle together. They'd snatched her from behind in Nick's garage. After Nick had fled into the house. The intruder had seen her but not Evie. Someone else had to be in the house. As the man grabbed her, she'd seen a blur of colour out of the corner of her eye. Evie. Smart girl. Moments later, it had been faint, but Kate heard the tiniest of clicks. Evie found refuge in the car. Kate stole a glance at its interior. The warm engine still ticked over but no sign of Evie. Kate prayed she stayed put. Her priority was to keep Evie safe. Nick could look after himself, couldn't he? Yes, he could. Kate forced herself to believe it.

As time passed, Kate's body tremored as fear took over. Her

bladder was suddenly full and she needed to pee. That would teach him, wouldn't it? Kate imagined the wee trickling down her leg and pooling over his sturdy boots. Instead, she focused on levelling her breathing. She needed to stay calm.

Kate smelled the stale and faint scent of tobacco lingering on his leather jacket. She imagined it was matched with dark pants, completing the typical tough-guy bikie look. Hair tickled the base of her neck. A long beard? It was hard to tell. But he had to be a bikie. One of the men Nick had acted for? Why were they here? So many questions…

Kate clenched her jaw and forced her jittery legs to remain still. In her head she uttered every profanity she knew. As a school teacher, she knew a lot. As the seconds ticked over, blood-fuelled frustration surged in place of her fear.

Bloody Nicholas Harding! Him and his good looks and chivalry and charm. And, dangerous life. She could have happily…

The bikie moved a hand around to her breast. She lifted her foot and slammed it into his boot. It didn't even make a dent. The man chuckled again and his chest pushed into her back as he took a breath. She didn't realise she was so funny.

'Ah, come on, love. We can have some fun.' And to prove the point that she was defenceless, he cupped her breast again.

'Yes, that's better,' he said as she instinctively moved her torso inwards. Her backside drove into his groin. Shudders of disgust swept through her as she felt the outline of his body. His rank breath on her cheek made her turn the other way.

Sirens wailed in the distance.

The man stiffened, and the world erupted into a cacophony of noise.

A commotion blasted from within the house. Sounds of furniture falling and cracking onto tiles, of glass shattering, the thump of fist against flesh and Nick's raised voice. He moaned. In pain? Her heart thumped harder. She had to get away from this thug and help Nick.

Then came the screams followed by capped boots stomping on hard ground and the wail of the automatic roller door being forced open. Kate wanted to cover her ears with her hands to block out the uproar. If she didn't, she'd disappear to that other place, another time and the trauma would engulf her. If that happened, she'd be physically here, but her mind would flee. Above anything else, she needed to remain alert. Otherwise, she'd be useless to Nick.

And Evie.

Her captor's hands dropped. Kate's palm flew to her sore throat, rubbing the spot to soothe it. She gulped in lost breaths and sussed out her surrounds. Walls of shelving sat on her left and the car to her right. There was no choice. She raced around to the rear of the vehicle. It was in her sights when a calloused hand seized her. The garage door creaked as it sliced into its spot on the ceiling.

She was pulled back and a sharp sting hit her square in the stomach; a knuckle landed in her soft folds. The ring on the bikie's right hand with its sharp edges pierced her skin. But the force of the blow doubled her over and air exited her lungs. The intruder was dragged backwards with force. With hands on knees Kate sucked in large gulps of air.

Bright, white light blinded her as she fell to the garage floor.

Evie screamed. Flashlights illuminated the square space.

'Get down! Be quiet!' a voice shouted.

A car door slammed and Kate tensed. Then she was dragged from the ground and into Evie's embrace and squeezed tight. Evie's body shook violently. Kate's heart thumped out of her chest and every breath spread splinters of pain throughout her body. The two of them remained crouched, heads cowered, too scared to even peek a glance around them.

A hand touched her shoulder and Kate reeled backwards onto her bottom.

'It's okay. I'm police. You can come out now.'

Evie shot up and ran out of the garage before Kate could stand upright.

'Dad!' she screamed. 'Dad!'

Kate moved as if in slow motion. When she stepped into the foyer, the whole place lit up. Twenty or more people filled the area, all jostling and busy with a job to do. Nick lay in a pool of blood with paramedics surrounding him. An officer held Evie back as she pushed her way through to be with her father.

Kate's legs gave way. The cold, hard tiles came up to meet her. She found comfort in their coolness against her hot skin and sat on her knees and placed her outstretched palms flat. Her aches forgotten. Her hair came loose and fell in straight strands around her face. It obstructed her view but as the ambulance officers moved around Nick's prone body, she wrenched her hair away from her face and saw him clearly. His skin was alabaster next to the red blood that had soaked his T-shirt. The medic yelled for assistance as he pumped Nick's chest. In the spot where she liked to kiss him when they made love. He had a mole there that she teased and tickled and made him laugh. It sat above his heart, near his left nipple.

Kate wailed, a deep, woeful sound. Even in the commotion, heads turned. She raised her cool hands to her face and swiped away the tears that fell, missing the snot that ran from her nostrils. She struggled to breathe as sobs wracked her, loud and ugly until hands grabbed her under the armpits and lifted her. Her legs refused to co-operate and remained bent in an awkward position, as if she remained seated. A soothing voice spoke into her ear, but she couldn't understand the words.

Two figures lay broken and dying in front of her. Ben and Nick. Both on hard, concrete grounds, with open wounds and flapping skin, and fresh, oozing blood with raised and panicked voices surrounding them. Evie turned into an image of a Greek local yelling in her native tongue. The men dressed in green overalls became Greek doctors attending to Ben's injuries. Strong arms gripped her tighter as her body crumbled. Uncontrollable trembling took over and she couldn't stop the shaking as her vision blurred.

Heavy hands dragged her outside. Once in the garden, the cool air slapped her in the face. She sat on a low sandstone wall bordering the driveway. A blanket was draped around her shoulders and a hot cup of tea placed into her hands. The sweetness of the drink eased her shaking. She took a couple of sips and then held tight to the heat it generated. Her head started to clear and Kate became aware of her surroundings again. The terrifying images faded, reality settling back in. Within minutes she shivered in the cool night air and pulled that blanket tighter around her.

A medic tended to her, asking questions she didn't feel like answering. Her body was not the concern. There wasn't anything the paramedic could give her to heal her mind and make the memories go away. Psychically, she was battered and no doubt her stomach wore a rainbow of coloured bruising but she wasn't injured. Nick was hurt. Or dying. She shuddered.

At some point Evie sat beside her. Tears welled in Kate's eyes when she observed the girl's stricken face. Evie's hair was a tousled bird's nest and her clothes were crumpled and her white jeans were splattered with spots of blood. She'd been close to Nick.

'How is he?'

'They're still working on him. They won't let me watch.'

'Probably best not to.'

'What will I do if I lose him?' Evie cried soundless tears that rolled down her cheeks and into her lap moistening her skirt.

'That won't happen. Do you hear?' Kate moved closer to join their blankets and share body warmth.

'He will be fine.'

'Kate, he was shot in the chest. He's unconscious.'

'I know. But the best people to care for him are in there now.'

They huddled together silently. The only other choice was to keep making reassurances and neither of them had the heart for that.

A few minutes later a stretcher was wheeled out with Nick strapped in. Tubes came out of his mouth, and sat in the veins of his bare arms. His eyes were closed. Evie jumped up but a man raced over to prevent her getting near.

'Evie,' he spoke softly. 'He's going to the hospital now. They'll look after him, okay? You know your dad, he's a tough bloke. He'll make it through this.' The tall man cradled Evie and turned to Kate

'Are you Kate?'

How did he know her name?

She nodded.

'Can Evie stay with you? As you probably know, her grandparents are in Toowoomba, but it's too late now for a trip out there.'

Kate nodded again. 'Yes, of course.'

'Evie, let's go and get your things. You can stay with Kate tonight. She'll look after you.'

The man led Evie by the arm and took her back inside. He took her through an alternative entrance to avoid the carnage in the foyer. Kate's mind should have been swirling with images and thoughts and confusion. But it cleared, went blank and couldn't capture a single thread. If she'd been asked her name, she wouldn't have remembered.

The man stood before her again with Evie.

'Okay, I am going to drive you to your place. Do you have a car here?' he asked.

Did she have her car here? She couldn't honestly remember. She shook her head, not knowing either way.

'Okay. I have a police car. Can you give me directions?'

##

Curtis Duncan placed an ice-cold gin in her hand. How did he know that was her favourite drink? Kate wrapped her fingers around it and let the condensation wet them. With Evie finally asleep, hours after they'd arrived back at her unit, she sat in her simple home with Nick's best friend.

Why didn't she know about him?

He knew about her, though.

Curtis had filled her in. Now, she felt more confused and upset. She fought to control the anger that swirled within her chest.

'So I have this clear. Nick has been receiving death threats for a number of months from the bike gang the Warlocks and tonight those fellows in the house were members of the gang and had come to kill him?'

'Yep.'

'You know that I didn't know about any of that, well, not the threats at least?' She ran her hands down her face, as if that would relieve her overwhelming fatigue.

'He didn't tell anyone.'

'He told you.'

'I'm his oldest friend and a cop.'

'And why are you here and not out trying to solve this crime?' Sarcasm dripped off her words.

Curtis had the decency to smile. 'For starters, Nick would be very worried about you and Evie and his priority would be the two of you. So I'm here to ensure that you are both safe and well in his absence. And secondly, I'm a street cop, running the beat, this is an investigation and it's in the hands of the detectives.'

He took a sip of his scotch.

'But this is only two guys, right? Because they've been caught it will end, won't it?'

'No, in fact, any of these members operate at the direction of their leader, that is how these gangs work and that is a fellow that Nick failed to keep out of prison.'

Kate's stomach lurched.

'But if he's in prison, everyone is safe, right?'

'No. We think he's the one behind this and he's in jail.'

They talked for a little while longer. Despite the reason for his visit, Kate liked Curtis and understood how he and Nick would be friends. They both had a cheeky streak to them; his eyes sparkled sometimes when he spoke. He had short, sandy hair to Nick's curly and long locks. But he had Nick's back and Kate was sure, Nick had his, too.

'Will you be okay?' he asked her.

'Yes.'

'I can stay if you want.'

'It's not necessary, we'll be fine.' Kate showed Curtis out.

Kate searched through her medicine cabinet until she found it. Her father had given the elixir to her after Ben's death. She'd become an insomniac and couldn't sleep. She'd used it religiously, for at least the first year. Now, she filled an extra-large portion in the medicine cup and drank it down. Before sleep took her, she knew she was certain about one thing – she couldn't go through losing someone again.

CHAPTER TWENTY-EIGHT

BIKIE LAWYER ATTACKED IN OWN HOME

Nick Harding, lawyer loved by crims was on the receiving end of the sort of treatment he usually defends last night. Harding returned home to be met by a Warlocks member ransacking his palatial abode. Clearly Harding didn't appreciate the intrusion as a tussle ensued between the men. Police reported the use of kitchen knives and a gun. It's unclear whether the gun belonged to the intruder or Harding. Whilst Jonno 'Jokester' Worthington suffered bruises and abrasions, he was captured by police. Another, as of yet unidentified member of the gang was also on the premises assisting Jonno. Harding sported a deep cut to his left upper arm and was shot. He remains unconscious in the Royal Brisbane Hospital.

Any attempts to speak with Harding's loved ones about the incident have been refused. He remains in a stable but serious condition. The Warlocks said that Jonno had been acting on instructions and had been brave as he stood up for the hood. Anyone who messes with the gang, messes with all of them and retribution could come from anyone, at any time. When asked what crime they accused Harding of committing, the gang representative went tight-lipped but gestured with his hands across his throat. Did the Warlocks threaten Harding and wish him dead? When asked if they would be continuing to seek revenge, the member joined other bikies and they rode off on their Harley Davidson motorcycles yelling 'wait and see'.

The Daily Quest will wait and see and keep an eye on this developing story. But the question begs – what did Harding do to raise the ire of the Warlocks? This paper has reported a link between Harding and the gang and his close association with them. How did Harding upset his loyal gang members? Was he unable to get one of his own off another heinous crime? Has Harding tried to regain his lucrative position of the Warlocks exclusive criminal lawyer and it's backfired?

Ironically, Harding has represented his attacker before, and was successful in having him acquitted of assault charges of the most vicious kind. Now the tables are turned and Harding is the victim. Would he defend his attacker and do his professional best to have him acquitted of the charge of assaulting him? It seems the boot is on the other foot at present.

***

Across town, Brittany and Lindsay Bartholomew sat on their paved terrace facing the Brisbane River. They ate a lavish breakfast spread at their wrought iron table and each had their own copy of *The Daily Quest* for perusal. People exercising traversed the river walk in front of their home. Neither paid them any attention. Brittany wore her trademark Dolce and Gabbana sunglasses despite the sun providing little warmth on the brisk spring morning.

She'd only reached page one.

'Oh, how terrible!' she exclaimed.

'Hmm,' Lindsay responded.

'The story about the lawyer, the father from school. He's hurt.'

'Yes,' Lindsay said rubbing his hands together after having placed his paper down to take another sip of coffee. 'What a scoop. No other paper has that story this morning. It's an exclusive. I've got us a source.' He tapped his nose with his index finger and his eyes sparkled with evil.

'It sounds dreadful. What about his daughter and his girlfriend, oh, you know, that mousy teacher from school?' Brittany feigned forgetfulness.

'They were present and at home at the time and were reportedly rushed from the scene. Saw the whole thing. The girlfriend sustained minor injuries.'

'And Nick's wounds are serious?'

'As the article says, my dear, he's unconscious. The bullet hit above his heart, near an artery I believe. Doesn't sound great.'

'No, it's awful,' Brittany said as she continued to read the paper.

***

Not far away, in Teneriffe, Kate collected two croissants and hot chocolates from Café de Flore and a paper as well. Evie had not yet woken, so she settled herself in the warmth of indoors and relished the hot drink and the flaky pastry. French food never failed to ease her woes. Unfolding the paper, the grasp on her drink slipped. A few hot drops scalded her bare thigh, exposed by a slip in her skirt.

Nick made front-page news.

Her appetite vanished. She put down her croissant and read the article. Tears rolled silently down her cheeks and she batted them away as quickly as they leaked in case Evie walked out. She was a fool; she'd underestimated the depth of the situation. Yes, she'd read the previous article; yes she knew he had a secret, but never did she presume that the mystery would be life-threatening and not only to Nick but those he loved. How could he have kept this secret from her? That's what hurt the most.

She'd imagined he might have had a secret second job; been an undercover agent assisting the police or maybe, he housed wrongly accused prisoners who couldn't afford legal representation. Maybe he harboured a desire to run for politics and it was all hush hush. What did she know?

Obviously, nothing.

The phone rang. It would be her mother. Kate refused to answer. In a panic, she formulated a plan, her desire for safety overtaking everything. She needed to get as far away from Nick and from Brisbane and as soon as possible. After Curtis came to collect Evie to deliver her to her grandparents, Kate would go home. She needed fresh air and peace and quiet away from the distraction of Nick. It was the right thing to do. But the images of him lying, hurt, in hospital wouldn't leave her mind. It broke her in two and she bent over and stifled her sobs.

***

Nick sat up in his hospital bed and yanked the covers aside. He watched the newspapers float to the ground with disposable coffee cups and other miscellaneous items that had collected upon the bed.

He wanted to get the hell out of hospital.

He had regained consciousness three days ago. He'd recovered, was sore in his upper torso and arm, but nothing that he couldn't handle. Standing at the hospital window, he watched fat raindrops fall against the glass and splatter. The weather suited his foul mood.

'C'mon, mate. Throwing a toddler tantrum won't get you released any earlier. Rest. Your body needs it, even if your mind won't let it.' Curtis placed a hand on his shoulder.

Nick shrugged away his hand. He wore the hospital issue white gown. 'I need to be with Evie to ensure she's safe.'

'Evie is safer in Toowoomba with your parents than being with you at the moment, trust me. Have you spoken to her?'

'Who?' Nick asked.

Curtis sighed. 'Lucky I love you, mate, otherwise I'd be out of here. Kate, and you know who I mean.'

'No. I can't talk to her. She can't be involved in this. It was a mistake in the first place, I knew it.' Nick banged his fist against the window frame and it rattled.

'She has rung the hospital every day.'

'Not to talk to me,' Nick responded, and in a softer tone. 'She hasn't asked to speak to me.'

'I spoke to her and she wanted every detail about your recovery and how you were. Is that the sign of someone who doesn't care?'

Through gritted teeth, Nick said, 'She can't care. I'm too dangerous. It's too risky for her to be associated with me. She needs and deserves safety and security and a nice life.'

'Mate, she was never going to get that with you, even without all this drama.'

'Exactly. And now it has to end.'

Curtis was quiet.

Nick held himself so stiff his jaw ached. A steely reserve had come over him since regaining consciousness. He'd demanded answers on Evie and Kate the moment he woke. Were they hurt? He'd asked for each minute detail about the incident and the police investigation. The hospital had called security such was the stir he'd caused. All hell had broken loose until Curtis had shown up to calm him down.

A nurse popped her head around the corner of his door. 'Phone call for you, Mr Harding, a lass by the name of Kate. Should I wheel you out?'

Nick paused, glanced at Curtis. He took a step toward the nurse but stopped himself, shook his head. 'No. Tell her I'm not available.' Nick gazed out the window again.

The nurse considered Curtis, who shrugged.

'I'm on a night shift tonight, I'll drop back in tomorrow,' Curtis said

Nick acknowledged his exit with a curt nod.

##

Nick was bored. He hated sitting around all day being treated like an invalid. Desperate, he pulled over the TV remote and switched it on. Daytime television only made matters worse. But then a news bulletin flashed up. Nick craned his head in interest–he'd missed the news the last few days. Presumably he'd been the headline, so maybe it was good fortune that he hadn't seen it.

Cameras rolled in front of a frantic scene outside the Brisbane Supreme Court complex. The new and modern building had only opened the year before. The distinctive eye mural adorning one of the garden walls outside the building came into focus behind the reporter. Nick knew that odd painting well. Reporters hounded a person heading toward the entrance.

'Mr. Ambrose, have you spoken to your client? How is Max Vincenzo feeling about today's proceedings?'

Unlike the other lawyers entering the courthouse, Mr. Ambrose stopped, turned and regarded the group of twenty journalists who all had their microphones poised for his response.

'My client is optimistic that the Court of Appeal will find in his favour and overturn his conviction and sentence.' The lawyer paused for dramatic effect. 'He will be acquitted.'

The pack of reporters went ballistic, shouting further questions, talking into mobile phones and taking notes. The prestigious criminal lawyer who had replaced Nick in representing the Warlocks presented as a smooth operator. His navy-blue pin-striped suit was immaculate and without a crease. The shiny bald head detracted from his words. It gleamed with oil and must have been slick to the touch.

'What argument will you be making to convince the court he was wrongly convicted?'

Ambrose smirked. 'You know I won't be revealing that to you before we've had an opportunity to present our case to the court. It will then become public record and you can access exactly what transpires in court today. I hope you do.'

'How is the bikie leader coping with life in jail?'

'He's coping fine.'

'Rumour has it that there's been rumblings with a rival motorcycle group. Do you have any comment on that?'

'I know nothing about that and if you'll please excuse me, I have to meet my client before we commence.'

Mr. Ambrose turned on his heel and entered the glass sliding doors where security prevented entry to the journalists. The footage then transitioned to a police panel van entering the back driveway of the court and claiming that Max Vincenzo was inside, arriving for his day in court.

Nick sat back with a thump. Would Max get off? If he was released from prison, Nick's life could potentially be over. He might be forced into witness protection and have to find a new identity, and Evie too.

His mind flicked to Kate. He had been right to push her away, she could not be dragged into this unholy mess. A hooded figure in prison issue overalls was manhandled from the van on the television and whisked away into the criminal entry to the court. The news bulletin then went into another story.

Nick had unwavering belief in the legal system. The charges against Max would be upheld; the crim's only hope was a reduced sentence. But even then, he'd incur the wrath of the Premier's VLAD laws; Max had to be up against it. Even if the bikie leader remained imprisoned, he'd been able to harass Nick from the inside. Would that continue after the appeal decision? The sick feeling in Nick's stomach wasn't from the hospital food. He knew nothing was for certain. Clients he'd been convinced were innocent had been sent to prison for lesser crimes than Max. Sometimes he did get it wrong. He hoped he wasn't mistaken this time, but even if he was right, would it be the end?

***

Angela squealed as the alpaca nibbled the toes on her bare foot.

Kate burst out laughing as they sat on her parents' open back deck seated in the sling back canvas chairs she'd lolled about in as a child. At every angle they were surrounded by the vast and sprawling hills of Bangalow. On the hobby farm, animals roamed free. Kate was used to it.

'Why do your parents have alpacas?' Angela asked after the animal had wandered away to follow its mates.

'It's Mum's newest project. These animals are the latest thing she told me. They are sorta cute though, don't you think?'

'Yes,' Angela agreed. 'Their fur is so soft.'

'Exactly and that is what they're for. They're the new sheep for Aussie farmers. It's a natural fibre and hypoallergenic and soft and durable and silky.'

'You sound like an advertisement,' Angela said.

Kate kept laughing, recalling the initial encounter with her mother. They'd had a similar conversation. 'I was given the low down from Mum when I arrived. She's devoted to them, like all of her ventures. It's a hobby at this stage but she hopes they'll breed and that she might spin the wool herself. She's trying out different options at the moment.'

'It's good to be passionate about something,' Angela commented and Kate sighed taking the remark personally.

'Sitting here right now, with you, the world is good. I mean, look at this place, it's idyllic. We're surrounded by rolling, verdant hills and birds are chirping and animals calling. Simplicity. This is what this life represents – uncomplicated.'

'Yes, and that is exactly why you moved away to uni in the first place and after you'd recuperated from Ben's death, you again returned to the city. This is a wonderful life, but not the one for you.'

'I'm not saying it is.'

'What are you saying then?'

'That I want a simple life.'

'Do you? Really?' Angela paused for a response. When Kate didn't offer one, she continued. 'Because, can you honestly say that part of the attraction to Nick wasn't that he was exciting and different?'

'After Ben died I only wished for a stress-free, safe life. One filled with modest pleasures. And that is the truth. I've achieved that.' Kate smiled, thinking of Nick. 'But look at Nick. He's not a humble straightforward sort of guy. I mean, he's so handsome. Women die for that, right?'

'Uh huh, oh yeah, he's a dish.'

'But, he has a very serious side. He's intense and intelligent and such a gentleman. The way he treats people, the way he treated me,' Kate raised her head to the sky and curled her body in on itself. 'So romantic. It was all of those things that attracted me. But yes, you're right, smarty pants, he made my life exciting and filled it up with events and conversations and moments.'

'He sounds like a catch to me. And that you're in love with him.'

Kate spoke as if she didn't hear the last comment. 'Yes, except that he's wanted by one of the most notorious motorcycle gangs in Queensland who want to kill him and won't stop until they do. And if that alone isn't serious enough, what about his lifestyle? He's a criminal lawyer. He's not going off to a low-key mundane job every day. The guy probably swims with sharks for entertainment!'

'How is he?'

Kate drained her coffee. The day grew warm and soon the heat would drive them indoors. She loved this place. Her safe haven. But Angela was right, she didn't want to live here. Kate wanted to escape here and visit and regroup to soak up the calming environment, whenever she needed or wanted to.

'Regardless of how amazing he is, he's dangerous to be around. It's not wise for me to see him. To ignore the issues would be to act like a teenager who cannot stay away from her bad boy crush despite knowing he isn't good for her. I'm not a child anymore and I need to be more sensible than that.'

'So sensible!'

Kate got the impression Angela held in her groan.

'And…' Angela prompted.

'I've rung the hospital and spoken to Curtis who's given me updates. He's awake and recovering. From all reports desperate to be out of there. I'm not surprised he's a terrible patient.' Kate paused as the herd of six alpaca walked across their path, followed closely by stray ducks and three lambs. 'But, Angela, you weren't there. You don't know what it's like. That scene, I've lived through it once and now twice and won't do it again. It was horrific.' Kate placed her head in her hands.

'He lay there like Ben had. I was convinced he was dead. Everything about the two scenes resembled each other–the chaos, the raised voices, panic and confusion. You don't ever recover from that sort of trauma. The body might but not your mind. I can't sleep, it is replaying every night in my head and I wake up in a cold sweat thinking he's dead. I can't live like that.'

'Have you told him?'

'I made a promise to myself that I wouldn't contact him. But I felt guilty. He was injured and I left. So I have asked to speak to him at the hospital. The nurse said he wasn't able to come to the phone. I tried again another day and received the same response.' Kate shrugged. 'I'm shocked. Why won't he talk to me? I mean, he's the one who lied. He's the one that could have told me the truth and kept me away. I wasn't sure what to think so I texted him. He hasn't responded.'

'How many times have you sent messages?'

Kate blushed bright pink. 'A few?'

Her legs cramped. She stretched them out after being curled under her body on the chair. 'Anyway, it doesn't matter. I have made my decision. I can't be with him. He represents everything I don't want. He's hunted for a start and plus, I'm his daughter's teacher!'

'You are absolutely right,' Angela concurred.

Kate stared at her friend, expecting anything but agreement. Before she could retaliate, her mother came outside. Kate brushed away the moisture on her cheeks. Her parents knew something was up, but she hadn't confided in them. Her mother was aware it had something to do with the 'bikie lawyer'. Kate had also spied a copy of the weekend Brisbane paper. She'd quickly discarded it when her mother wasn't looking.

After the trauma they experienced after Ben's death, the thought of any harm coming to Kate made her parents immediately fraught. They, too, had been through the nightmare before and she couldn't do it to them again. After Ben died she'd been in a bad place, for a long time. They had witnessed her day after day refusing to leave her bed, to get dressed or even eat. It had been a difficult time for them. How could she ever subject them to something like that again? Let alone, herself? Next time, she might not survive.

'Okay, what are you girls going to do today? Do you want an

alpaca lesson or to weed my vegetable patch or feed the chickens? We've tons of jobs to do.' Her mother smiled.

'You know what, Mum, we are heading into the markets. Angela hasn't ever been and she can't come all this way without attending one of our major attractions.'

'That's right, Mrs. F. But what about Kate and I source products and we'll be on for dinner duty tonight? Sound okay?'

'Perfect, love. Make sure you get a bottle of red to go with whatever you're making.'

'You're a woman after my own heart. It goes without saying.'

Kate didn't contribute to the exchange. She pulled out her phone and checked for messages. Nothing. All that she said was true, but her heart ached nonetheless and she couldn't help but wonder why Nick didn't make contact. At least to let her know he was okay. Despite her good sense, she had become wholeheartedly attached to Nick Harding and she grieved for his company; his touch, that smile and oh, those eyes. Was she in love with him? She'd heard Angela's comment but ignored it. She didn't what to answer the question. What would be the point?

Nick had pushed her away so obviously the feelings were mutual. They were toxic for one another. And, he was a liar. Thank goodness they had not become more serious. She'd continue on with her stable and secure life, focusing on her career and job and her students. Kate had great friends and had loved deeply already–she'd be all right. How many people got to experience such enduring love, not only once, but maybe twice? The only thing that mattered now was her safety. Right? She convinced herself. But that didn't stop the sobs forming in her chest, and the cavern opening up there, making it impossible to feel whole.

CHAPTER TWENTY-NINE

'Cheer up, buttercup. Why the sad face?

Evie didn't acknowledge her aunt. She sat on the low front stairs of her grandparent's home in the country town of Toowoomba. The grass was corn-yellow and the sun tinged red any exposed skin, regardless of the time of day. The stairs faced a worn old picket fence that kept the house from acres of space. In the distance, a car engine rumbled.

'C'mon Evie, don't be sad. You haven't been out here to visit for ages. We love having you again and it makes Gran and Pops happy.'

'Yes, me, too. I'm happy to be here and see you, but I should be at school. I'm missing out on work and spending time with my friends. Plus, I need to be with Dad, he's sick.'

Lizzie shook her head. 'He's not sick, he's recovering in hospital and he's feeling a okay from what I hear because he's causing havoc with the poor medical staff with his whinging and whining about being released.'

'I should still be with him.'

'And what good would you be with him in hospital and you at home with no one to care for you? He'd be worried, and because you're here with us, he isn't and that means he can get well more quickly. Right?'

'I guess so.'

'Yes, that's right. Isn't it holidays soon anyway?' Lizzie said as she fanned herself with her Akubra hat.

Evie grinned. 'No, we've not long started term four!'

'There's that smile I've been missing. Gran has her lady friends over for lunch today and Pops has to check out his friend's tractor that needs repair, so it's you and me. What should we do?'

Evie shrugged.

'You are exciting, aren't you? We could go to the movies, out for lunch, play cards… I don't know. What do you like to do these days?'

'I can do all those things in the city,' Evie said as she eyed off her aunt. 'I know! Dad never lets me go horse riding because he says it's too dangerous. But he's not here, right, so let's do that.'

'You're cheeky. I love that your eyes are now sparkling at the talk of mischief. Let's do it. You'll be safe with me, I'm a well-equipped horsewoman no matter what my big brother says. And, this is one of my favourite things to do so we are both winning.'

Lizzie rose. 'Let's go and you can get changed. I have jodhpurs you can borrow and boots that will fit. Today you will commence 101 in horse husbandry. Maybe if you love it enough you'll come out and visit more often. Perhaps you can even have a horse.'

Evie squealed as she re-entered the house.

***

The only good thing about being stuck in the hospital was twenty-four-seven access to the coverage of the appeal. Nick bordered on the obsessive, but it kept him sane and focused when otherwise he'd be pulling out the hairs on his arms one-by-one. Today, his nerves jangled. The judgment was to be handed down. The melee outside the court complex had reached dizzying heights as a pack of reporters staged a standout ready to pounce at the announcement.

Nick knew a select few journalists would be in the courtroom, but the others had to wait for their colleagues, or someone else to deliver the news. Whilst the court technology had improved, it didn't include live streaming of the case. Damn, Nick would've liked to hear the defence submissions.

What would Max's flash new lawyer argue?

Currently as an invalid, Nick had plenty of time to formulate what he would have proposed. He had to control his itchy fingers from pulling out a laptop and knocking up his own arguments. He could almost mouth the words he'd say, they formed so fast in his mind. But, of course, Max had engaged a senior barrister, the most expensive sort, to appear on his behalf along with his smooth new lawyer. He wasn't taking any risks. He wanted this appeal to succeed, and badly. He knew how Max ticked. Nick had, after all, spent a lot of time with the guy.

Max had never admitted his guilt. He'd denied that he'd even been involved in the crimes he'd been convicted of–torture, deprivation of liberty, murder. Nick raked over the facts and couldn't accept that Max and his team of lawyers would have appealed on the basis of a miscarriage of justice or that there'd been an error of law. It would be laughable to argue that the verdict was unreasonable or couldn't be supported based on the evidence.

Or was it the case that Nick now considered the matter through rose-coloured glasses? At the time it had been difficult sifting through the gory details of the offences–it had been horrific, even to his hardened ears. The papers reported it as a drug deal gone wrong and most likely, it had been. The young dealer had chosen the wrong gang to provide with poor quality drugs. The kid wouldn't live to regret it, he was dead and the sad fact was he'd been tortured for hours before released from his misery. The only glaring question for Nick was–did Max actually kill him or had a subordinate done the dirty work? Max had never passed blame or implicated one of his own. The injuries sustained on the victim could have been inflicted by one or more persons.

Nick slammed his fist onto the soft hospital mattress. He wished he had the material to read again with a fresh set of eyes. Not his problem now, but it sure did feel like it was. If Max was acquitted, Nick was in deep shit. If Max's sentence was affirmed, he'd be sent back to jail and presumably, Nick was safe but that didn't provide him with much comfort. His attention drifted back to the television as a breaking news bulletin came onto the screen. The by-line at the bottom read *Gang boss did it and sentence confirmed.*

Nick released the air he didn't realise he'd been holding. Okay, this was a good thing. He kept his eyes peeled to the TV. Mr. Ambrose exited the court carrying his officious briefcase accompanied by two barristers in their formal horsehair wigs and flowing black capes. The elderly senior counsel was to be the spokesperson as he was paid the most. Nick smiled as he observed the lawyer in another of his pinstriped suits, black this time, standing behind the SC. Mr. Ambrose bit his lips, as if holding back words, and scowled and menaced reporters who stood too close. Nick had the sense he wanted to be the honcho up the front doing the talking. A dozen microphones were shoved into the barrister's face. Words were called out to him, questions, comments and opinions. He ignored them all.

'Obviously, our client is extremely disappointed with this outcome. He maintains his innocence and says that justice hasn't been served here today. We will be convening a meeting with him as soon as possible to discuss his options on an application for leave to appeal to the High Court.' With that he nodded and the group of three men walked away. No doubt heading to drown their sorrows after the loss. Nick commiserated with them on that. Nick hated losing. He knew how they must be feeling.

There'd be no application to seek leave. That would be stupidity. But, no doubt, the legal team would vigorously discuss it. Toss up the pros and cons. Money would be no object, unless of course, it became apparent that they were being paid by crime money like Nick had been accused. What would they do then?

The coverage continued. One reporter stood live at the scene. After a brief report confirming the news, they flashed to a pre-prepared package. Max's confirmed sentence merged into a segment about the State's worst offenders and those Max would be mixing with at the Correctional Centre. Footage of the police van carrying Max was captured speeding down the highway en route back to jail. The female journalist standing at the side of the road surmised what Max must be experiencing. Nick hoped that Max wasn't thinking of him as he sat cuffed in the back of the paddy wagon.

What did the verdict now mean for him?

***

'Evie Harding?' Kate called the roll in home room. Still no Evie. As her students left the room to head to their first class of the day, Kate added papers to the already burgeoning pile at the side of her desk. Evie needed to attend school. At this time of term, the new units were being delivered and exams would follow weeks later. With all that she missed, it would be hard to catch up. Placing her hand on the work she'd set aside for her, Kate realised she'd have to make contact. It was for her student's sake. If any other student didn't attend school for an extended period of time, she would call the parents. Decision made, Kate accepted that she would call Nick this afternoon, after her last class.

##

Kate enjoyed playground duty. It provided an opportunity to observe the girls in relaxed states and mixing with their peers. High school permitted a more restrained environment; unlike lower school, children didn't run around chasing balls or playing made up games. Instead, they sat huddled in groups talking or had their eyes glued to their phones. Plus, duty allowed Kate to be outdoors on gorgeous summer days when the sun shone and a gentle breeze sometimes blew. It also meant she avoided idle small talk in the school staff room.

It had become hard to admit she had nothing planned for the weekend. Her life was now back on track and quiet, safe and stable. She should be ecstatic, but she wasn't. Kate rarely felt jealous of others going to the latest films or drinking the night away at chic new bars. Post the Nick fiasco, she'd reverted to her steady life. But, somehow, everything had changed. Whilst her chosen path provided comfort and certainty, strangely, it felt oddly dull and empty and void of all colour.

Kate took small steps, pacing slowly, letting the sun soak into her skin. Suddenly, she shivered and a cloud of gloom descended upon her.

'Have you seen the news?'

Kate spun around and her heart sank. There were few things that could sink her mood, but Brittany Bartholomew was one of them.

'Hi Brittany. How are you today?'

Kate ignored the fact that Brittany didn't greet her and by the look on her face, obviously had salacious gossip to deliver. Brittany held a copy of *The Daily Quest* in her hand and waved it in Kate's face.

'It's all over the paper. It covers the appeal proceedings and the decision.'

Kate stood dumbfounded.

Brittany stamped her foot. 'Don't you read the newspaper?'

Kate shook her head.

'Me either, excepting there's always multiple copies lying around our place. And how could one not read this about our poor Nick.'

'I guess I don't have time. And plus, I can access all the news I require via social media.' The last bit wasn't entirely true. She rarely read news on the Internet, but Brittany didn't need to know that. Sometimes it was necessary to hit where it hurt and this was their family business after all.

'Anyway,' Brittany said waving her hand. One finger sported a large, sparkling diamond ring and bright pink nails matched it. She also wore a bright-coloured fuchsia bloom in her French roll. Kate had to agree, she was a spectacle.

'Nick's former client, some might say friend.' She shrugged flippantly. 'Went to appeal this week but didn't get off. He wanted to be acquitted but was sentenced to a longer jail term. He even had the violent offender laws enforced and it's likely he'll never be released.' Brittany wore an odd smirk that caused her lips to sit at a bizarre angle.

Kate's mind spun as she tried to digest the words. She heard - Nick, bikie, appeal, jail. Was Nick going to jail?

Brittany continued. 'What do you think this means now for Nick? Will he continue an association with the bikie gang, *the Warlocks*, or will they still be seeking revenge?'

As the seconds passed with no answer from Kate, Brittany's face screwed up, her lips went tight and her eyes narrowed. She wasn't as attractive as a moment ago.

'Oh, c'mon. Why do the two of you always act so coy? You must know.'

'Are you interviewing me, Brittany? Is that what you're doing? So then you can go back and feed this information to your husband and he can print it in the paper as an exclusive? Why are you even telling me this?'

'You are the innocent, aren't you?' Brittany purred. 'If I were you, I'd be very worried. This gang is not to be messed with. They will track you down, Kate, if they haven't already. They will hurt you to get to him. That is, unless he can stop it by perhaps cutting a deal with them…'

Kate blanched.

Brittany giggled, obviously happy to have caused this reaction.

'We could have been great friends, you and I. But no, you chose the path of sleeping with Nick and favouring his daughter, and now look where you are. I could have helped with your career. But, no, not now. It would be a terrible shame if that gang found you, wouldn't it?'

Kate's mouth hung open.

'Are you threatening me, Brittany?'

'Me? Don't be so silly. I'm simply stating the facts. Of course, if Coco-Sage delivers straight As this term, things might all turn out differently.'

With that, Brittany turned and left Kate standing gob smacked in the school ground. Every encounter with Brittany Bartholomew had the earth shifting beneath her feet. Kate pulled out her phone and Googled the appeal. It splattered across each news feed. As she read, her mouth dropped and her throat went dry. Holy shit! She'd made the right choice to stay away from Nick Harding if this was the fellow he was mixed up with.

***

Despite the situation Nick found himself in, Kate was determined to do the right thing by Evie. It was her job, her responsibility. Kate stared at the time, again, pressed out the creases in her clothes with her flat palms and sipped her water.

Her heart rattled in her chest.

She was being ridiculous she knew. But butterflies fluttered in her tummy at the prospect of ringing Nick. Would she put herself at risk even contacting him? His number remained punched in her phone and she pressed dial.

***

Nick scrunched up the piece of paper and slam-dunked it in the waste-bin across the room. He'd sat at his desk for hours, doodling images and playing with words and wasn't thrilled with any of the ideas. Lying for days in the hospital bed with little to do but think, he'd made a decision. His professional life could not be on hold any longer. His job was his identity, so intrinsically tied up in his self-worth that not being a lawyer was destroying him.

With the appeal over and Max imprisoned for his lifetime, Nick had to move on, right? He wasn't convinced, but felt he had no choice. He'd commenced putting out leads, talking to people he knew in the legal industry and it was a fair summation that his reputation was tainted. Whilst in conversation people lauded the recent events as heroic, exciting, even amazing, but that hadn't meant they wanted him working on their team. A few were brutally honest–you are a liability, a risk, we can't take the chance, whilst others lied. There were no vacancies or business was slow and they couldn't employ more staff, particularly not at his rates.

He understood.

But that didn't solve his problem.

Nick would go mad if he didn't start applying his brain. Should he approach the Department of Prosecutions and go to the dark side and actually put criminals in jail rather than defend them? Even he wasn't desperate enough for that.

So, he'd decided to commence his own firm. He had doodled logos and firm names for most of the day.

'Mrs. Travers, would you engage a law firm called *Get Me out of Jail Quick?*' he yelled out to his housekeeper as she strode past his study. The older lady paused, feather duster in hand, and looked at him aghast.

'No, Nick, I would not. That sounds shonky.' She didn't wait for him to bother her with further strange questions and walked away to complete her dusting.

There was a current trend of modernising law firms and making them relatable to the general public. Gone were the days of having firm titles after each founding partner so that five names rolled off the tongue. Even his old firm had two names and that was enough. In the end, Nick chose simple *Harding & Co*, and as his by-line, *specialist criminal lawyers*. He avoided the word partner as he didn't know if the business venture would even get off the ground, let alone attract enough work for him to add a partner. This name allowed him to be flexible into the future.

He sat back and typed the name on his screen and made it bold so that it jumped out at him. He liked it. For the first time in months, a frisson of excitement uncurled within. Life had been unbearably shit. But this, it could be his new beginning. He kept idly drawing. A blossoming rose formed on his note pad. He'd loved to use a single red rose stem as his firm icon. Adrenaline pulsed through his veins as he violently scribbled over the image until not a speck poked through. He'd have to be an idiot to in any way identify with the Warlocks. What an irony that he was forever linked to the gang logo and wore it close to his own heart every day. He touched his bicep. Instead, he'd use a play on his name or the firm initals.

His mobile rang. Nick snatched up his phone and answered it without checking the caller ID.

'Hello, Nick. It's Kate Penrose from Trinity College.'

Her voice came out stilted and formal but still familiar. His words clogged in his dry throat and his stomach swirled. Nick found himself mute. Sitting back in his leather chair, he imagined her fingers tantalising his skin, his hands running through her hair and their hungry lips devouring each other. It aroused him in a matter of seconds.

'Nick?' she prompted.

'Yes.' His voice squeaked so he cleared his throat.

'Evie is absent from school. She needs to attend as she is missing out on a significant amount of work this term. Exams are a number of weeks away and I fear she will have difficulty catching up.'

His mood collapsed then. Kate rang about Evie. Not to speak to him or to ask how he was. The tiny spark that had ignited went out as if doused by a bucket of water. His arousal followed quickly thereafter.

'Evie?' he said stupidly as if trying to remember his own daughter's name.

'Yes, your daughter, Evie.'

Despite the cold tone to her voice, this was the Kate he knew. Forever ferocious about doing the right thing and upset with people who didn't. Meddling, you might call it, but it came from the right place. Nonetheless, he sighed. She didn't always know what was best.

'Yes, she's been absent. I'm not sure it's best for her to return yet. I need to keep an eye on her.' He banged his palm against his head. That made it sound like they were still in danger, but maybe they were? Nick didn't want to give that impression to Kate. Why? He didn't know. It wasn't like she would be coming back to him. They were not together and there had been a reason for that. Reality hit him in the gut like a punch. Plus, she'd fled, and run away like a scared child.

Anger bubbled through his veins at the memory. 'Kate, I will decide when it is appropriate for Evie to return. She's actually been spending time with her grandparents as she hasn't done that for at least twelve months.'

Never one to back down, Kate interrupted him. 'Yes, but it's been a month.' Her kind voice returned. 'I'm sure you'll agree that is sufficient time to catch up with Grandma and Grandpa.'

God damn this woman!

He paused. Had it been four weeks? He tried to count the days in his head. Was she right? Nonetheless, he wouldn't back down. Nick used his professional voice as this was a call from his daughter's teacher, nothing more than business.

'Mrs. Penrose.' Kate took an audible intake of breath and he immediately regretted the formality. But he'd gone too far and couldn't stop now. 'You understand there has been a situation of a serious nature. Evie is taking the time she needs to recuperate and spend quality time with her family. I will send her back to school when she's ready.'

'When she's ready or you are ready?'

The ice-steel tone pierced his heart. Why was it okay for him to be terse, but not her?

'Is that all, Mrs. Penrose? Because I am otherwise engaged.'

Kate hung up.

Nick threw his phone on the carpeted floor. Then he swept his arm across his desk causing every piece of paper, cup and folder to crash to the ground in a mess. He hung his head in his hands, his excitement about his new firm forgotten. Now his mind filled with the vivacious beautiful teacher once more.

CHAPTER THIRTY

Kate spied them and a knot of tension formed in her stomach. Nick and Brittany stood on the opposite side of the school crossing. Her fingers crept up and tugged on her right earring. The morning had been a terrible rush. Dark dreams had interrupted her sleep and she'd missed the alarm. Now, she still felt disheveled and hadn't yet regained her equilibrium. And, of all the earrings she randomly pulled out of her jewellery tray that morning, she wore red roses. The only other pair that may have been more symbolic would be the witches or black cats. She imagined Brittany's head bobbing on the witch and cat bodies and allowed herself a tight smile.

As the crossing indicator beeped, Kate paused. Students pushed past her in their hurry to cross. But, Nick outside Trinity could only mean one thing–Evie had returned to school. Yes! Her morning improved instantly and she smiled wider. Evie's faithful parent had recommenced his tried and tested routine of escorting his daughter to the school gate.

Bet Evie loved that.

Kate commenced to walk with the remaining throng of students and Nick caught her eye. He didn't smile, or frown, his features remained impartial. Kate's facial muscles itched to move but she held them steadfast. If he couldn't muster up a pleasant greeting, neither would she.

Despite that resolution, she couldn't stop her heart hammering with each step as she drew closer to him. He stood directly in her path.

Words raced through her mind of what she might say but as her foot hit the curb, Brittany slinked up closer, distracting him. Kate blew out her breath. Saved by Brittany. She'd never thought that before!

Nick turned his head to look behind him and up the street and trailed his hands through his hair. But Brittany kept talking, leaning in close with a hand on his arm, never stopping her ceaseless prattle into his ear. Brittany's free hand gesticulated in the air, discussing her important topic. As Kate reached the school gate, Nick held up his hand, making a gesture to Brittany. Kate couldn't control her grin as Brittany stepped back.

Kate would have loved to hear what he'd said. Was he polite or rude? The gesture revealed more rudeness than civility. Either way, Nick strode off, presumably towards his car. It didn't matter, Kate had class. The tingles that had spread through her body upon the sight of Nick, evaporated. She'd have to get used to running into Nick Harding and her body would have to adjust, too.

'Girls, spread out! C'mon. Are any of you taking this seriously? Okay, stop. Go and run around the track.'

Kate barked at the team of volleyball girls she attempted to train. The girls acted like they had lead in their feet. Kate wasn't cheerful and fun today, either. She rode her team and worked them hard until their complaints rang out. As they wiped sweat off their brows, Evie approached her. She hadn't spoken to the girl all day despite having taught her in three classes.

A stabbing pain throbbed in her chest. Evie reminded her of Nick and each time she gazed at the girl, her emotions ran wild. She'd get over it, she felt sure. Kate had forgotten in those few short weeks, how beautiful Evie was. The girl glowed as she sat beside her with her golden curls pulled back into a messy ponytail and porcelain skin and those blue eyes. Another knife twisted into her heart.

'Hey, Miss. Are you okay?'

'Oh, hi, Evie. Yes, I'm fine. How are you? Happy to be back at school?'

Evie groaned. 'Yes, I'm loving it. I wanted to come back weeks ago but Dad forbade me.'

She'd known it; she'd been right all along. Stubborn Nick.

'How is your dad?'

Evie's forehead creased and her eyes narrowed into slits, but she didn't ask the obvious. 'He's okay. He's working hard again.'

'Working? He's back with a firm?' Kate asked.

'No. He's decided to start his own firm. It's all fresh and new and just getting off the ground. He's super excited about it, though. He's been in a much better mood since making the decision.'

Kate deflated as all the air left her lungs. Nick had made a life changing decision and she didn't know about it. And nor should she, as they were no longer together. Still, it hurt. But, Nick was now free to do whatever he liked.

'Yes, he's not one to be idle, is he?'

Evie shook her head so her curls bounced.

Kate knew she'd been in a bad mood all day after having seen Nick this morning. Unusually, she'd been unable to recalibrate her mood. No wonder everyone kept asking her if she was okay.

She was about to ascertain if Evie needed a lift home, but the girl ran off to join her team mates who stood around bantering. As a group they huddled together, laughing. A good thing–driving Evie home would be a mistake. Kate sat back on her haunches, near the stands overlooking the field they'd been training on. The night chill had kicked in and took away the heat of the summer day. Kate welcomed the reprieve.

After seeing Nick and Evie again, her emotions commenced their rollercoaster ride once more. Her thoughts were riding a fast train and she couldn't catch them or make sense of how she felt. Without the two of them around, she'd been able to pretend they didn't exist. But reality made life tough. Having them right in front of you knocked out all pre-conceived ideas about how you thought you were coping.

Kate let her shoulders roll downwards in a posture that she'd admonish her students for. A light touch to her shoulder made her roll them back out and sit up straight.

'Hey, what's up?'

'Hey. What are you doing here?'

'Like you, my love, I've been convinced to take a year twelve volleyball team. However, unlike your group, mine actually know how to play and it didn't take them long to work out that their coach didn't. It was a shambles. I had to get one of the more responsible girls, and one that wouldn't advertise my failings, and ask her to tell me the rules!' Angela laughed.

'Nothing ever bothers you. Even when you are completely out of your depth and don't know what you are doing. You keep going.'

'What other choice is there?'

'I saw Nick this morning. Evie is back at school. Seeing them was like a knife tearing through my heart all over again. I have to admit, it caught me by surprise. My reaction, that is. I thought I was coping. Actually, you know what it feels like? It's like I've suffered the loss I was so desperate to avoid, except Nick is still around and every time I feel okay, I see him and my life gets tumbled upside down like clothes in a dryer! Is that weird?' Kate released a laugh that caught in her throat and came out strangled.

'No. Not at all.' Angela sat with her on the ground and draped an arm around her shoulders.

'You're the one who makes everyone think you're so tough and indestructible. Are you telling me you aren't?'

Kate offered a weak smile. 'You know what, I think I'm losing either way. My heart is already ripped to shreds. Now that Nick is gone, I recognise that he was all exciting and dashing and before I knew, life had become amazing again. Now everything is dull and grey and oh-so boring!' Kate gave a little sob.

'But what you were missing was love, not fun. Isn't there a way you can work it out? Talk it through at least? Surely it doesn't have to be all or nothing? Your choices don't have to either be an exhilarating life lived on the edge or a solitary and safe but tedious existence? Plus, didn't you say that the fellow that's been bothering him has been jailed indefinitely?'

'Yes, but it's not that simple. He was in jail while causing all the problems, so being incarcerated isn't an impediment to leaving Nick alone. Plus, Nick has frozen me out and made it very clear that he doesn't want me as part of his life anymore.'

The team of girls squealed as they threw the ball around.

Kate sighed, that's exactly what she'd wanted them to do during practice.

'I miss her, too. Who'd have thought?' Kate gestured toward the tall, lanky blonde girl.

'Maybe give him time and perhaps you can try again?'

Kate nodded. 'The whole situation is stupid. The thought of voluntarily putting myself in danger with him makes me frantic with fear but the prospect of not spending time with him and Evie again, also makes me feel wretched.'

'Usually, I'd make a smart comment about love being scary, and it is by the way, but this situation is more serious. You need to think about things carefully.' Angela commented with a shrug. 'Either way, honey, you are miserable. Want to take care of one another together and be happy or miserable alone?'

'I'm afraid it's not only up to me.'

***

'Tell me you've caught the news?' Curtis burst in on Nick.

'What? Hi, mate. What are you on about?'

By way of response, Curtis turned on the television in Nick's living area. Then, without asking he went over to the bar and poured them both a double scotch. The news bulletin echoed around the open space. Until that moment, Nick had been engrossed as he had been all day, in setting up his new firm: the website, facilities, leasing office space and registering the company name. When consumed with a task, like being in the middle of a legal case, Nick became oblivious to the outside world. As a result, he hadn't turned on the radio or watched the television. He hadn't even played his favourite tunes.

Leader of the notorious Warlocks motorcycle gang, Max Vincenzo, has been murdered. Found dead in his jail cell just hours ago, it is alleged that he'd been stabbed in the chest a dozen times. It's asserted that a war had been brewing between rival gangs behind bars. Arch enemies, The Hells Angels' leader had been incarcerated in the high security section of Wolston Correctional Centre, the area Vincenzo was transferred to after losing his appeal. Tensions were already heightened as other gang members had been squabbling for weeks. Apparently an argument over a hairbrush set off the incident. With Vincenzo's death, the jail is in lockdown for fear of further reprisals.

Nick stared at the screen. He gulped his drink. The news footage scanned to the headquarters of the Warlocks.

Chaos. Members brawled in the run down old tin shed. Chairs flew as divisions surfaced over who should be the next leader. The reporter stated that no agreement could be reached and members were turning on each other and threatening to abscond to other gangs.

'Is Max really dead?' Nick asked.

Curtis nodded. 'Yep, stupid old fucker. Can you believe it?'

'I almost can't believe it without evidence, like his body, you know. Is that weird?'

'No, not at all, given what you've been through.'

'I don't want to get my hopes up.' Nick hung his head to regain composure., 'But could it even be possible that the whole gang will go under?'

'It's conceivable. Consider the history. You'll remember the Taylor Boys? Similar story, once their leader was killed, they couldn't hold it together. Vicious fighting occurred, they ended up mostly killing each other and for those that remained, it became a liability to be associated with the name. Could happen again. Why not?'

Curtis refilled their glasses.

'If it was Max Vincenzo calling the shots and causing all that trouble for me, I should be in the clear then.'

'Let's drink to that.'

Nick was cautious to celebrate but a heavy burden lifted from his shoulders. Instantly, he felt lighter, freer. Even if the gang maintained a vendetta–the vendetta was Max's anyway – the rest of them would be clueless to execute it. They weren't a smart bunch. Max had been the brains. Nick had been given a fresh start. Evie would be safe, now and forever. He'd make sure of that. There's no way he'd give up being a criminal lawyer, but he would not represent any more bikies or anyone associated with that gang-like mentality. His prospective future clients would be carefully vetted and he'd ensure his ego remained firmly in his back pocket. Infamy and being a notorious criminal defender were no longer on his agenda. There were many good people who made simple mistakes: doctors and nurses in the course of saving lives, teachers, drivers having one too many drinks when they thought they were safe to get behind the wheel. He'd seen many lives changed irrevocably and forever by lack of judgement. Unfortunately, a whole bunch of the community required his legal help. He'd make a list of who and who he wouldn't act for and stick by it. He'd ensure these were not just words. Nick made a solemn vow to himself. One he would stick to. At this moment, he felt resolute, hopeful and an urgent sense to protect his future over took him. He would not commit the same mistake again.

'Let's drink to this whole sorry saga being over and getting on with your life,' Curtis raised his glass.

'And, to the poor bugger who clocked Max one, let's raise a drink to him, too. No doubt he'll now rot in prison for the remainder of his life if he wasn't already.'

As the news sank in, Nick wanted to celebrate. He didn't know what the future held, but at the moment he felt jubilant. He and Curtis stayed in, watched the footy and drank. By the early hours of the morning they were singing the team song of their favourite club, also victors that night. As he sang that song, tears sprang into Nick's eyes and he cried like a baby.

##

Narrow rays of dawn sun peeked through the curtains as Nick lay awake in his downstairs living room. Curtis had collapsed after one too many scotches and snored noisily from where he'd landed on the opposite couch. Nick couldn't sleep. How could he after such news? He imagined the murder of Max in his mind a hundred times. Having witnessed plenty of testimony from accused killers, he could visualise the act. The part about blood spurting out of Max's chest might have been dramatised. But as the hours passed, it wasn't Max who consumed his thoughts: it was a pixie who wore crazy earrings and a perpetual smile despite the pain and tragedy she'd suffered. He'd always felt illuminated in her presence because of her ability to make others happy. Kate Penrose's constant upbeat mood was infectious. Her smile radiated warmth in all directions along with those sparkling chocolate brown eyes. Nick recalled her luscious locks falling down her back when it wasn't restrained in a loose ponytail or bun.

Nothing had changed, though, had it? Whilst a buoyant life force, Kate still craved a *normal* life whatever that was. But in her words-a stable, secure existence that didn't allow for hiccups or lapses from the well-travelled path. Up to now, he'd led a life filled with surprises and had operated in fifth gear. Admittedly, he'd slowed down after Evie had come to live with him, but not in his professional life. Yes,

227

in his personal life he still rode his Harley Davidson and drank too much and bought expensive things, but the risks he didn't take in his private world, he executed in his work. He'd become cocky and pigheaded and he realised now, with the grace of hindsight, thought he was indestructible; a dangerous combination, particularly in the world of the law.

Yep, he'd become a cocky, arrogant bastard.

Rather than refuse to act for potential clients when that frisson of fear mixed with excitement had cut through him in initial interviews, he'd relished it and begged for more and thought no matter what, he could do it, he could get this person off their charges, be the hero, be the saviour. If it hadn't been for the disaster that became Max, he might still think that. He'd be given a scare, and survived, and now, the future would be different. Nick had almost died and left Evie without a mother and a father. What had he been thinking? The shady world of his clients had corrupted him.

No longer.

Perhaps in his new firm he could train future lawyers and leave the excitement of court appearances, bail hearings and cell visits to the next generation. He could be a mentor and guide them along the slippery slope of criminal law. Maybe with his help, they could avoid a fall like his. These thoughts led him to a more content place. But agitation rose up within him. His legs jiggled and his mind whirred. He'd stuffed up with Kate. She'd arrived at the wrong time in his life. Could he make amends or was it better to let her go?

CHAPTER THIRTY-ONE

The audience of girls yawned, fiddled with their badges, picked their fingernails or had quiet conversations with their neighbours. Even Kate seated at the rear of the school assembly hall had to still the urge to tap her feet and drift away into daydreams.

Mrs. Peterson spoke for at least forty minutes on the virtues of hard work, good grades and responsibility and with those three objectives, the students would have choices in their futures. Kate agreed with the principal's sentiment but on a sweltering thirty degree summer afternoon in a hall that wasn't air-conditioned, the message was lost. And they still had the school awards to complete.

The scent of summer holidays lingered in the air and the students could taste freedom. Eventually, Mrs. Peterson sat and the deputy principal stood at the lectern to run the remainder of the program. Kate clapped too enthusiastically as students she taught were awarded academic prizes for being top of their year. Despite music not being one of her primary subjects, it had grown on Kate. She planned to approach Mrs. Peterson to continue teaching it next year.

Year Seven English award goes to Evie Harding.

Even though Kate knew of this prize-Evie had blitzed her peers in English-she still swelled with pride and joined in the loud applause. Evie's shocked expression demonstrated her genuine surprise but she couldn't hide her luminous smile. Despite any recriminations that might follow, Evie had earned this award and Kate did not experience even a flicker of guilt about her relationship with the student. Kate forced her eyes ahead and focused on each recipient. She would not glance around to look for a handsome lawyer.

Moments later Evie was awarded head flautist. Kate reserved her clapping now. She didn't want to witness Brittany's reaction. She could imagine her fury that Coco-Sage did not receive any awards.

At the end of the ceremony, special mention was made of teachers transferring to new schools or retiring. Warmth radiated through Kate at being part of this school community. She'd grown to love Trinity College: her friends and peers and the job she'd carved out for herself. After zoning out briefly, she tuned back in to listen to Mr. Jefferies announce Angela Zimmerman as the new pastoral leader for year ten next year. Kate patted Angela on the back as she strode to the stage to be acknowledged for this promotion. Kate was proud of her friend. Angela was a great teacher and would be a wonderful leader plus her fun teaching approach would assist her in the role.

Mrs. Peterson returned to the microphone for the next announcement. Kate sighed and readied herself for another speech.

'Now, we are to make special mention of a new teacher to our school this year. She's been a burst of fresh air and brought a voracious don't get in my way attitude to her teaching and to the school. She's been committed in every aspect of school-life from coaching netball, to running stalls at the fair, to taking over all of the music lessons for year seven when Mrs. McAndrews fell ill. Her students are taught to generate their own opinions and to stand up for what they believe in. She has been a welcome hurricane, even though, I can certainly say, that she and I have not always agreed. I am of course, talking about Mrs. Kate Penrose.'

Applause exploded around the room.

What? Did Mrs. Peterson say those wonderful things about her? In the crowded hall filled with students, parents and staff, all eyes turned toward her. Mrs. Peterson continued. 'Mrs. Penrose is being awarded the Head Teacher of Year Seven and next year will lead a new program for children identified as in need.' Kate remained seated as her feet felt stuck to the floor.

'She's being shy. Come on up, Mrs. Penrose.'

Kate rose. The crowd of young girls squealed encouragements, urging her on. She forced one foot after the other to reach the stairs leading up to the stage. Mrs. Peterson drew her in for an unexpected congratulatory hug and handed her a mini plaque to hang in her office. The ceremony ended and the year twelve student body threw their dress hats into the air and shrieked. If Kate wore one, she would have catapulted it as high as she could, too.

She held that plaque to her chest. It had all been worth it: the hard work, dedication and commitment to these students. Even when it had proven difficult. Mrs. Peterson had been right, hard work did pay off. She turned her trophy around to view it at all angles. It validated her decisions, her choices, those dark hours and tough times. She had done it.

'Miss! Miss!'

A group of her year seven girls surrounded her in a circle and cuddled her as they danced and sang with joy. Kate joined in with her own tears of happiness.

The mood was jubilant. Students talked in booming voices to their classmates. They ate their way through caramel-covered popcorn, cupcakes iced blue in Trinity College colours, spring rolls and other food laid out on the narrow tables lining the far side of the hall. Now that the formalities were concluded, the students celebrated the end of year. Freedom from alarm clocks clanging at early hours and the tyranny of school uniforms was only moments away and everyone, even the staff and parents were excited at the prospect of summer holidays.

Still reeling from her own achievements, Kate sipped on iced lemonade and chatted to students about their holiday plans. She became deliberately vague when asked about her own summer break. Then, behind her back came the distinctive clatter of stiletto heels on the corked surface. It came closer. The steps rang out hard and fast. The student she spoke with looked over Kate's shoulder and her eyes widened. Kate turned.

And faced Brittany Bartholomew. What would a day at Trinity be without an encounter with Brittany? And, damn, she'd almost escaped for the summer. Kate stared at her. One look and she knew disaster was about to strike. Brittany's face was puce and her forehead tried to crease but it's tightness only pulled her eyes towards her brow forming a shocked scowl. Her eyes narrowed into squinting slits.

'That tops off a great year, then, doesn't it? You've had your way. You've successfully denigrated my daughter the entire year. Her self-esteem is in tatters and she believes she has no future because she didn't succeed in her first year of high school.'

Oh, the exaggeration!

Brittany growled the words at Kate. All those in the immediate

231

diameter paused mid-sip to focus on the woman wearing the bright pink Armani suit. Brittany poked her index finger in Kate's face. 'How could you? You were happy to sleep with your boyfriend and then award his daughter not merely the top English award but also flautist. Your loyalties are not divided are they?' Brittany didn't stop to catch her breath. 'I am frustrated with this pathetic school. I'll be making a formal complaint against you.' Kate took a step backwards as Brittany closed the gap between them. A waiter carrying a tray of drinks walked by. Brittany grabbed a flute of champagne and tossed it in Kate's face. Fizzy bubbles rolled into Kate's eyes and over her mouth giving her a taste of the good quality drop. She stood stock-still as the droplets rolled over her chin. The liquid sank into the strands of hair surrounding her face. Kate rubbed her eyes to clear away the moisture so she could be ready for what Brittany had in store next.

'That is enough.' A deep and authoritative voice resonated form behind her. It matched a lanky frame and stood between her and Brittany. A hand rested on her arm as if to restrain her, but next a handkerchief was placed into her palm. After mopping up her face and clearing her vision, she realised Nick was standing beside her, his face a storm cloud. His friend Curtis stood in front.

Nick used his hand to persuade her away from Brittany. Despite Curtis standing between them, Brittany bustled to either side of him, trying to reach Kate.

'Get out of my way!' she hissed.

Curtis placed his grip on her shoulders, preventing her movement. 'I said that is enough. If you do not desist from your name calling and your assault, I will arrest you.' Curtis spoke in a calm voice.

Daggers shot from Brittany's eyes. 'And, I said, get out of my way! I have not finished my business with *her* and it has nothing to do with you.'

Curtis released one arm and moved around to extract his police identification and along with it, a pair of handcuffs. Brittany twisted in his grip, trying to break free. Nick went to stand on the other side of her to prevent her liberation.

'I have witnessed you assault this teacher by throwing a drink in her face. You have further proceeded to verbally assault her with witnesses present. I give you one last chance. You may now leave the scene without speaking any further to Mrs. Penrose and exit the school grounds and I will not charge you. Your other choice is to continue and I will arrest you now and place you in handcuffs and escort you to the police station for questioning. What do you choose?'

Brittany actually paused and deliberated. Her face scrunched up as if she was struggling to control herself. Kate caught her breath. If that woman was let loose, well, one could only imagine what vehemence she could unleash. But then, as if common sense took control, her features dropped, and she commenced to move away, but not before throwing a menacing glare in Kate's direction.

'Oh, and one last thing. I will formally record this incident. If you approach Mrs. Penrose again I will charge you for stalking, intimidation, assault and defamation, so let this be your warning. This ends now. And that includes if your husband prints an article in his paper.'

Curtis watched to ensure she left the building before turning to Kate. 'Geez, Kate that woman really hates you.' He laughed as if it was just another incident in the course of his duty. Kate blew out the breath she'd been holding.

'Thank you for your help, Curtis.' She kissed his cheek. 'I was about to give her a mouthful and defend myself, I am capable, you know, but you prevented me the embarrassment. Would you have arrested her?'

'Absolutely but not charged her. Even though wearing a glass of champers can be assault. I would have done it to scare her and make the behavior stop. It's a shame, could have been fun escorting her out of here in cuffs!' Curtis collected a drink and downed it. 'And, for the record, I know you can look after yourself, you're a tough chick, but sometimes it's nice to have help.'

Kate smiled at the truth of his words.

'I'll do a quick run around to make sure she isn't lurking in a dark recess of the school.' Curtis moved away.

***

A few metres away, Coco-Sage moved in to stand beside Evie. The girl stiffened, expecting a double whammy from both mother and daughter. Instead, she said, 'My mother is full-on isn't she? I'm sorry about all that. It's embarrassing. She thinks that I'm a superstar at everything, whether it's music, sport or school work. The pressure! It's hideous. But, that was humiliating and I'm sorry. Well done on your awards, you deserve it. I don't have any quarrel with you or our teacher. Let's be friends, okay?'

Evie stood mute, uncertain. Was she for real? Or would the real Coco-Sage emerge at any moment?

'I'll give you a call and we can catch up over the holidays.' Coco-Sage strode away and Evie turned to her friend and they both shrugged. Evie searched for Mrs. Penrose but her father had led her outside. They were deep in conversation and she didn't want to interrupt them.

***

Kate crumbled once Brittany had left the scene and Nick led her outside to the quiet balcony. She shook off his grip.

'I could have handled that myself.' The confrontation and Nick being here,
suddenly overwhelmed her and instead of thanking him, she was annoyed. Did Nick Harding think he could waltz on in and save her when it suited him?

'Yes, you could have. But as Curtis said, why can't friends help you?' Nick paused. 'I remember this balcony. I had a penchant for that potted plant one dark night many days ago,' he said with his lips curled upwards.

Kate's spine slackened. She let him draw her in close and hold her tight until the last of her sobs subsided. When she came up for air, she placed her hand on his chest to create space between them.

'What do you think she'll do now?'

'Brittany?' Nick shrugged. 'She's persistent, we've learned that. After bullying you all year and not getting what she wanted, I thought she'd give up. But she never did. So, I guess, she'll either devise a new evil plan or next year she'll come back a respectful and more considerate parent because the embarrassment will be too great. The entire school witnessed that scene and it didn't paint her in a good light. Best case scenario is that she'll try her luck at another school where her daughter might shine.'

'That would be good,' Kate said. 'Here's your handkerchief, all wet and dirty I'm afraid.'

'Um, it's okay, you can keep it.'

She twisted it around her fingers and avoided looking at him. If she didn't, she'd be powerless. But she couldn't resist the urge and when she did, her body flooded with warmth and her arms longed to reach out to him.

'How are you?'

'Besides being assaulted by the parent who hates me most in the world? Okay, I guess. I was acknowledged for my teaching.'

'Yes, congratulations. I knew you were great. It's well deserved. All those times you bulldozed me into making decisions. The principal was right, you are tenacious and always take the moral high ground.'

'Hard work does pay off.' She nodded. 'Evie mentioned you are working again?'

'Yes. The new proprietor of Harding & Co stands before you. I don't actually have a client yet, but I'm working on it.' Nick laughed. 'I'm going to be very selective in who I represent.' Nick mentioned his hopeful client base from the list he'd made up and memorised. 'You see, Kate, I got greedy and over-confident and thought I was indestructible. That nothing would happen to me, that I would continue to be this hotshot lawyer and be given accolades for my success rate in defending clients. I was warned, by those more experienced than me.' Nick looked down at the tiles, remembering. 'But I was too stubborn to listen. My colleague told me acting for the Warlocks and being their exclusive criminal defender would lead to trouble and he was right. It took me a while but I've learned my lesson.'

Kate nodded. 'I'm pleased for you. You give everything a hundred percent so I'm confident the new business will be a great success.'

'I've had a lot of time to think lately.'

'Mm.' Kate swiped a white wine off a passing tray and sipped it, her throat dry.

Nick declined.

'You're right. I give everything I do my all, I'm intense like that. When I met you, the timing was wrong. I'd received a number of threats already and yet, here I was meeting this beautiful teacher taking a keen interest in my daughter and not at all scared off that I had a thirteen-year-old to start with.'

Kate smiled but remained quiet.

'But I couldn't help myself. You're so delightful and happy and have this unique ability to shine in the darkest of times. Our time in Vietnam, wow, that was incredible. We got to know each other, didn't we? But that incident.' He shook his head. 'I couldn't let you become involved in that situation; it was dangerous. I had to protect Evie and couldn't let you be dragged into that mess when you didn't need to be anywhere near me. You understand, don't you, that I couldn't subject you to it, take that risk?'

'I do, Nick. But you lied. You kept it a secret from me all that time. That was unfair. If it wasn't safe for us to be together, you should have been upfront about it before anything happened. It was worse, finding out that way. At least, if I'd known, I could have made my own decision.'

'Yes, you're right. But you would have run away then instead of later.'

'I didn't run away. First of all, you lied and then for my own safety I stayed away and when I tried to speak to you, you froze me out. You didn't return any of my messages if I recall correctly.'

'Okay, it's been a real balls up. But, the reason I'm talking to you, is that Max Vincenzo—I won't assume anymore that you don't know who he is—is dead. And everything is different now.'

He stopped to let that news sink in.

'Dead? I know he wasn't successful in his appeal. Strangely enough, Brittany Bartholomew told me. Can you believe it? She was out to score more points, I guess.'

'Yes, dead. He was murdered in jail last week. Since then the gang has totally imploded with in-fighting and brawling and disagreement and they've gone bust. They no longer exist.'

Kate remained silent, refusing to help him along. He had to talk.

'My priority was always to keep Evie safe and then I grew to care for you and had to keep you safe, also. There is no threat to me now, or you or Evie. There is nothing keeping us apart.'

'Nothing?' A fire stirred in her belly. 'Is it the case that when the first lucrative client comes along who is less than squeaky clean, that you are going to say, oh no, thank you, I'm sorry. Your case is worth millions of dollars and is complex and interesting but I can't help you?' Kate mocked him.

'Ouch. Okay, I understand. But that's not a fair example. What's the danger in that case? If the person isn't a biker or drug mule or have vicious criminal associations, then that case sounds fantastic.' Those blue eyes twinkled at her as he grinned.

'I cannot stop being a criminal lawyer. It is who I am and you have to accept that. But I do promise not to get a big head and believe I'm a hotshot and act foolishly. Here's the thing–I have remained on good terms with my old partner, I can even run dubious clients past him. If he says he would act, it's a sure-fire good client. He never acts if he's uncertain. You'd never meet a more ethical and professional lawyer.'

'That sounds good. But what about on weekends–will you be skydiving and riding your motorcycle and living life on the edge?'

'You do have a certain image of me, don't you?'

She nodded in earnest.

'I have never been skydiving, nor engaged in life threatening activities as a pastime. You can check with Curtis if you don't believe me. I do have Evie and if anything happened to me, she'd be an orphan. The thought of that cuts me in two and I'll do anything to avoid that. You have my word.'

Hope blossomed in Kate's heart. It filled up with longing and need and want, ready to burst. She took one small step toward him. It acted as an invitation. Nick met her halfway and their fingers intertwined at their hips. The slightest of touches. And with that one stroke, she was sure.

How could she possibly stay away from this man? And, more so, why did she want to? 'I tend to avoid all activity so perhaps we can meet somewhere in the middle and live a fun and balanced life.'

'If I get to do that with you, I couldn't be any happier.' The desire flashing in his eyes made them turn cobalt-blue. The intensity she was used to simmered in those pools once more. She'd desperately missed it.

'Let's live vicariously through your clients because they have extraordinary existences.'

'They sure do. Does that mean I can kiss you now and you won't hit me?' Kate brought her lips up close to Nick. She could feel his warmth and smell the sweetness of his breath. She inhaled deeply. 'I'd never hit you,' she said before smothering her mouth over his.

As their lips touched, Kate was lost. Starved of his caress, she ran her fingers through his hair and held the base of his neck. He placed his hand on her hip, gently holding her to him whilst his tongue tenderly pushed her lips apart. Kate did not want the kiss to end, and when he eventually pulled away, he placed her head to his chest and she listened to his deep breathing. She wanted Nick Harding by her side, always.

'Can you move in now so we can be together, always?'

Kate lifted her head then, and shoved him gently with the flat palms of her hands to his chest. Nick placed his hands over hers and drew her in toward him again. Kate snuggled into that embrace with her heart full and feeling the most protected she had for a long time.

Nick gave her a steely glare and said, 'I love you, Kate Penrose and I promise to keep you safe, always.'

And Kate believed him with all of her heart.

EPILOGUE

Kate stroked the Rolex watch one last time before rolling it down her wrist. It continued to tick as she placed it into the box. Next, she extracted the euro coin from her pocket and without further thought, placed it amongst the other items. For the last time, she extracted the sickly green poncho and held it to her nose and breathed deeply. Plastic. The only smell that remained was of age and the slightest hint of mildew. Kate took one last look at the contents and closed the lid. These items of her former life with Ben would forever hold a place in her heart, but she didn't need them anymore.

'Kate! Pizza's here,' Evie screeched from the downstairs level. Kate smiled; she wouldn't ever get sick of hearing her voice reverberating around the house, her home. Pushing the box across the carpeted floor of the bedroom, Kate found a place under her side of the bed. The bed she now shared with Nick. Once it was securely in place, she rose and rushed out the door, urged on by the smell of melting cheese, but more importantly, Nick. She'd heard him arrive home and she couldn't wait to see him.

ACKNOWLEDGMENTS

This book challenged me in many ways. I can say that it is the best book I can make it at this time in my writing career and I do love Kate and Nick. I've have so much help in producing it and it is a joy to finally send it out into the world. The list is endless but to specifically mention:

My fantastic editor, mentor and friend, Annie Seaton, your ongoing support and guidance is invaluable to me. Thank you. For my beautiful cover, Lana Pecherczyk at Bookcoverology, another amazing design. To my neighbour, Liana for her proofreading skills. To my book club friends who have been enormously supportive – you all inspire me and make me laugh and I value your friendship. I love our monthly meetings! To my writing group who offer their support and encouragement, finally I have found writing friends!. To the author friends I have made along the way, thank you for being part of my journey and reading early drafts of this book. Enormous thanks to all of the authors who continue to produce so many fantastic books and for making my to-be-read pile so large I will never have time to read them all, but mostly, for providing hope that that I might one day, be just like you.

Also, a shout out to everyone who purchased Unexpected Delivery and left reviews and encouraged me in my writing journey.

And lastly, and most importantly to the people in my life: Justin, Scarlett, Eloise and Mitchell for tolerating my endless hours tapping away at the computer and when I'm not writing, reading. Love you all very much.

ABOUT THE AUTHOR

Leanne Lovegrove is a lawyer, wife and mother and a lover of romance and reading. Her law career has caused her addiction to coffee but provides her with countless story ideas. Leanne lives in Brisbane, Australia with her husband and three children. Illegal Love is her second novel.

You can find Leanne at:

www.leannelovegroveauthor.com

FB-Leanne Lovegrove-Author

Insta-Leanne Lovegrove-Author

OTHER BOOKS
Unexpected Delivery

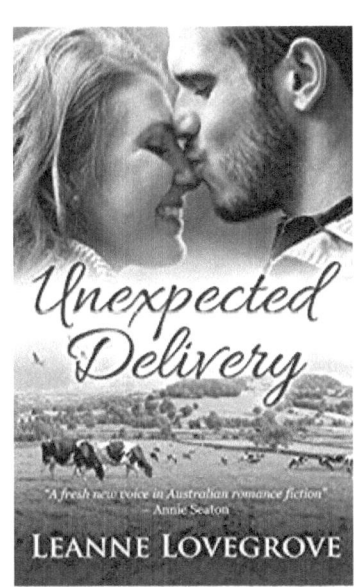